Treasure Preserved

It's action all the way in this classic and witty whodunit centred round the fate of the 19th-century Round House whose survival can wreck a multi-million pound development in a South Coast resort. A dozen interested parties are for knocking it down. They include an Arabian oil sheikh, a sexy English Lit. drop-out from Sussex University, the head of a construction company, and a romantic novelist. And where does Canon Tring's languorous young wife fit into all this? You may well ask!

Only Louella, Lady Brasset, is committed to keeping the Round House standing; she believes it to be the joint creation of two famous architects, Sir John Soane and William Butterfield. But four hours after Treasure promises her a stay of execution on the house, it's Louella who's blown up—and another death follows. Double accident—or double murder?

David Williams's new novel offers a twisting plot, red herrings galore, and a tale peppered with delightfully drawn characters, not forgetting Dung the dog. Of course Treasure finds all the answers, but only after doing battle with a monster demolition machine, a bizarre chase through the sleeping town, and a hair-raising confrontation on the windswept pier.

For Mary e Mike

DAVID WILLIAMS

Treasure Preserved

A Mark Treasure novel

Affectionately

David Williams

March 1983

COLLINS, 8 GRAFTON STREET, LONDON W1

William Collins Sons & Co. Ltd
London · Glasgow · Sydney · Auckland
Toronto · Johannesburg

First published 1983
© David Williams 1983

British Library Cataloguing in Publication Data

Williams, David
    Treasure Preserved. — (Crime Club).
    I. Title
    823'.914[F]   PR6073.I42583

    ISBN 0 00 231928 4

Photoset in Compugraphic Baskerville
Printed in Great Britain by
T. J. Press (Padstow) Ltd

— including doctors!

This one for Morris and Joy West

CHAPTER 1

'Saints alive! I've got it!' snapped Lady Brasset in crisp Bostonian, and only more or less to herself.

She looked up sharply from the faded handwriting she had been studying. A notice on the wall spelled SILENCE in letters big enough to emphasize serious intent.

But it wasn't the printed stricture that troubled Louella Brasset. Her outburst had been intended strictly to mark private jubilation. Her composure was recovered only after she established she was still the only occupant of the reference room. It was not a much used section of the Tophaven Public Library. She had been alone there practically throughout the two weeks of her researching.

In Louella's firm view — and she never entertained the other kind — the place was most always empty because there was too darned little to refer to in it. And that was something she aimed to take up with the proper authority in due time. Right now she had more urgent business on hand.

None of the private diaries, boxes, folders and papers arranged on her reading desk had come from the open shelves. They had been especially and inconveniently produced from Archives on demand.

According to George Sims, the Chief Librarian, Archives — meaning things, not a specific place — ineluctably denoted material no one in Tophaven was ever going to want again. Yet for one fool reason or another he was charged to keep everything so designated on the premises, and never allow it to leave them.

The Sydney Marshford Papers were Archives. They had been bequeathed to the library half a century earlier by Randolph Marshford, the last in a short line of Sussex minor gentry. A bachelor, Randolph had died in a run-down pension near the old casino in Nice. His funeral had been at that municipality's expense — but unwillingly, and definitely not in recognition of the fortune he had dissipated within its boundaries. No one else could be found to pay.

Like most Archives, the Papers had first been housed in a secured storeroom next to the reference room on the first floor of the library. Over the decades, though, they had been demoted. For the previous fifteen years they had been in the attic on some 'temporary' shelving erected while the building was being redecorated. Like the shelving, the Papers had stayed there undisturbed. Only a catalogue entry witnessed their existence.

Although the building — scheduled for replacement — was Victorian Gothic with a high-pitched roof, retrieving the Papers had cost the middle-aged if reasonably athletic Sims a graze on his head and a bruised elbow. The wounds he had stoically dismissed: not so the desire to know why the sixty-eight-year-old American-born widow of a Ministry of Defence senior official needed the material in the first place.

It went without saying her Ladyship wasn't going to tell him or any other Council employee — not until she was ready to strike. His anxiety became daily and genuinely more acute.

Louella Brasset was the scourge of officialdom: the serene champion of countless inconvenient causes and alleged innocent victims of local bureaucracy. Her purposes and powers were ignored only by the determinedly unwary.

There was a general understanding that anyone in local government who detected Louella engaged in private ombudsman activity had a duty immediately to alert the targeted department. The lady was well aware of this. It explained why she was not sharing her current intentions with harmless George Sims of worthy reputation, being a night school lecturer and a youth club leader. It explained also why harmless George Sims, a constant worrier, was spending most evenings after the library closed studying the Marshford Papers even more assiduously than Lady Brasset did during the days. After all, Louella knew what she was looking for.

To date, and for the life of him, Sims could find nothing that made the Papers valuable or remotely relevant to the affairs of present-day Tophaven.

It followed, of course, if the improvident Randolph Marshford had believed his grandfather's diaries, letters, contracts, bills, tradesmen's circulars, not to mention the most totally unremarkable memorabilia, had been worth anything at all, he would never have willed them to the library in the first place.

The social historians, professional scandalmongers and the simply curious who had examined the Papers when they first became available had evidently shared Randolph's opinion. No one had produced a biography or published the diaries. There had been no learned monographs, no deferential references in doctrinal theses to what might have proved a rich source of mid-nineteenth-century minutiae. There had been nothing in the racier Sunday newspapers: no saucy titbits; no sensations.

Sydney James Marshford, gent. (1797-1869), had been husband, first, to Lucy, and father through that union to Charlotte, Grace, Penelope, Emily, Victoria, Alice, Louise, Alexandra and Beatrice. A year after Lucy's untimely demise in 1867 — she choked on a cherry stone while returning from Goodwood Races — Sydney, then seventy-one, had married Sarah Castle, a spinster of thirty-seven.

Against the odds, in several contexts, Sarah had produced a son, Albert. Her husband praised divine intervention, though if you took the word of a jealous parlourmaid at the time, the second coachman deserved most of the credit.

Through the testimony of his diaries, Sydney had been a Godfearing man, a loving husband and father, astute in business, rich through his own diligence, a philanthropist, a careful patron of the arts, and a generous local benefactor.

Reading between the lines of those same diaries, other possibly less commendable traits emerged. Sydney had made something approaching a profession out of combining self-righteousness with self-advertisement. He had been strangely—though not apparently improperly—obsessed by womankind, and—this inescapably—he must have been a deeply boring man.

Most of what, by 1860, had become the prosperous Sussex seaside resort of Tophaven had been Marshford family sheep-grazing land at the end of the previous century. Brighton, some miles to the east, had owed its popularity to the Prince Regent. Tophaven, a much later developer, owed everything to the new railway which, in turn, owed everything to Sydney Marshford.

It was Sydney who brought a spur of the iron road across the chalk downs in 1847 when railways were temporarily out of fashion. It was Sydney who had thereby overridden the opposition of other local landowners: most had turned conservationist some time after unwittingly selling Sydney prime parcels of land at what had seemed irresistible prices. And it was Sydney alone who engineered the creation of a whole town on his inherited and acquired acres—albeit a haphazardly arranged development at the outset.

Brighton had been endowed with gracefully plotted Georgian squares and crescents. Tophaven had broken out in rashes of boxy, stuccoed villas, and streets of high, redbrick terraces; the whole, for many years, sadly lacked cohesion.

At first the only plan seemed to have been Sydney's scheme to become as rich as possible as quickly as possible. That he tempered this with lapses into and later regular commitment to showy benevolence was not to do with underlying virtue: it was social ambition. The church, the town hall, the library itself were erected at Sydney's expense. Such sponsoring increased his standing in the county and should have increased the eligibility of his team of daughters.

'My girls are rich in talents if deficient in what passes for beauty: a transient thing, beauty,' he confided in his diary in June 1858 when Beatrice, his youngest, was already eighteen, and not one of the brood married off.

Sydney commissioned Sir Charles Barry to design the church, and Isambard Kingdom Brunel the town hall. Both of them were offered fees too large to turn down but not large enough to justify their producing wholly original work.

The church closely resembles one of Barry's London clubs in the Italianate manner: it was 1856 and for liturgical reasons the architect had long gone off ecclesiastical Gothic.

Predictably, Brunel's town hall—now demolished— looked like nothing so much as a Brunel railway station.

The library was the work of an enthusiastic amateur, the then Archdeacon of Chichester, the cathedral city nearby. He was a friend of Sydney's and one who fancied his capacities as a natural, untutored architect. The man's faith was misplaced, at least in this connection, as George Sims was given to confirming frequently and even vehemently when he injured some part of his anatomy while labouring in the labyrinthine attics and basements.

All three buildings came after the railway and lay to the south-west of the station. The land there, running down to the sea, was taking on the semblance of a homogenous community by the late 1850s. All monuments to Sydney's benevolence and affluence carried plaques with the name of the architect in very small letters, probably at the request of most of them, but with Sydney's name much larger.

It was the plaques that had first put Louella on the scent.

'Archive material may only be photostated under supervision by a member of the staff, Lady Brasset.' The Chief Librarian smiled nervously as he quoted the rule verbatim. 'It's a question of the age of some of our more precious possessions.'

He could hardly believe his luck. She wanted copies. He gazed rapaciously at the small stack of material she had brought down and placed on the counter. The coin-operated copier was just across from where they were standing in the ground-floor lending library.

'In case somebody damages your Gutenberg Bible, you mean?' Louella Brasset smiled back disarmingly.

She was still a handsome woman — middle height; neat, slim figure; taut, tanned skin. Her white hair was cut short and loosely waved. She was wearing an oatmeal cardigan and a darker brown skirt, both in cashmere, under a three-quarter length sheepskin coat. The single row of graded pearls suggested good taste without affecting opulence. Louella didn't tailor her appearance to overawe people like George Sims: her presence did that automatically.

'I'll do these for you myself,' the librarian volunteered. He had only one assistant and she was having her tea. 'How many copies? I'm afraid they're 10p each.'

She opened her handbag. 'Figured you couldn't split a five pound note . . .' She watched the beginnings of a protest to the contrary. In the circumstances Sims would have offered change for the Kohinoor diamond. '. . . so I brought my parking meter statch.' She jangled the contents of a long red purse.

'Very thoughtful.' They moved across to the machine. 'I'm still wondering what particular aspect of Sydney Marshford's life . . .'

'Fascinating man. Real original. I just need one copy of all these. The diary pages have paper markers. Oh, and the letters . . . How about I feed the money in if you'll handle the delicate part? Want to watch those bindings.'

He was too busy memorizing dates — there were no page numbers in the diaries — to make more than noises of acknowledgement.

'Say, if you're interested, you can make copies for yourself. Or just keep the markers in.'

Sims looked up with undisguised admiration. You had to face it, she was a good loser.

Louella accepted the show of undeserved homage. She had spent the previous hour upstairs hand-copying the letter and the short diary entries she really needed. The originals were still in the reference room.

She had toyed with simply taking the letter. No one had shown any interest in it for fifty years. No one was going to miss one tiny letter at this stage. Then she had changed her mind. Her late husband had been a lifelong exponent of the rule of law. There had to be standards. More to the point, having to own up to pinching library property could land you in court — and court was where Louella expected to be heading, but strictly on the side of the angels.

She thanked Sims for his help, and tucked the prints into the large envelope she had brought for the purpose. They were copies of things she had chosen almost at random. Only she had made sure they provided no connected commentary on any particular subject. They were aimed at keeping the librarian puzzled for a bit longer.

Today he made no attempt to follow her to the hall where she regularly enjoyed a cigarette before leaving. Usually he went with her and without any finesse tried digging for leads about her Marshford interest. Now she watched him hurry up the stairs clutching his spoils and even before she had left the lending library. He was in pretty good shape too: took the steps two at a time.

Lady Brasset took a last deep draw on the nearly smoked cigarette and stamped it out. Then she got into her Austin Metro and drove it out of the library car park: she never smoked when driving. She turned right at the next corner along the Parade, and left at the T-junction shortly after. This brought her out on to the Esplanade.

It was nearly five o'clock and the mid-November night was closing in. She would still be in time to catch Cynthia before she left the college. The two discoveries were much too important to relegate to a mere phone call. Louella Brasset had a strong sense of occasion. Anyway, Cynthia seemed to be out most evenings: she never really said where. Could be the reference to the lease—the Trings' lease—didn't mean anything. It was worth a try though: let the lawyers figure it.

The route took her past the pier. It was still intact, not like the one at Bognor Regis just up the coast. It sprang from the western end of the wide promenade that paralleled the road on the seaward side.

In summer, along here, there were flags and fairy lights and deckchairs and children in swimsuits and harassed mothers in Marks & Spencer sundresses. Now there were just a few old ladies exercising dogs. Everything was put away, the ice-cream kiosks shut up, the pier closed for the winter, the children's roundabout in the old bandstand battened and canvassed till spring.

There was life still on the other side of the road—shops just closing, pubs just opening at the pier end—and the old Embassy cinema that had managed to survive without becoming a Bingo palace. There were free Monday matinees for pensioners, transport provided if required. Louella had organized that herself—after a battle with the penny-pinching Council. There weren't as many takers as there should be, after all her trouble. People ought to be more appreciative: she was strong on obligation.

The two star Prince Regent Hotel was on the next corner. It was a favourite of Louella's: original double-bow windows rising through three floors—and with pepper-pot tops. The upper floors had jutting balconies with delicate, wrought-iron balustrades. It had been a private home once, the principal house in the tiny eighteenth-century village of South Wallerton—now the unidentified eastern edge of railway age Tophaven.

The Prince Regent was a statutory listed historic building—Grade Two and starred. You'd need more than money and influence to get that knocked down. Louella nodded confidently at the thought. The starred listing had been mostly due to her vigilance years ago.

After the hotel came two guest-houses, a nearly anonymous betting shop, a not very serious retailer of fishing tackle who also sold cut flowers, and a quite large monumental mason's yard with rows of assorted virgin gravestones, their sombre impact lightened by a few bird baths and one immense ornamental well. The bogus well had been there for years. Live sea-gulls regularly perched around it, lending a kind of authenticity while unfairly detracting a bit from the bird baths.

It was here the Esplanade turned sharp left and headed inland, becoming an unglamorous main road. Louella didn't follow it. Instead she drove straight on into Sandy Lane—a rutted, narrow way that ran beside the seashore unflanked by a promenade. The only indications of civic interest were a cul-de-sac sign and a peeling street nameplate that had obviously not been included the last time Tophaven had renewed such things.

The lane ran for three hundred yards before ending with a farm gate, fencing, and a homemade no parking sign. Beyond was a meadow—a caravan site in summer, but empty now except for four threadbare beach donkeys leaning over the gate waiting for something to happen.

There were three buildings set back at uneven intervals along the way.

The Beachcomber Hotel was nearest to the main road but still too far from the town centre and the march of progress to be a paying proposition. With sixteen rooms, one with private bath, it was the heavily mortgaged and partly modernized property of the nearly bankrupt Mostyn and Esta Daws. Louella drove past the miserable garden in front of the whitewashed building with its jumble of gables and unbalanced annexes added in a more prosperous era. The Daws she considered targets for pity and charity—she more than he: he being a basic fool.

Next came a pair of semi-detached houses called Three Winds and South View. Typical, mid-'thirties seaside villas—flat-roofed, steel-framed windows, pebble-dash rendered—they nearly fronted the roadway. The speculative builder who put them up had hoped to make a fortune with a hundred similar pairs, but his business had failed along with his plans for the Wallerton Estate.

Three Winds was owned by Commander Nigel Mane, Royal Navy, retired. He was fifty-seven, a widower and jobless. His youngest and unmarried daughter Tracy lived with him. He was hurrying to post a letter at the corner box as Louella drove by. He waved after recognizing the car.

Next door, at South View, no doubt Lancelot Elderberry was tapping out unenduring literature for consumption by that diminishing army of females for whom his romantic novellas provided innocent escape from unimpassioned reality.

Few of Elderberry's readers would have guessed he was an overweight bachelor with personal propensities hugely at variance with those of his dashing heroes. Few of his readers knew he was a man at all. Five *noms de plume* protected his privacy, disguising his formidable output as well as his gender and identity.

Louella, a confidante, approved of his books and their high moral tone. She also approved of Lancelot, even after the incident with the dreadful young man. She continued to believe it had taught Lancelot an enduring lesson. But for her he might have been publicly vilified over something very unsavoury—unjustly, of course, or so she had chosen to believe. She and Lancelot took tea from time to time: he had a marvellous talent to amuse.

Louella was still thinking of the author when further on she turned into the drive of the Round House. Good; there were lights burning still on the upper floor. Cynthia's Cortina Estate was parked outside.

The moon was out now. It cast interesting shadows on the building, then the lights of the Metro swept the whole façade. People were entitled to call it hideous—people without the imagination to figure how it ought to look: how it looked when first built.

Louella hurried up the steps and pushed open one side of the panelled door. She had quite a surprise in store for Cynthia: a double surprise. Her pace was even livelier than usual.

It would have been more symbolic of events to follow if Lady Brasset's step had been funereal; her features composed for tragedy, not joyous tidings.

'Cynthia,' she cried from the stairs, 'it's Louella. Darling, I'm never going to get over this.'

And in a terrible way, she was right.

CHAPTER 2

'Again. Success to Sandy Lane Towers.' Tony Quaint, the fifty-year-old Managing Director of Roxton International Construction, Ltd., raised his nearly empty glass of Château Latour '61, drained it, and hoped for more.

Perhaps there was a brandy coming, or better still, some port first. He was glad now he hadn't refused the third Scotch before lunch. There was no doubt these Arabs meant to do the right thing: just needed instructing on the form.

Quaint knew all about doing the right thing. He had started his career as a regular army officer, switched to public relations, and ended up in the building industry. He had gone to the top of Roxton's more or less from the start. Being married to the Chairman's daughter made up for his lack of background in the industry.

'I am drinking to that.' Sheikh Mhad Alid ben Haban also emptied his glass, doing credit to the wine if not to his religious scruples. Meek by nature—and in appearance when dressed in Western clothes—he looked to his other guest expectantly.

'To Sandy Lane,' murmured Mark Treasure conventionally. The urbane Vice-Chairman and Chief Executive of Grenwood, Phipps and Company, merchant bankers, lingered over the sip he took from his glass. He was again examining the swathes of alternating black and white silk splaying out from high above the table and down the walls.

A perfectly sound Adamesque dining-room in a house not a stone's throw from the Albert Hall, London, had been expensively decorated in this way enduringly to simulate a large and exotic desert tent.

Treasure couldn't rid himself of the impression he was attending a rained-out garden-party.

'Since Seawell Developments are now owning planning permission, you start in earnest tomorrow . . . er . . . Tony?' asked the Sheikh. He regularly pressed his business associates to call him Ali. This helped him to get over his shyness at addressing them by their first names. As the eleventh in the line of the Emir of Abu B'yat's fourteen brothers and half-brothers, he was weighed down with a sense of inferiority. He was not even moderately rich.

Seawell Developments, Ltd. was owned and guaranteed by the Emir. The pale, bearded, twenty-nine-year-old Sheikh Mhad Alid was paid a not very handsome salary to direct it. True, he had the house to live in, an English butler, and several other servants. He had Grenwood, Phipps ultimately overseeing the financial affairs of the company. Best of all, he had avoided an arranged marriage with someone he didn't care for — and who he suspected cared even less for him.

Six months before, the Emir had paid off Ali's debts on condition he gave up power-boat racing. They were not considerable debts by the standards of other families who owned oil wells, nor was power-boating as expensive a hobby as some followed by other members of his own family. Even so, he had been pretty embarrassed financially at the time. Now he was committed to perfecting his English and making Seawell Developments into a viable long-term investment.

Quaint had been watching the butler replenish his glass — not before time and not over-generously. 'Tomorrow is Saturday, Ali,' he said, a touch patronizingly. 'Not that we won't be working weekends on part of the contract.' It depended on what kind of winter was coming. It was a fixed price job and there was an agreed completion date. They could be working Bank Holidays before this one was done. Quaint was well aware of the perils.

After Roxton's had landed the complete contract they had moved on to the back of the site, starting work there a month before official planning permission had come through that morning. There had been financial risk, but it had paid off. They had cleared nearly a whole row of condemned dwellings and laid out trenching and conduits for services to the whole site.

Treasure stirred his coffee. 'Seawell will be doing completions on buying out the existing Sandy Lane buildings now, of course. Shouldn't take long.' He paused. 'Except the lawyers tell me even when you own all the freeholds you'll still have a laggard leaseholder *in situ* for the remaining weeks of a lease.'

'The Round House,' Ali grumbled. 'The leaseholder, a retired holy man. A priest. He won't go until December the twenty-fifth. Christmas Day? It is some religious . . .'

'Quarter Day,' said Treasure, smiling. 'Nothing to do with his being a holy man, as you say. At least, I shouldn't think so. Most leases expire on one of the four Quarter Days . . .'

'Except in this case it's a formality that should have been dealt with ages ago. By the freeholder,' Tony Quaint broke in irritably. 'The owners of all the properties can't wait to take the money and run. Canon Tring—that's his name—he's just being bloody-minded. Got it in for the freeholders . . .'

'The Rackburn & Claremont Insurance Company,' Treasure offered.

'That's right. Doesn't like them or Seawell for some reason.'

'Tring is the only leaseholder involved, I gather,' said the banker. 'The others are freeholders in occupation. Seawell are dealing with the freeholders, of course. In the case of this Round House, that's the insurance company, whom I admit I'd never heard of before. They've tried bribing Canon Tring,' he added.

'To bribe is allowed?' Ali demanded, throwing a meaningful glance at Quaint.

'I was speaking figuratively. The insurance company offered the chap money in compensation for the last weeks of his lease. Perfectly normal and above board. He won't play, though. So now they sell out over his head, and Seawell have to wait for occupation till Christmas.'

'His wife, she teaches girls there. It's a school.'

'So I understand, Ali,' Treasure continued. 'Actually it's a secretarial college.' He had been well briefed, even though the lunch had been arranged at short notice — on a whim of Ali's. It was to celebrate the receipt of formal planning permission from the Tophaven District Council.

The Sandy Lane development was not an especially big project. The first phase called for an investment of just under six million pounds. The site was bounded by the sea frontage to the south, and ran back inland nearly a hundred and fifty yards to the row of abandoned cottages on a side road. Seawell's offer to demolish the cottages and replace them with high standard municipal housing at less than cost, whatever the decision on the rest of the project, had endeared the company to the local authority.

It was no concern of the Council's that it was Quaint's company that would carry the loss on this piece of loaded public benevolence — but it was one of the reasons why Roxton International had been awarded the whole contract by Seawell. Immediately, this involved building a wide, six-storey block of expensive apartments intended for affluent retired people. The block was to include an indoor swimming pool, gymnasium, sauna, hairdresser's, small shopping mall, garage and restaurant at ground and basement levels. There were to be some individual homes bordering the sheltered gardens to the rear, plus two hard tennis courts.

Subject to some minor stipulations, Roxton were also to

be given the contract if and when Seawell got permission to build a marina to the east of the site. The development company already had an option to buy the twenty acres of farm land at the end of Sandy Lane—dispossessing the donkeys.

Altogether, Quaint had good reason to feel content about events so far—even though Tophaven was only a curtain-raiser. Real success depended on Roxton getting contracts for projects in Abu B'yat itself.

Treasure had not been involved in the financial detail. Gerald Head, one of the bank's three Managing Directors, was responsible. It was Head who should have been at today's lunch, except he was in Scotland. Treasure had volunteered to stand in. It had been a good opportunity to show interest. Sheikh Mhad Alid had been flattered—as intended.

The Emir of Abu B'yat had a special regard for Treasure. He trusted the banker implicitly and had charged him with personal responsibility for all the Emirate's financial activities in Europe. In these terms, Tophaven was small beer, but Treasure had kept in touch on the affair from its inception.

He had no very formed opinion of Ali, though having met most of the Emir's close male relatives he considered this one potentially the best of the bunch. A youngish 'retired' speedboat enthusiast with no other known eccentricities was preferable to the alcoholic and the womanizer (brothers number four and seven) who had in turn directed Seawell previously. They had both been recalled by the Emir—a sensibly strict and circumspect Muslim who deplored moral shortcomings in his dependants, especially overt ones.

Had he been the host today the Emir would certainly have countenanced the serving of alcohol for his guests—and disapproved of the parsimonious habits of the butler. Treasure wondered what the Ruler would have made of the 'tenting' installed the year before by brother number seven, apparently to impress a girl-friend. The Emir was a student of European architecture, though it was not a subject he chose to discuss with a European—particularly one as well informed as Treasure.

The banker switched his thoughts to Tony Quaint whom he was meeting for the first time. Roxton was not a company of huge repute. Gerald Head had considered it right enough for the Tophaven contract: hungry enough had been the expression used. Their 'in house' architects were good; Treasure had to admit as much after seeing their designs.

Using a builder with competent staff architects had appealed to Ali: it saved money. Even so, the bank had pressed for the retention of independent quantity surveyors.

There had been no problem with the local authority planners about the development. The town needed the work and the income Sandy Lane Towers would generate. The short British summer no longer provided a traditional living for a small holiday resort. More light industry, more affluent permanent residents and a piece of the booming South Coast yacht marina business: these were the triple aims of the Council and the Tophaven Chamber of Commerce. Seawell Developments had welcome resources and connections.

The problems and delays had been with Whitehall. The Department of the Environment noted Sandy Lane was classified as Green Belt land—latter-day holy ground. Also the Minister had had enough of marinas for the time being: the things seemed to take up more shore than sea. The Minister happened to be a golfer: he was also a nominal Presbyterian who outwardly regarded with suspicion developers who ingratiated themselves with local councils by building municipal housing below cost.

Permission for Sandy Lane Towers had now been grudgingly approved. Outline planning permission for the marina was being held over until the first development was complete.

Treasure thought Seawell had done as well as could be expected—perhaps better. If the Towers project was a success, that would be time enough to see about funding the marina—and to assess the tried capacities of Roxton International. The short-term problem on this Round House, though, he found irritating and somehow evidence of inefficiency. Because the place couldn't be knocked down for two months the whole operation was being delayed into a deep winter start.

'You might have had a go at the retired clergyman yourself,' he remarked to Quaint.

'I have. Went down personally. By appointment. He wasn't about. Bloody typical.' Who could doubt the impending demise of organized Christianity, he implied, when that sort of thing went on. 'His wife saw me instead. At their home. That's not the Round House. Bit of all right, as a matter of fact. The wife, I mean.'

'But she . . .'

'Can't be more than mid-thirties. Second wife, I'd think. Quite bowled me over, I can tell you. Expecting some old biddy . . .'

'Please? What is biddy?' Ali put in, gold pencil poised over a gold-edged pocket notepad. He had kept both by his place through the meal, making entries from time to time.

'Opposite of sweet little chick, smashing bird . . .'

'Or attractive young woman,' offered Treasure more helpfully. 'Biddy is old American for an Irish maidservant. Old biddy means . . .'

'This wife of the holy man—she is Irish?'

'Forget it, Ali,' said Quaint firmly. 'Before I saw her I had a good look at this Round House. Secretarial college is an overstatement. Place is empty. Ground floor at least. Couldn't see upstairs. She said that's all they use now. Running down. Nobody lives there. Just a day school.'

'Is the house actually round?' This was Treasure.

'Sort of. The top floor, anyway. Pretty ghastly place. Proper hodge-podge.'

'Excuse me . . . ?'

'Mess, Ali. Proper mess. I offered her a hundred a week on top of whatever the insurance company would pay. That's if she'd give us possession when planning permission came through.'

'She's not buying this? Perhaps you are not giving enough?'

'It was hardly up to me to offer anything, Ali,' Quaint snorted, twiddling his empty glass, and thinking the Arab wouldn't have asked the question if it had been Seawell money on offer. 'It's a school. They have twelve-week terms. I checked. She admitted they close down for Christmas. Nothing doing there after December tenth. Anyway, I pushed it up to two hundred a week. That was two weeks ago. I was guessing we'd get building clearance about now.'

'Still no sale,' commented the banker. 'D'you think I could have some more coffee, Ali?'

'She pretended to be shocked. She had obligations to her pupils, their parents and so on. How could she fore-shorten their course? — all four of 'em!'

'Are there really only four?' Treasure sounded doubtful.

'That's all. She admitted it when I pressed her. Anyway, she wasn't buying. Couldn't advise her husband to surrender the lease. Matter of principle.' He snorted to indicate principle was not his strong suit. 'Fact is, of course, even if she vacated after the end of term we'd be almost into building industry holidays, and they're effectively two weeks.' There were more snorts as commentary on this probably communist-inspired liberty. 'It's the time between then and now we need. Long-term weather forecast says fine for the next four weeks.'

Treasure knew about the time clauses in the contract. There were to be penalties for late completion, bonuses for an early finish. The official start date had yet to be named. Any extra working time Quaint could win now would be to Roxton's advantage. 'Are the other houses on Sandy Lane ready for demolition?'

Quaint nodded. 'Ali will own the freeholds by Monday. Could have 'em today if he wanted. The hotel on the corner won't be closed till after Christmas. Very generous arrangement for the owner. He still gets his price now. Place is off the main site. We'll be using it as site offices later. Then there's a pair of semi-detached houses. Owners are contracted to give vacant possession seven days after they've got their money.'

'That's the arrangement, Mr Treasure . . . er, Mark,' Ali corrected bashfully. 'When we get building permission we pay. Not before. Our price is over market rate. But they have to go fast, these people.'

'They can all afford to move to the Savoy on what they're getting,' grumbled Quaint. 'Same applies to the hotel people. As for this Round House. Phew! The Seawell price for that is wild.' He caught Treasure's frown. 'Well, it's pretty high. Probably justified in the circumstances. Anyway, if we could have knocked that down and the semis straight away we'd have been well into main foundation work in two weeks. As it is . . .' He shrugged his shoulders.

'And no one lives in the Round House,' Prince Ali repeated innocently—or, at least, without inflection.

'No, they don't,' Quaint replied promptly, made as though to add something, changed his mind and finished his coffee.

*

'If you could drop me on Piccadilly. Opposite the Ritz'll be fine.'

Treasure had given Quaint a lift after lunch: they were in the banker's Rolls. Henry Pink, the chauffeur, had taken the Carriage Road south through Hyde Park.

'No trouble to take you to your office. Berkeley Square, isn't it?' He understood the Mayfair headquarters of Roxton International was little more than a prestige suite. The working offices were south of the river. He supposed it was marginally valuable to Roxton, with its corporate pretensions, to have a West End address. It had impressed Ali, and, more surprisingly Gerald Head from the bank.

Treasure considered such business ploys outmoded and not worth the expense. He took a different view on Rolls-Royce cars.

'I'd as soon walk the last bit.' Quaint was a big man—an inch taller than the six-foot banker and ten years or so his senior: the face was florid and the large frame running to fat. He had spoken earlier of playing Rugby for the Army twenty-five years ago. Now he looked as though the two-hundred-yard length of Berkeley Street was more exercise than he took most days. 'Unless you'd come in for a brandy? Ali was a bit light on the extras. Claret was good.'

'But not much of it. No, I can't stop. Another time, perhaps.' Treasure smiled. His companion had consumed three-quarters of the single claret decanter by himself. 'Butler's possibly converting to Islam.'

'Or on the fiddle. Shifty-looking. Wouldn't trust him with my shopping-list.'

'It may just be Ali's frugality,' Treasure offered charitably. 'Consumables are provided with the house, but I think our young sheikh is kept on a pretty tight budget.'

Quaint glanced sideways at the speaker. 'Er . . .' he hesitated, then seemed to make up his mind . . . 'that was something I wanted a word on, as a matter of fact.' He stopped again, then nodded pointedly at the chauffeur.

'That's all right,' said Treasure quietly. From experience he trusted Henry Pink not to register business confidences—even those he understood. The one that followed he never heard, since Quaint had dropped his voice so low.

'We're paying Ali two hundred thou. Half now, the rest on completion. There's a matching deal on the marina contract.'

'You mean a personal payment?'

Quaint nodded. 'It's above board . . . in a sense. Audit proof, if you follow me. He's got one of those all-purpose consultancy companies in Zürich. They're invoicing us for architectural services.'

'Are they indeed? And it's Ali's company? Nothing to do with Seawell or Abu B'yat?' He thought he knew the answer to this already. If there had been an official Abu B'yat-owned consultancy in Switzerland he would have heard about it.

'It's his private outfit all right. Nothing to prove the connection, though. Sinking fund for a new toy boat, I'd say.'

'That's probably sharply apposite.' Treasure avoided showing his extreme displeasure at the news.

'He told me we'd get detailed invoices. The first one came last week. Very er . . . creative.'

'But nothing in writing between you and Ali?'

'Nothing.'

At least the young sheikh was not as naive as he appeared in at least one important area—even if the fact did him no credit.

'You've told Gerald Head?'

'No. Didn't seem necessary. Didn't affect our getting

the contract.' Quaint had expected to note undisguised doubt on the banker's face. 'Ali raised it after our bid had been accepted.'

Treasure supposed he would have to take the man's word on that. 'And you're telling me now?' They were approaching the Ritz. He raised his voice to speak to the driver. 'Go round Berkeley Square, will you, Henry?'

'Gerald says you're Mr Big with the Emir. If we do the right job in Tophaven, will it put us on the inside track for work in Abu B'yat?'

The car was moving slowly down Dover Street. 'It might, yes.'

'Nothing better than that?'

'A bit better, perhaps. Ali's told you something different?'

'Very different.' Quaint leaned sideways, closer to Treasure. His elbow pressed hard into the wide armrest between them. The camelhair topcoat increased his bulk so that his size and proximity were almost menacing. 'Look, we'll be lucky to break even on Sandy Lane.' This was delivered in a desperate undertone. 'If, if the marina goes through, we'll be better placed to make some sort of profit. Not much. The real pay-off has to come from work we get in the Emirate. There's a new hospital scheduled for next year, an airport, an industrial complex, God knows how many housing projects . . .'

'All subject to the usual tendering.'

'Tendering my foot. Ali's promised if we make sure Tophaven comes in on the nose, including his cut, he can fix it we get twenty million-plus in work out there. In the next three years. His percentage will stay the same.'

'Then it's up to you to decide whether he can deliver.'

'You don't believe he can?' Quaint fell back on to the seat. Now he looked strained and exhausted.

'Honestly, I've no idea. These people can be very inscrutable. I get along fairly well with the Emir. It's still a pretty arm's length relationship.'

'Does Ali rate with him?'

'Higher than any of his other brothers. Not as high as his sons, but they're none of them through with higher education yet. Depending how well he does in London, it's possible Ali could go back as Development Minister in a year or two. That would certainly give him the clout to do what you want.' Quaint made no immediate response. 'Go round the square again, Henry,' Treasure ordered.

'No, driver. Let me off here. Thank you, Mark.'

Pink stopped the car appropriately outside the Barclay Rolls-Royce showroom. He got out and held a rear door open.

'Suppose I should have kept my mouth shut,' muttered Quaint, preparing to leave.

Inwardly Treasure agreed. 'I'll respect the confidence, but with your permission I'll tell Gerald Head what you've told me.' His tone allowed for no option.

The big man nodded. 'But not the Emir?'

Treasure hesitated. 'Not the Emir. If I wanted to change my mind on that I'd tell you in advance.'

'It's just we've got so much riding on this business. A real commercial footing in the Middle East. It's a lifeline. You understand?'

Treasure's instinct was to understand Roxton International had more riding on Ali's promises than was corporately prudent. Aloud he said. 'Seems you've got phase one in the bag. The rest could fall into place. Goodbye.' He held out his hand.

CHAPTER 3

Merchant banks are a dying breed: people have been saying so for more than a century. Rival institutions have grown fat trading on the merchant banker's traditional preserve—notably in the lending and underwriting of venture capital.

But raising the wind through the Treasury, an insurance company, or even a High Street bank will never be quite like borrowing from a Rothschild or a Baring or a Schroder. It's the personal touch.

Cosimo de' Medici had the nuances figured when he got the idea moving in the fifteenth century: he was also right about keeping the scale big—and the riff-raff out.

It's true that not all the banks these days carry the family names of the dynasties that once funded kings and wars (sometimes both sides) and new countries—even new continents.

It was after World War Two that the family bankers—who might be termed the Gentlemen—decided seriously on the good sense of introducing talented outsiders into their folds—people who might be called the Players.

In no time the Players were assimilated and became indistinguishable from the Gentlemen. Equally the Gentlemen became much better Players—proving, or disproving, the adage that heredity is all, whichever conclusion you prefer.

Mark Treasure joined Grenwood, Phipps after Oxford, the Bar and the Harvard Business School. He was made Chief Executive just before his fortieth birthday. He didn't behave like a 'high flier': but he performed like one.

Lord Grenwood, now in his late seventies, is the great-grandson of one of the bank's co-founders. He is non-Executive Chairman because it gives him something to do, keeps him out of his wife's way, and because he is the biggest shareholder. It also sometimes gets him into situations he'd much rather avoid — as at 3.15 p.m. on Friday, November 15, the day Treasure lunched with Prince Mhad Alid and Anthony Quaint.

'Are you sure Mr Treasure's not back yet . . . er . . . my dear?' the aged Peer enquired of his secretary in an agitated stage whisper. The girl, whose name he had forgotten — again — was new, pretty, bright and not at all experienced. She had been chosen — in compliance with Lady Grenwood's secret standing instruction — for possessing all those qualities.

His Lordship had little work for a secretary, but without one he would have felt uncared for and definitely less needed. His wife ensured the job was filled by a succession of young lovelies who would in turn boost his morale until they became bored, and moved along armed with better commercial credentials than before. It was an arrangement that suited all concerned. There was no hanky-panky involved. Her Ladyship would have found hanky-panky tiresome: she knew, also, that it would unnerve her husband.

The present incumbent's name was Jennifer. Her boss was with her in her own office: the door to his was firmly closed. There had been no reason for whispers: the other room was sound-proofed.

'Miss Gaunt, Mr Treasure's secretary, said he'd be here any minute, Lord Grenwood.' Jennifer looked prettily perplexed — something she'd been good at even before attending the Oxford & County Secretarial College: today, though, it wasn't enough.

'Well, Mr Head will have to do. Send for Head.'

'He's in Scotland.'

'Is he? Damnation. I mean bother.'

Jennifer, whose father was a Major-General, smiled, indicating that she was used to strong language.

'I hear you're looking for me.' Treasure appeared from the wide, carpeted corridor.

'My dear chap, thank heaven you've arrived,' muttered the Chairman, literally wringing his hands. 'There's a . . . there's a female in my office.' He paused. His lower jaw moved up and down but no words came. He was ordering the further outrages that had befallen him; his hierarchy of horrors. 'She's American. Name's . . . huh? . . . name's . . .'

'Lady Brasset,' put in Jennifer.

'That's it. Old Jimmy Brasset's widow. Scarcely acquainted, I assure you.' Lord Grenwood paused as though expecting a rebuttal. There was none. He went on. 'Off her chump, I'm afraid. Huh? He wasn't much better. Remember that gaffe he made with . . .' He looked from Treasure to his secretary, then back again. 'No, you wouldn't. Too young. Both of you. That was about knocking things down, too. Huh?'

'This Lady Brasset wants something knocked down?' Treasure was used to helping the thread of Grenwood's discourses to unwind.

'Certainly not. Didn't I tell you? Preserved. Not knocked down. Absolute opposite, my dear fellow. Huh? Didn't get her drift at all to start with. Not sure I've got it now.' He blew his nose loudly before reverting to his still muffled narrative. 'I ask you, what can you do about a house in Tophaven? Ghastly place, anyway. Whole town should be knocked down.'

'This is to do with the Sandy Lane development?'

Grenwood lifted both arms in a gesture of astonishment and relief. 'Got it in one, Mark. That's the place she said. Sandy Lane. Knew you'd have the facts. Assuming there were any. Been stalling her till you got here.' He looked at his watch. 'Where've you been? Never mind. None of my business. Sorry I asked. Huh? It's just that you're usually back earlier. Miss Gaunt said . . .'

'I was delayed. D'you want me to deal with Lady Brasset?' — whatever that might involve.

The Chairman nodded vigorously. 'Better go back in. Said I needed a wash. She'll think I've fallen down the plughole. Or gone home. No more than she deserves.' He paused before the door of his office, turning about to face Treasure again. 'Knew her husband, you see. Very slightly. Not a chap you'd cultivate. Sent up a message an hour ago. Her, not him. He's dead . . . Well, you know that. Had to see me. Matter of life or death. What could we do, Mark? She was waiting in there after lunch. Making phone calls!'

The 'we' was evidently meant to include and in some way excuse Jennifer. Treasure guessed she had admitted the unwelcome lady without authorization. Even so, if the visitor had no appointment she should have been kept down in reception until whoever it was she wanted to see had personally approved her being let loose.

So much for the bank's strengthened security arrangements if they could be bypassed by elderly ladies, Treasure mused. This was before he had met Louella.

'Proof positive the Round House was designed by Sir John Soane in 1793, and probably executed by William Butterfield in 1841. That makes it a principal work by two principal architects. Possibly unique. How about that?' Lady Brasset inhaled deeply on her cigarette.

She had removed neither the dark ranch mink coat nor the matching Cossack-style hat. The coat was open and arranged carelessly to set off the white wool dress with the gold metallic thread. She sat forward and upright, the expression alert, the voice controlled and assured. The long cigarette-holder she used like a conjuror's baton with smoke effects.

Treasure considered the quality of a Hepplewhite leather wing chair was seldom challenged by an occupant. On this occasion the lady was more than a match: she even had better legs.

There were four such chairs set around the drum table across the room from Grenwood's imposing partners' desk. Treasure guessed it had been Lady Brasset who had chosen to sit at the table rather than risk any attempt by Grenwood to dominate from the business side of that desk.

'Soane? Soane? Did he design . . .' His Lordship's voice faltered hopefully from the depths of his own chair.

'The Bank of England, Berty,' put in the lady. 'Even you ought to know that, darling. The English surely do their geniuses too little honour. Still, there are compensating virtues in your case, my sweet.'

The easy intimacy that governed Lady Brasset's relationship with Grenwood was entirely unmatched by Grenwood's nervousness in the presence of Lady Brasset.

'Soane's Bank was replaced. The style of the present one's similar, though,' Treasure offered. 'Lady Brasset's right. Soane was a genius. Probably the most original architect of his time.'

'Eighteen er . . .'

'Seventeen fifty-three to eighteen thirty-seven, Berty,' Louella prompted.

'His interiors were better than his exteriors, though.' This was Treasure again.

'John Nash for outside. John Soane for in. Isn't that right, Mark. I may call you Mark? You know the Soane Museum?'

He nodded. 'In Lincoln's Inn Fields. His own home. And it fuels the adage you quoted.'

'I was there this morning. The façade's better than you

think. It needs studying. The whole place is the most compact temple to culture and the visual arts I guess I know. Makes the Frick in New York look unwieldy, with a lot less to see. And that's just a town house, too.'

'They're both nice,' Treasure added in the cause of good Anglo-American relations.

'Agreed. The lady librarian at the Soane was just peachy. She let me handle their own copy of *Sketches in Architecture*. That's Soane's 1793 book. Huge thing. Plates Thirty and Thirty-one show the Round House. Just like the letter says.'

'I find it curious that a work of distinction . . .'

'Hasn't been spotted, Mark? Listed? Protected?' She interrupted in a tone less outraged than expected. 'Isn't it the truth? But it's fallen on hard times. OK, it's a Soane building. The chances are the outside never was its strongest feature. Right now, with all the added bits, it looks like a roughly circular workshop with a flattish kind of lighthouse pushing up through the middle. It's an eyesore. It's why the guy from the local authority took one look and never went inside.'

'You mean it was checked?'

'A few years back. I've seen the report. It just says "post 1840, extended 1941" and that's it. He never looked inside. Not that it would have made a deal of difference. What the Navy did to it in the war was rape it.'

'But buildings were usually put back . . .'

Louella shook her head. 'Not this one. They added bits on when it became a WRNS secretarial school, and a secretarial college is what it stayed after the war. Custom built, you might say. Lot of the plastering was knocked about. Some of the decoration got boxed in. Still is. There's an inside colonnade that's a honey.' She was feeding Treasure's interest. 'And that's only the half. It's all there for the uncovering. Resurrecting.'

'But nobody's troubled because functionally the place suited.'

'That's about it. Canon Tring, sweet old man. Guess his family's owned the lease since the Flood. Place was sub-let in 1946 when the Navy handed it back . . .'

'Sub-let to whoever started the secretarial college?'

'Right. Two ex-Wren officers. They needed it exactly the way it was. Might have closed three years back when they retired.'

'Except Mrs Tring, your friend, decided to keep it going herself.'

'She'd been a competent secretary. Married to a man a hell of a lot older than herself. Figure she was bored. And you don't exactly live like a Cardinal on a Church of England pension. The Canon was vice-principal of some theological college.'

'Does the Canon have a private income?'

'Some. I guess not much. The school was to provide the little extras. Trouble is, it hasn't paid.'

'So Mrs Tring hasn't been spending a lot putting the Round House back to its original glory?'

'Tell you the truth, Cynthia isn't exactly an architectural buff. Also, you have to know the lease reverts to the freeholders this Christmas . . .'

'So you can hardly blame her for taking no action. At least in that connection.' Treasure nevertheless had ample evidence Mrs Tring was every bit as redoubtable as Lady Brasset when it came to defending the house to the last ditch. Still, it seemed her reasons were bedded in loyalty to her friend rather than in aesthetics: at least he could now account for her obduracy. He excused himself for a few moments to telephone his secretary from the outer office. When he returned Lord Grenwood was speaking.

'I really don't understand your part in all this, Louella.' It was the first time the older man had addressed his visitor by her first name. 'And I still don't know what you expect us to do. Huh?'

'I've told you once, Berty. Heaven's sakes . . .'

'If I could summarize, Lady Brasset?' Treasure cut in. He was under no illusions about the purpose of her visit. She wanted an assurance. He was ready to give it to her, but he needed information before he could give it unreservedly. Reiterating the facts for Lord Grenwood would fill the time while his secretary did some devilling.

'Go ahead, Mark.' She took out another cigarette and waited for Grenwood to light it.

'Earlier this year you read about the Sandy Lane development in your local paper. Long before that you thought the Round House was special. You've already tried to get the local authority to list it with the DoE, the Department of the Environment, as a building of historic value . . .'

'But no one was buying,' Louella interrupted. 'It wasn't finished till 1841 so it didn't get automatic listing like everything built before 1840.'

'And the local preservation group wasn't interested, nor the Georgian Group . . .'

'It isn't strictly Georgian.'

'Quite. And the Society for the Protection of Ancient Buildings . . .'

'Helpful, and looking into it . . .'

'But as yet . . .'

'I'm going there next.' She glanced at her watch. Grenwood looked encouraged.

'So you decided to do your own researches. Delved into the Marshford Papers.'

'Marshford built the town.'

'And is known to have been a snob about architects.'

'He liked getting top names at beginner's prices.'

'But he didn't care or know too much about design . . .'

'Just so long as he got a name for the plaque.'

'You say there's no plaque on the Round House but it was never intended as a public building. He built it as a small private school for girls.'

'Young ladies. And who could blame him with nine of his own to educate . . .'

'Leasing it to a Miss Darlington.' Treasure ignored the interpolation. 'She founded the Darlington Academy for the Daughters of Gentlemen. It survived till 1939.'

'It was just a while before Sydney Marshford became a railway baron, but not before he knew there'd soon be a demand for that kind of place.'

'He was probably aiming to get his daughters educated at a cut price. I see that.' Treasure smiled.

'Got nine girls out of sight and hearing for a good part of the day,' said Louella pointedly. 'And rid his house of governesses who bothered his wife socially. Says so in his diary. He also had something going with that Miss Darlington. Cheated on his wife, Berty. That's what I think.' She wagged her head at Grenwood, who wagged back with less certainty.

'It's apparent, from what you've read, he believed the Academy had to be housed in a superior sort of building. Something that reflected refinement . . .'

'That's it, Mark. Not a schoolhouse. Something graceful but not over-large. In those days education for girls didn't extend beyond the basics. They didn't need much space or apparatus. Just a piano and some needlework frames. Shocking, really.' She seemed to address this remark to Grenwood who looked shamed and somehow guilty.

'You think this was Marshford's first venture into patronage of architecture,' Treasure pressed. 'And whatever his later ploys, this time he opted for a young man. The W.B. referred to in the diary . . .'

'Almost certainly William Butterfield,' Lady Brasset interjected quickly.

'Irritating of diarists only to use initials. Anyway, Butterfield, or whoever it was, doesn't satisfy Marshford with his first three submissions. But it's Marshford who suggests he asks Sir J.S. if he can copy an old plan in his book *Sketches in Architecture*, published 1793.'

'So there can't be any doubt that Sir J.S. was John Soane.'

'I agree, Lady Brasset.'

'Not very original title. *Sketches in Architecture*,' observed Grenwood gratuitously.

'The sketches were original,' Louella retorted briskly.

'You say the copy letter you found from Marshford to W.B. sets out the situation clearly. W.B. must have had to swallow a lot of pride. He was accepting congratulations for copying a cast-off design.'

Lady Brasset bridled visibly. 'Just remember Butterfield was twenty-two at the time. Probably no patrons, no important buildings to his credit. The Round House was an adaptation, not just a copy . . .'

'And young W.B. with his way to make took the soft option. It's credible.' Treasure responded. 'And if it was Butterfield . . .'

'Later the acknowledged leader of the Gothic Revival. Architect of Keble College, Oxford . . .'

'Keble!' exclaimed Grenwood. 'All red brick, like a railway station. Nobody liked . . .'

'. . . If he and Soane collaborated on a building —' Louella totally ignored his Lordship — 'and if that building's still standing, it's probably, almost certainly, unique.'

'Collaboration's a bit strong.' Treasure smiled. 'Soane was dead two years before you say the place was started.' He paused. 'Pity you don't have that letter handy.'

'Darned thing. Comes of trying to be too clever. Went to all the trouble of copying it by hand, then left it in the library. Must have done. Went back after seeing Cynthia

Tring. Place was closed. Getting old, that's my problem.'

'Not at all,' Treasure offered gallantly. 'We all do these things.'

'I'm always forgetting things,' put in Grenwood: nobody disagreed.

'But the original copy letter's safe with the Marshford Papers,' said Treasure. Lady Brasset nodded, aware that her own copy could be there with it but on top of the pile, signalling its importance. It all depended on whether Sims bothered to go through what she had left on the desk: whether he had been content with the stuff she'd fed him.

There was no other explanation she could think of for what she had done. Cynthia's desk had been covered in papers as usual. At first they had thought she had put the copy letter down there during her excited arrival.

Now she wished she had delayed leaving Tophaven till the library re-opened. It had become clear here at the bank and earlier at the DoE that her story lacked credibility without that key document. Again she racked her brain about where else she might have left it—who else she might ring . . .

'Pity Marshford didn't include the whole salutation in the copy.' Treasure broke into her silent recriminations. ' "Dear Butterfield" would have been very satisfactory.'

'It was a while before carbon paper or copying machines. I guess making copies of anything was a chore. Later Marshford had a clerk. Several clerks.'

'And there's nothing turned up at the Soane Museum to suggest Soane wrote to Butterfield in 1836?'

'Not so far, Mark. Maybe there was no correspondence. It could have been done verbally. Butterfield could have called on Soane at Lincoln's Inn Fields. Soane was an old and important man. Maybe an assistant handled the whole thing for him—once he'd given his OK. Butterfield wouldn't have been keeping records of his correspondence at twenty-two years of age. The facts are . . .'

There was a knock on the door. Miss Gaunt, Treasure's staid and resourceful secretary, entered quietly. She handed her employer a folded, typewritten note, and, without acknowledging the presence of the others, left as quietly as she had arrived.

'The facts are,' Treasure repeated after scanning the note, 'without much doubt the Round House is based on a Soane design adapted after his death by someone else, possibly Butterfield. On the strength of that, Lady Brasset, you want our word we'll do everything in our power to see nobody demolishes the building over this week-end, nor before the DoE inspector visits the site next week as promised.' He paused. 'You have our word. I'm sure Lord Grenwood will confirm that.'

His Lordship sat up looking first startled, then stern. 'Indubitably,' he pronounced. 'Wouldn't think of doing anything else,' he added with the assurance of a man who had studied every nuance.

Five minutes later Louella had left. Treasure returned to the Chairman's office after seeing her off the premises.

'You handled that brilliantly, Mark,' said the old man, now securely installed behind his desk. 'Like some tea? Won't take a moment for Fiona—' he consulted the notepad before him—'I mean Jennifer to get some.'

Treasure shook his head, and walked over to a window. It was raining outside. 'She seemed happy enough. The thing's not our business, really. Anyway, since Canon Tring won't give up his lease till Christmas, she's quite mistaken in thinking the developers could knock down the house now. She'd been scared by those reports of buildings demolished on the eve of preservation orders being served. Understandable, I suppose.'

'You gave her peace of mind. Huh? Heartening she came to me . . . er, us, in the circumstances. Got the names of all the companies involved—Seawell and . . .

and Roxton, is it? Didn't trust the others. Said so before you came in.' Lord Grenwood looked around the large office for fear of interlopers before adding: 'Between you and me, she and I had a mild flirtation once. Years ago. Country house weekend stuff. Perfectly harmless, really, but her ghastly husband twigged it. No end of a fuss. Far more than she warranted . . . I think.' He had hesitated, the light of reminiscing in his eyes. 'Fine figure of a woman still. Huh?'

'Certainly.' Treasure smiled and dropped into a chair, his expression indicating preoccupation with matters more pressing. 'Afraid I shan't be bringing much peace of mind to Sheikh Mhad Alid when I ring him in a minute. If the lady's theory holds up, the whole development could be in jeopardy. Seawell have no certificate of immunity.'

'From interfering busybodies? Is there such a thing?'

'Very much so. Result of the conservation movement getting so powerful. Till recently property developers had a justifiable complaint. A developer gets building approval. Plans reach the expensive stage. Along comes a conservation group demanding last-minute spot-listing for an historic pile on the site. If the DoE agrees, the building's listed. End of development. Or else plans have to be curtailed, altered . . .'

'But you mentioned this immunity business . . .'

'That's the way things were. Nowadays the development company can apply for a certificate of immunity. Once granted, it means no existing building on the site will be given statutory protection for a period of five years. Much fairer. The builder still has to get planning permission, of course.'

'Which you said our Arab friends got this morning.'

'Mmm. And with a certificate of immunity it wouldn't matter if Lady Brasset had discovered Inigo Jones built the Round House. Trouble is, they never applied for one.

Miss Gaunt rang Seawell while we were talking. They're vulnerable as hell. I gather the building is slap in the middle of the site. It's got to come down.'

'What if the DoE says it's to stay up, dear boy? Government interferes in everything these days. They'll be listing Odeon cinemas next.'

'They have, as a matter of fact.'

'Good God. So what's the criterion?'

'In this case it'll be broadly "a principal work by a principal architect". The one Lady Brasset quoted.'

'So if this Soane chap . . . ?'

'A copy of a Soane design wouldn't qualify, unless it was remarkably handsome. This one evidently isn't. But if it's by Butterfield.' Treasure shrugged. 'It'll still depend on the quality. There are plenty of good buildings of his about. Churches mostly.'

'Mark, aren't you involved in the National Trust or something?'

'Or something. Yes.' Treasure nodded. He was on the council of a charity pledged to protect historic churches.

'There you are then,' said Grenwood confidently. 'This is right up your street. Tell at a glance the place isn't worth preserving. Or the opposite, I suppose,' he added without enthusiasm. 'I mean, shouldn't you take a look? Your chum the Emir might be much obliged. Huh?'

Treasure had been thinking on similar lines.

CHAPTER 4

'You were the gentleman whose secretary . . .'

'I'm sorry?' Treasure had difficulty catching the whispered words.

The mousy woman behind the reception desk at the Beachcomber Hotel, Tophaven, reddened and tried

again. 'You were the gentleman whose secretary rang this
afternoon. Mr . . .'

'Treasure. That's it.' At first glance he'd put her at
forty: now he thought a faded thirty.

There had been one other car in the drive; a red
Porsche, which had seemed as much out of place as the
Rolls.

The main hall was larger than he had expected—a
nearly empty square with archways leading off to left and
right. The reception desk was on the side opposite the
main entrance, with a wide staircase to the right. There
were some basketwork chairs and glass-topped tables.
Carpet in serviceable mottled green ran in all directions.
The ubiquitous flock wallpaper was also green.

There was background music, something Treasure
deplored on principle, made worse because it was Bach.
Doubtless the management aimed to prove it was
cultured—but succeeded only in establishing it was
doubly perverted.

The woman was fumbling with a sheaf of registration
cards. She had extracted them en bloc from a wooden
slotted contrivance. She pushed a lank strand of hair
from her eyes. 'If you wouldn't mind—' She could tell
from his expression she was mumbling again—'wouldn't
mind,' she repeated at the top of her voice, 'filling in . . .
Oh dear!' Most of the forms had slipped from her grasp
and scattered on the floor in front of the banker. 'Please
don't trouble . . . Thank you very much . . . Sorry . . . So
sorry . . . Oh Lord!' She had nearly dropped them all
again. She handed him back one of the cards he had
picked up.

'Still only . . .' She cleared her throat. 'Still only the
single booking? You'll be sleeping alone in the double
room.' Her effort to achieve audibility provided the
statement with the resonance of a station platform
announcement. 'I mean . . .'

'Afraid so. My wife's in New York. Long way to come for the weekend.' He wondered why the British troubled with such feeble jocosities on occasions like this.

'Did your secretary explain . . . EXPLAIN—' she improved the volume—'we have to charge the double rate, less the breakfast charge, that is?'

'She did, yes,' he lied. Miss Gaunt would not have wasted his time on such trivia. 'I wanted the private bathroom, you see.'

The only three star hotel in Tophaven had been full: a bird-watchers' conference. The Prince Regent, a more modest establishment, was closed for redecoration. In any case his business was here in Sandy Lane. It was only for one night.

He had come down almost on impulse, driving himself. He could have waited till morning: in fact he liked being at the seaside whatever the time of year.

'The room has a sea view?'

'Oh yes.' It was her first immediately audible offering—and fully assured: did he think he was in Leamington Spa? 'It's a very nice room. Pity your wife . . .' As she spoke she absently allowed the ballpoint pen she was thrusting at him to trace a line over the back of his hand. She drew in her breath: her whole body froze in horror.

'Well, at least we know it works,' observed Treasure lightly, while trying without success to rub out the mark. He took the pen gingerly.

'Shocking waste of the bridal suite. Bet you get offers, even without breakfast. 'Evening, Mrs Daws. Sorry I'm late. Meeting still on? Shall I do reception or bar? 'Evening Mr . . . Oh! Mr Treasure. We've got the carriage trade tonight!'

The tall, lissom girl had long jet-black hair: when she looked up from reading the registration card her eyes seemed nearly as dark.

She wore dangling gold hoop ear-rings, no make-up, a red cotton shirt, tight blue jeans, and, it appeared, nothing much else. She was about twenty. The surprised glance at the banker quickly blossomed into cool appraisal. It then ripened into an expression he believed was calculated to disturb: anyway, it did—agreeably so—though he steeled himself not to acknowledge the fact.

This much registered in the few seconds it had taken for the girl to appear from behind Treasure, duck under the reception desk flap, and take up position beside the little dowd he now knew was the owner's wife.

'Tracy, I don't think you should . . .'

'Be so forward with the guests, Mrs Daws? I know. I only do it to the dishy ones, Mr Treasure.' She looked him steadily in the eyes. 'Have you had dinner, sir?' She gave an obsequious bob, fluttering her eyelashes.

'On the way down, thanks. I'm glad I was in time for the cabaret.'

The girl stiffened, ran her hands, palms outwards, up the sides of her body, then flung them high in the air. 'Olé!' she cried, snapping her fingers. She held the provocative pose for a second, then relaxed. 'That's it for tonight. Two shows on Saturdays.'

'I can't wait.'

'You are terrible, Tracy,' mumbled Mrs Daws before disappearing into an office at the back.

'Which means I'm in charge till she gets over her embarrassment. I'll show you your room. You're married to Molly Forbes, aren't you? Mrs Tring said you were. How blissy. I think she's marvellous.'

The girl snatched a key, ducked under the flap again, grasped Treasure's case and led the way to the stairs.

'Bar and dining-room through there,' she called over her shoulder, pointing to the archway on the right. 'Residents' lounge and sun loggia and boring view of the esplanade on the other side. Furniture's a bit thinned out in places. They're closing down soon. No lift and you're on the second floor, but it is the best room.'

'I was lucky to get it at short notice.' They both chuckled. He had yet to spy another guest. 'You don't have to carry my bag, you know.'

'Part of the inclusive service. No tipping allowed either. Also it's good for my deportment — and your male chauvinist residuals.'

'Then you should balance it on your head and give us both the promised benefits.'

She did, holding the bag with both hands. She turned around, ascending the next half flight backwards ahead of him. 'I deduce you're a bottom man,' she chided, but staring resolutely on a plane a foot above his head.

'And you're entitled to your erogenous if erroneous opinions. You're a model or an actress?'

'I'm Tracy Mane from next door. Part time bar-keep and receptionist at the 'ole Beachcomber. Drop-out from English Lit. at Sussex University. Currently shorthand and typing course at the Round House up the road. Hopefully heading for acting school in New York city in January.'

'Good for you, except that's a tiresome misuse of the word hopefully — even for an English drop-out.'

She poked a tongue at him. 'Pedant. Exactly like my father.' They had reached the second floor. She lowered the case.

'I take that as a compliment. It also introduces a seemly element into our relationship which it has so far lacked.'

'You mean you don't like me chatting you up.' Treasure winced. 'OK, flirting with you. Or else you don't like girls.'

'I'm inordinately fond of girls. One in particular. I married her.'

'Ouch!' Tracy unlocked a door and led into the room.

She dropped the bag, pulled the curtains and did a pirouette in the centre of the floor. 'Like it?'

He nodded. The place had been modernized fairly recently. It had the standard ready-built fitments of the kind that made it difficult to distinguish one lesser hotel room from another.

'Bathroom's through there. Shall I check the mattress?'

'That won't be necess . . .' He was too late. She had taken a backward leap on to the double bed and was lying in the middle of it, arms behind her head.

'Very commodious, as Mrs Daws would say.' She laughed, 'D'you feel compromised?'

'Not with the door open.'

'Aha! There's no one else on this floor.'

'Then I still don't feel compromised. If you're that desperate you could always try screaming.' He began unpacking the few things in his bag, purposely unconcerned.

'You're a cool one. Are all merchant bankers like you?'

'They're often less individual than some part-time hotel receptionists I've come across. So you know I'm a merchant banker.'

'*The* merchant banker. The one Lady Brasset saw this afternoon. You don't think I'd be offering free ravages to passing commercial travellers do you? Take me! Take me!' she cried melodramatically, kneeling up on the bed, waving clasped hands before her. 'Take me, but please pay my Daddy the money for the house.'

'I see.' Treasure swung out the chair from the dressing-table-cum-writing desk and sat in it, facing Tracy. 'So before I take advantage of your generous terms . . .'

'Which you're not going to because you're not doddering enough — or starved enough . . .'

'Or daft enough to take you seriously.'

'You should, though. I'd do anything, absolutely anything, not to have Daddy disappointed.'

'About the sale of your house to Seawell Developments? Hang on to your virtue. So far as I know he'll have his cheque shortly.'

'You sure? Oh God, are you sure?'

'Could be tomorrow.' He was fairly certain all the conveyancing had been pushed through that afternoon. The Rackburn & Claremont he knew had been paid off already. 'Tell me how you know Lady Brasset came to see me.'

'Easy. She rang Cynthia Tring from the Society for the Preservation of Ancient Buildings . . .'

'Protection, actually.'

'All right, Protection. Cynthia happened to be out. I took the call. I had to do some measuring for Lady Brasset. One of the rooms. Cynthia runs the secretarial college. What's left of it. There's only four of us, but she's insisting we're allowed to finish our course.'

'Before Christmas?'

'Mmm. That's when the house is supposed to come down, isn't it? Except Lady Brasset said it's going to be officially preserved or something.'

'Protected. She's applying for it to be listed.'

'Which means it can't be knocked down.'

'Not necessarily.'

'But it could? And that could mean no development after all. That's what Daddy thinks, and Mr Daws, and Lancelot Elderberry—he's the gay old cuddles who lives next door to us. They all think Lady Brasset's crazy. It's why they're meeting downstairs now. Council of War, with Denis Pitty. He's the lawyer who acts for everybody. Is that why you're here? Lady Brasset says you've promised there'll be no demolition till the Government have decided.'

Treasure paused before replying. 'Nothing Lady Brasset has done or is doing is likely to affect anything but the Round House. I'll be glad to tell your father and the others if you like.'

'Please.' Tracy quickly got up from the bed.

Treasure reasoned Ali couldn't have changed his mind since their conversation on the telephone at four. When first told of Louella's machinations the Arab was certain the whole development would have to be abandoned, that there was no point in buying the freeholds. Seawell having no certificate of immunity, he agonized, had been a piece of gross negligence for which he was responsible. He had predicted the Emir would disown as well as fire him — or worse.

The banker had dispelled most of the despondency. It wasn't certain the Round House would get a listing, and if it did, it might not be a high enough listing to make it sacrosanct. Failure to apply for a certificate of immunity had clearly been an oversight: without doubt a certificate would have been issued if it had been applied for at the proper time. The powers that be took account of such things.

If the worst happened, the Round House might somehow be 'built into' the development. Meantime, ownership and evidence of intention counting for a good deal in British law, Treasure advised completion of all conveyances.

It was then that the banker had definitely promised to go himself to see the Round House next day in return for a promise from Ali that no attempt would be made to destroy the place. If, as Treasure suspected, the building had little aesthetic merit, he committed himself quickly to bring pressure to bear to have Lady Brasset's intervention quashed.

Ali had been hugely encouraged by the last intention. He had asked how big the bribes would be. Treasure had answered briskly that merchant bankers didn't bribe people: they just knew the right people to approach when requiring the removal of unnecessary obstacles.

The banker hadn't mentioned he also had it in mind to meet Cynthia Tring—to see what could be done on the subject of the lease.

The fact of the matter was, it pleased Treasure to accept a complicated challenge which seemed beyond the capacities of others. A resolute individual could solve problems of the kind presented more quickly and efficiently than a whole raft of corporations and lawyers. He had not forgotten he was due to visit Abu B'yat shortly. How he came to straighten out a little local difficulty in Tophaven would make amusing small talk with the Emir.

'Mr Treasure, this is my father, Nigel Mane. Daddy, this is Mark Treasure. I just left his bed.'

'How very nice for you, my dear. How d'you do, Mr Treasure. Trouble is, I'm as unshockable as Tracy's unbelievable. What'll you have?'

Commander Mane had detached himself from the group of people around the tiny bar counter as Treasure entered. He was a big man, bronzed, muscular and athletic-looking, with a strong handshake to match. While Tracy poured the whisky Treasure asked for, from behind the bar, her father started introducing him to the others.

'You haven't met Mostyn Daws? Mine host, as you might say. Owns the place.'

'But not for much longer, thank the Lord. That's if Tracy here got you right.' Tracy had come down ahead of Treasure. 'Pleased to meet you, squire. Sorry I wasn't around when you arrived. Room OK? Tracy did the honours all right, did she? All the comforts of home? Eh? Eh?'

Treasure shook hands. He didn't like much about Daws—not his greased down hair, his blazer with the bogus-looking crest, the overgrown handle-bar moustache, the way the fellow leered at Tracy, alluded to her as though she weren't present *and* addressed him by his least favourite fawning salutation. He felt sorry for Mrs Daws.

'Met the wife, did you? Tracy said so. When you arrived?' Daws went on with his ceaseless interrogation as Commander Mane tried to introduce the others. 'Frightened little thing, I expect you thought? Eh? Right too, squire. Wasn't like that when we came here. Oh no. Eight years ago. Three years after we were married, that was. No, I tell a lie. It was four. Tophaven's done that to her. Tophaven.' Perhaps it had done something to Daws as well. 'Full of the old upwards and onwards, then we were. I still am, of course, but it's done for Esta. Oh dear me, yes.' Head and eyebrows lifted heavenwards in despair. 'Mortgaged this place thanks to a bit of money Esta came by. Put with mine, of course. Called the Sea View in those days. I ask you?'

'Quite so,' replied Treasure, hoping for rescue. He stared about the bar. The decor, presumably altered after the change of ownership, did little unmistakably to evoke the new name as opposed to the old. The bit of driftwood attached to one wall, and the short length of tarred fishing net over the entrance to the dining-room constituted the only likely testimony to change: they could hardly be adjudged evidence of a metamorphosis. One could as easily come upon driftwood while earnestly seaviewing as stumble over discarded nets while idly beachcombing.

'Escaping from the rat race, we were, squire.' So they went beachcombing instead: the diatribe seemed unstoppable. 'I was assistant area sales supervisor with DDH—you know, the pet food people? One day I said to Esta, "This isn't what it's all about, love," I said. "We can do better than this," I said, even though I was up for promotion. Run-down hotel. That's what we want. Build it up from scratch. Personal service. Eh? That's what brought us here. Poured money in the place. And what's the Council done?' The question was rhetorical: there was no pause, only repetition. 'What's the Council done, all the time we've been here? Put the rates up. That's all the Council's done. And what's the Chamber of Commerce done . . .?'

'Very little, I expect,' Treasure broke in firmly, looking over Daws's shoulder. 'You're Mr Elderberry, I expect.'

'Indeed I am. Commonly known as an old fruit,' the fleshy Elderberry offered wanly, along with a limp hand. 'How d'you do. Perchance my infamy has gone before—but sadly not before time.' There was a coy, slow twist of the head. 'Has this gorgeous creature been spreading calumnies about me? I do hope so.' Now there were benign smiles for everybody and quick glances from one face to another through large, round spectacles.

Mr Elderberry favoured colourful clothes—a pink shirt, a loosely tied yellow silk cravat, a bright blue velvet suit. The long double-breasted jacket was done up on all four buttons. This accentuated the girth of the wearer as well as exhibiting a certain kind of courage.

Treasure had the impression Elderberry might go pop at any minute. 'She said you were an accomplished writer.'

'The sweet child. Remind me to put you in a book, lovey.' A podgy hand dabbed at the cravat.

'I keep reminding you, Lancelot,' Tracy giggled.

'No character yet that does you justice. Some day. Some day, lovey.'

'*How can my muse want subject to invent,*' Tracy quoted with mock despond.

'That's Shakespeare, isn't it? One of those smutty sonnets, forsooth. See what education does for them, Mr Treasure? Taking rises out of their elders and betters. Well elders anyway.' The writer sniffed, then smiled archly. 'Yes, I turn an honest coin or two in the pulp market. Not what it was, though. Or I'm not. Only just keeps the predators from the threshold.' He sounded as though he meant the last comment.

'You've lived here long?'

'Nearly thirty years. I had a friend, dear friend. We shared the house. He passed away. But that was some time ago. Always been meaning to move. Haven't had the energy, I suppose. Not without an incentive. Not like now with the development money coming. And then, I do so love the sea.'

'Not to mention the sailors,' said Daws in an aside loud enough for everyone to hear.

Elderberry sighed. 'That was a remark in very poor taste, Mostyn.' He glared at Daws. 'But I'll forgive you. Mr Treasure, you haven't met Denis Pitty.'

'So sorry,' broke in Commander Mane. 'Never finished the introductions. Denis is solicitor for all of us.'

Treasure shook hands with the fourth member of the group who had been standing behind Elderberry. He was about the banker's own age and build; fair, crinkly hair, broad forehead, strong chin. The heavy black-framed glasses added a touch of solemnity to otherwise dashing good looks. The hand-tailored, dark grey pinstripe betokened success, as did, in another context, the approving glances of Tracy Mane.

'He's lawyer to Canon Tring too. Denis works for all the best people,' said the girl from behind the bar.

'Well, I seem to cover the waterfront, don't you know? We've met before. With respective memsahibs. You'd hardly remember. Devilishly crowded first night party. At the Dorch. One of your lady wife's first nights. Topping. Great privilege.'

Pitty's chortling and top-drawer accent struck Treasure as over-contrived. The same applied to the outdated idiom. At a guess, the lawyer was artisan progeny made good in a profession—and full marks for that, if not for the affectation.

'Thank you. I'm sorry I don't recall our meeting. Your wife well?'

'We've since divorced, actually. Incompatible careers. She's in public relations. Needed to be in the Smoke. In jolly old London.'

'And you've settled for a lucrative practice away from it. Can't blame you for that. Did you leave a London firm?'

'No. Always been here. Was a partner with a local show. Ribert and Glens. Set up on my own nearly four years ago . . .'

'Denis is a real success story,' put in the Commander. 'Two offices in Sussex now. Another planned for Hampshire.'

'Legal work here's mostly conveyancing, but there's a lot of it in these retirement areas. And there's still time for the odd spot of golf.' He pronounced it 'goff'. 'Didn't you play for the Varsity?'

'For Oxford, yes. Long time ago.' Treasure assumed a man so singularly well informed must just have looked him up in *Who's Who*.

'Down here for a game?' The lawyer put the leading question casually enough.

'Not really.' The reply produced no evident surprise from anyone.

There was silence for a moment.

'Tracy's just told us you say the Seawell scheme's still on, despite Louella Brasset's meddling.' It was the Commander who spoke.

'So far as the sale of your properties is concerned, I don't believe there's been any change of plan.'

'Thank God for that,' said Daws with feeling.

'That goes for all of us,' added Mane.

'Oh, indeed it does.' Elderberry nodded vigorously.

'I should add I've no special authority in the matter.' Treasure shrugged. 'I did happen to speak to Seawell this afternoon.'

'And you do happen to be their valued adviser, what?' put in Pitty.

'They've completed on the purchase of the Round House in double quick time.' This was Daws. 'Chap at Ribert and Glens heard on the grapevine. That's Denis's old outfit. Told me this evening. They used to act for the freeholders, years ago. Isn't that right, Denis?'

The lawyer nodded.

'The Rackburn & Claremont Assurance Company,' Treasure remarked, a touch of comedy in his expression.

'One man and an office boy somewhere north of Selfridge's by the sound of it. Bet they've made a packet on the Round House,' commented the Commander.

Daws agreed. 'I heard they picked up that freehold in a job lot in the Depression. 1931 or thereabouts. With more than half a century to run on the lease, peppercorn rent, hard times.' He made a clucking noise at the back of his throat. 'Must have got it for the proverbial song. Eh? D'you know how much, Denis?'

'I'm hardly in a position to say.'

'Never looked it up? When you were with Ribert's?'

Pitty ignored the question. 'Anyway, Mr Treasure, I've just been assuring these good people Seawell are hardly likely to treat them any differently from the insurance company.'

'Except they've already coughed up their lolly. Eh? So why haven't they paid us off too?'

'I suspect, Mr Daws, because the Rackburn's advisers were easily available in London at very short notice.' Treasure didn't add their lawyers had probably just been quicker off the mark than Denis Pitty.

'I tried to reach Seawell Developments this afternoon. The moment we heard about Louella's activities. News to all of us, I may say,' the lawyer volunteered pointedly. 'No luck. Probably close early on a Friday.'

Treasure had talked to Ali at four on the telephone. Perhaps Pitty had got a wrong number.

'Are you going over to see if Louella has just cause or impediment to stop you knocking down the Round House, Mr Treasure?' It was Elderberry who put the question.

'Let's say I . . .' The banker did not complete his intended bland reply.

Mrs Daws had appeared through the archway from the hall. She was deeply agitated. 'Mr Pitty, could you come to the phone,' she implored. 'In the office. It's Mrs Tring. About Lady Brasset.'

Pitty turned about to face the speaker. 'I wonder what Louella's been up to now,' he began. His expression changed when he saw the look on Mrs Daws's face.

'There's been an accident,' she uttered, but nearly inaudibly: the awful tremor was still there in her voice.

'What kind of accident?' Commander Mane asked above the exclamations of the others.

Pitty hurried out.

It was Elderberry who spoke before the confused Mrs Daws could find more words. 'Oh dear. I have a perfectly dreadful presentiment.' He put his glass down on the bar and ran a hand across his brow. 'It's come over me like a cloud. She isn't dead, is she? Don't say Louella's dead.'

'She's dead,' confirmed Mrs Daws, the whispered tone easily discernible because of the hush that had followed the chilly prophecy.

CHAPTER 5

'Seems she left the gas on, unlit. Went to London on the early train this morning. Got back here at eight-fourteen. Opened that door with a cigarette in her mouth, or else she was lighting one, more like. Lighter was on the floor. Then boom! Blast blew her back out against the garage wall. Brick, it is. Died instantly, I'd say. Got her to hospital, of course.'

The heavily built, close to retirement Police Constable Stock had delivered his summary in a quiet monotone. He was standing with Treasure and Denis Pitty in the scorch-streaked kitchen of The Cottage, Penn Lane, a mile and a half inland from the centre of Tophaven, and effectively part of the village of Colston which began officially a few yards further on.

It was nearly 10.00 p.m. The banker and the lawyer had stopped on their way to the Trings.

Seated in a corner of the room was a very fat, bespectacled young man with short-cropped hair and dressed in blue overalls. He was reading a paperback copy of *War and Peace*. He had been identified by the policeman simply as George, an Emergency Service fitter from the Gas Board. George had acknowledged this fact with a cautious glance at the speaker. He had then continued reading without looking at the others.

'Gas Board Supervisor's on his way. There'll be a formal investigation. For the inquest. Not much doubt what happened, George says. Here in minutes, he was. Very sensitive, the gas people. Very touchy about explosions . . . and fatalities.' The constable paused.

George had looked up at the mention of a superior's expected arrival, and considered the rest of PC Stock's commentary. 'Had to make safe, I did. That's all.' He went back to his book, then looked up again. 'Make safe. That's official procedure. I done it.' He looked belligerently at the faces of all three listeners as though expecting questions; there being none, he abandoned himself to Tolstoy.

The policeman sighed. 'Never did see her Ladyship without a cigarette. Except in the car. "Never smoke when driving," she said to me more than once. Had a fear of fire. If there was an accident. Fire. Funny.' He shook his head and stared around the room.

The kitchen was about nine feet by ten, not counting a short, open passage leading to the outside door. The door, half blown off its hinges, was the side entrance to the small, thatched dwelling. Treasure and Pitty had come in through there. Outside there was a slightly angled covered way that bridged the few feet to the side door of the garage.

The cooker was on the wall opposite the passage. There was an internal door to the right of it. George was seated close by. What was left of the single window was in the wall to the left. It looked out on to the front drive. The sink was under the window, abutting on to a string of matching units that continued round the room on both sides. There was a small table in the cramped central area with one chair: George had the other.

'I'd have thought gas would have found a way of seeping out,' said Treasure.

'Before this place was modernized it very likely would have, sir,' the policeman observed sadly. 'Four hundred year old, it is. Or so they say. Cavity brick walls, though. She had it done up before she moved in. That would be five years since, wouldn't it, Mr Pitty?'

'Bit more.'

'You're right. Year after her husband died. When she gave up the big house. No expense spared here. Double glazing. Cavity insulation. Electric central heating. Wouldn't have gas. Only for cooking. More expensive, of course. Then everything was draughtproof. She hated cold. American, of course.' This last was offered to explain a predisposition to hedonistic indulgence.

'What about air-bricks? Ventilators? Aren't they required by law?'

George stirred at Treasure's question, but it was Stock who answered. 'S'right, sir. And too many people close 'em up or bung something in them this time of year. Her Ladyship did, by the look of it.'

Despite the burn marks on the walls and other surfaces, the blown-out window and the general signs of disaster, the covered strip light over the window was still functioning.

To the right of the light was a metal ventilator in the wall. It occupied the space of two bricks—or it would have done if its bottom half had not been bent away from its housing by the blast. It consisted of a standing part and a sliding shutter for moving across to close the ventilating slits. It was a familiar enough piece of equipment. The policeman pointed to it and continued.

'Ventilator's shut, see?'

'Could have been caused by the bang.'

'Could have, Mr Pitty. I said as much to George here. Not likely, he said. Nearly impossible.'

'S'right,' George confirmed suddenly and without looking up.

'There's another one down there,' said Stock. He pointed to the object just above the skirting-board on the wall opposite the cooker, near the passage. 'That's closed too. Undamaged. There's no accounting with explosions. But George says if the owner closed one vent she'd likely have closed the two. For the winter.'

All eyes involuntarily turned to George. He swivelled his triple chin, which protruded tightly from the top of his overall, so his gaze could fall directly on the offending ventilator. He removed his steel-rimmed glasses, blinked, then put them on again.

'S'what I told you.' He nodded at Stock. 'Not approved,' he added, surprising the others.

'Meaning they don't list that kind any more. The ones with shutters,' the policeman elucidated. 'These were fitted before they were taken off the Gas Board's approved list.'

A lift of the eyebrows indicated the overweight fitter had noted and sanctioned this enlargement on his last imparted intelligence.

'And she left a switch on the cooker turned on, but forgot to light the burner.'

'That's the likeliest explanation, Mr Treasure. Funny thing with this sort of explosion. Some parts of a place look like a hurricane went through. Other things you'd expect to have gone up are left looking normal. The cooker. It's like new.'

Everyone except George considered the gleaming white enamelled cooker.

'Would the explosion have ignited any burner switched on?' asked Treasure. There was no movement or word from George.

'That's a good question, sir. We think we've got the answer. Pretty definite,' replied the constable. 'Like Mrs Tring told Mr Pitty on the phone, old Mr Fairfax and one of his sons from Longacre Farm, they heard the blast. Reckoned it came from here or hereabouts. Came down in their Land-Rover straight off. It's a tidy half-mile. Young Terry Fairfax had the bits of fire out while his Dad did what he could about Lady Brasset. Rang for the ambulance and fire brigade within five minutes of the bang. They'd noted the time. It was the thatch they were worried about, of course. After her Ladyship, that is.'

'And the cooker?' Treasure pressed.

'Ah. First thing Terry did was pull down the curtains. They were burning. He didn't try the lights in case of sparks. Well, you can't be too careful. So he was working nearly in the dark. He remembers a newspaper burning on top of the cooker. Come off that shelf there, I expect. He pulled it away. Stamped it out with the curtains. He didn't check the burners. Not specially, but he's pretty certain one was on. Lit, I mean. Thinks he switched it off.'

'So an unlit burner would have been lit by the explosion? That could happen?' Treasure was more surprised than querulous.

'It could do, sir. It could do, George said.'

There was a more than momentary silence while George indicated he did not intend affirming this alleged but unwitnessed and perhaps now regretted speculation.

'It still seems to me that turning on a gas tap, not lighting it, and leaving the house with it still on is so unlikely as to be . . .'

'Unbelievable,' put in Pitty flatly. 'I absolutely agree. And Louella was no dimwit. You met her today, Mark. One of the most intelligent women I've ever known. And pretty alert still. For her age.' He paused. 'But what other explanation is there?'

'An ordinary gas leak?' hazarded the banker.

'There's no leak,' came the firm voice of George from the corner. 'Test'll show.'

'She left in a hurry, sir. Without her breakfast.' Stock broke the lull in the exchanges that seemed always to follow George's rationed pronouncements. 'It was laid for but not eaten. There's some smashed crockery that went over with the table. Clean, it was. I've put the bits on one side.' He looked towards Pitty. 'She'd have caught the seven thirty-four to London.'

'That's what she told them when she phoned the college. Mrs Tring mentioned it.'

'Right, sir. That's an early rise for Lady Brasset, I'm thinking. Perhaps she overslept. Came down late. Started to make breakfast. Reckoned she didn't have time. She'd filled the electric kettle. Maybe in the rush she turned the gas on under her egg saucepan, thought she'd lit it, hadn't, and didn't notice when she left.'

'What egg saucepan?' asked Treasure.

'That one, sir, on the draining-board. It was on the floor by the table. Water all round it.

'No egg?'

'Perhaps that was it, Mark,' put in Pitty. 'She fills the saucepan. Puts it on the cooker. Turns on the gas. Thinks she's lit it. Goes to the fridge for an egg. At that point decides there's no time after all . . .'

'Comes back later to a gas-filled room. Steps inside. Lights a cigarette . . .'

'Outside.' George had spoken. He looked from Treasure to Pitty, then at the constable. 'She'd have lit up outside.' This time he nodded before returning to his book.

'He was telling me before you came, sir. A room full of gas wouldn't have blown up. You need five to fifteen per cent of gas in the air for it to be dangerous, like. Less or more than that is actually safe. Funny thing.'

'So once she opened the door . . . ?'

'Even a crack, sir, concentrated gas from inside . . .'

'Pours out to join clean air outside. So in a split second there's the right volume of the two constituents for ignition.' Treasure was dimly recalling an elementary rule of physics. 'That's assuming she's smoking or lighting a cigarette.'

'Which she would be, sir. Once she was out of the garage. She keeps petrol in there for the machines. Once at the back door she'd be lighting up.'

'Well, we can't be absolutely certain . . .' Pitty began.

'But the constable said they found a lighter on the

floor,' said Treasure, mildly surprised the lawyer needed the point repeated.

'Of course, of course. Makes it all pretty clear, I'd say.'

'Mmm. And it's not likely anyone entered the house while Lady Brasset was away, Mr Stock? Daily help?'

'Comes Tuesdays and Thursdays, sir. Happens to be my missus. Very cut up about this, she is, and that's a fact. Her Ladyship was a true friend. To both of us.' The policeman shook his head. 'Gardener comes Saturday afternoons only. Not much ground here. Lot of hedging, though, for privacy. Eddie Jacks does it. He's the postman. They have half days Saturdays now. Regular.' There was no envy in the voice, there being benefits and drawbacks in every job.

'This is Colston village proper. The Trings live here in the old vicarage. It's just up on the right. Oh, that's the police house where the admirable Stock abides.'

'Being the village bobby?' asked Treasure.

'That's right. Damn this rain.' Pitty slowed the Porsche and peered through the windscreen, looking for a gate opening. 'Colston's under two miles from Tophaven. Natives very conscious of the separation, though. It's not much of a village, even so. Back way to Chichester, really. Louella regarded herself as Colston, not Tophaven.'

'Except her civic pride . . .'

'Extended to both places. Yes. Here we are then.'

He had stopped the car at the end of a short drive. Treasure took in only a glimpse of the house as he dashed for cover. The outline was of a small Georgian building, two-storeyed and stuccoed. There was a projecting central porch supported by columns. An illuminated bell push was the only sign of occupation.

'Blast! Left my side lights on,' cried Pitty, going back to the car after pressing the bell.

When the door swung open there was only a dim,

reflected light from an inner doorway. The woman's arms
went around Treasure's neck. 'My dear, what took you so
long? . . . Oh!'

'Cynthia, this is Mark Treasure,' said Pitty, appearing
from behind the banker. 'Saving electricity, are you?' He
reached inside and snapped on some switches. The porch
and hall were now brightly illuminated.

Tony Quaint had described the lady as 'a bit of all
right'. Treasure thought this, if anything, an
understatement: but then Quaint had not enjoyed benefit
of warm, anxious embrace.

'And you think those gas people will leave the place
secured? Louella has—' Cynthia Tring gave an impatient
jerk of the head—'I mean had—such lovely things. It's all
so awful. I still can't believe . . . accept what's happened.'

The movements of her body were quite as expressive as
the emphasis in her naturally husky voice.

She was not a flawless beauty, and she was too nervous
to be serene, but she owned a presence Treasure found
wholly engaging. She had a developed talent for gently
emphasizing her best features. The tapered hands stroked
the softly waved, ash blonde hair. The slim fingers
caressed the outstretched chin and long bare neck—or
absently explored the cleavage that showed above the V
of the low-cut sweater.

While she spoke, her shoulders were restlessly
declaratory. Her legs, which were rivetingly good, she
crossed and recrossed frequently—but again without the
suggestion that these were conscious movements.

Altogether Mrs Tring appeared to be hardly type-cast
as wife for a long retired clergyman.

'We left the workers at it. Doing the window. Re-
hanging the door,' Pitty volunteered. 'Old Stock was
absolutely committed to stay till they're done.'

'A Supervisor brought a whole team of able-looking

chaps. Heaven knows where they came from at this time of night. Anyway, they seemed competent.' Treasure added assurance.

'Seemed competent.' The Reverend Canon Algernon Tring was given to repeating the last words of others. 'More whisky, Treasure?'

He was the only one of the four standing. He was tall, about six foot three, but stooped, with the preoccupied demeanour of a scholar. His dark suit hung about him loosely. His neck was several sizes too small for his clerical collar. The flesh on his face and head clung to the skeletal shapes beneath. He was a gangling, spectral image of a man.

'No more, thanks. Doing very well,' replied the banker, nursing his glass.

'Doing very well . . . Sad business.' The Canon continued to hover.

The atmosphere reminded one of living-rooms in country parsonages circa 1930 — all chintz covers, rugs over polished boards, some nearly good pieces of mahogany, a few unremarkable still-lifes, a log fire burning, but no central heating.

'Can't be too careful with cigarettes,' the clergyman added absently while producing a silver cigarette case from a side pocket. 'Smoke, anyone?'

'I wish you wouldn't, Algy.'

'Wouldn't?'

'Smoke. You know what the doctors said. It'll shorten your life.'

He considered his wife's comment for a moment, then took out a box of matches. 'Top you up, my dear?' His question was punctuated by a hideous cough following the first deep inhalation on the cigarette.

'You see? Yes, please. Not so much tonic. And Denis needs a refill.' She turned to Treasure. 'Louella was a dear friend, Mark. I may call you Mark?' She paused for approval.

'Of course.'

'It was ghastly at the hospital. Nothing to be done, of course. I just couldn't go back to the cottage. You do understand, my dear?' The question was directed at Pitty. The endearment was put casually enough. Treasure wondered if it had been meant to disarm others: notably himself.

The embarrassing greeting on the doorstep had been lightly dismissed at the time—so lightly as to have put in doubt its special intimacy. The two men were the same height and build. Only Pitty had been expected. How easy it had been to mistake Treasure for him. And that had been that.

'You saw her this afternoon, Mark. She looked well? Of course she did.' The eyes opened wider. 'So dedicated to ideals. A lovely, lovely person. Mr Stock rang me straight away. Knew how close we were. That was thoughtful.'

'Very,' Treasure agreed.

'Very,' echoed the Canon.

'She'd complained about the cooker. The pilot lights weren't working properly.'

'She'd complained?' Pitty leaned forward in his armchair.

'When I was there.' Cynthia went on. 'Lunch on Sunday. Algy went to Chichester. For the High Mass in the cathedral. A friend took him. They had lunch there. Louella and I were snacking in her kitchen. She got angry when two of the pilot lights didn't work. Angrier still when she rang the gas people. They said it was Sunday and pilot lights weren't an emergency. Could she ring Monday. Quite right, of course. But it didn't please Louella.'

'I wonder if she did ring again?' Treasure asked pointedly.

'Being Louella, almost certainly.' It was Pitty who answered.

'Almost certainly,' said the Canon. 'Very determined woman. Remember once . . .'

'You think it would make a difference? If a repair was ordered and hadn't been done. In terms of liability?' Cynthia interrupted her husband.

'No. It'd help explain how the accident could have happened,' the lawyer replied.

'. . . Question of extending licensing hours for the pub in the village. Coronation. Or was it one of the Royal weddings?' The Canon was continuing with his own subject.

'You mean she could have pressed the button forgetting the thing wasn't lighting?' It was Cynthia again.

'Or else realized it wasn't after turning on the gas. Gone looking for a match . . .'

'Didn't find one. Got involved in something else . . .'

'Realized the time. Abandoned breakfast . . .'

'And left for London thinking everything was switched off.'

'That could be it.' Cynthia completed the almost practised exchange with Pitty.

'Perhaps it was the Silver Jubilee,' the Canon still ruminated aloud.

'What was that, Algy? Well, perhaps it doesn't matter.' She smiled warmly at her husband before turning to Treasure. 'She'd have been touched to know you'd been so faithful about your promise, Mark. She rang me, you know. I'd popped out. Had to leave a message.' She sighed. 'My last chance to have talked with her. She described you as devastatingly male, apparently. You know how she talked?'

'I thoroughly enjoyed meeting her. Great fun.' He paused. 'I ought to admit, Denis knows already, I didn't come down solely about the promise. I wanted to look at the Round House. At the stuff Lady Brasset unearthed at the library. Also . . .'

She broke in on his hesitation. 'Also to get us to give up that wretched lease straight away.'

'Perhaps that too, Mrs Tring. Yes.'

'Cynthia. Please call me Cynthia.'

'Very well, Cynthia. In the circumstances you possibly feel even greater loyalty to Lady Brasset. I mean over supporting her aim to keep the Round House standing. The lease is your own affair, after all. I wouldn't have intruded tonight . . .'

'Except I invited you,' Pitty interjected. 'You were the last one of us to see Louella alive. She obviously took to you.'

'Algy and I won't be crusading for the Round House, Mark. There are other reasons why I don't want to give up the lease before the end of term.'

'Which I respect,' the banker interjected.

'Thank you. Otherwise we frankly thought Louella's fixation about the place a little misplaced. We also thought it was over ages ago. Until last night. Just one of her causes. Some were good. Others, like this one, rather curious. Architecturally the Round House is hardly remarkable.'

'Hardly remarkable.' This time there was sadness in the Canon's echoed words. 'Another whisky, Treasure?'

CHAPTER 6

Treasure rinsed away the toothpaste, then bared his teeth at himself in the bathroom mirror. This involved his having to stoop. Were Beachcomber Hotel bridegrooms expected to be undersized—or just too tired to stand up properly? Very droll: he took some deep breaths. Now only his chest was reflected in the mirror.

It was just after 6.00 a.m. He had asked for a call at

7.30: should have known better. He always woke early at the seaside.

Outside it was still dark. By the time he had shaved, showered and dressed there ought to be light enough for him to inspect the Round House before breakfast. He had a key.

The circumstances of his visit had changed dramatically with Lady Brasset's death. Put bluntly, the problem had been simplified enormously.

So Louella had been alone in wanting the place listed. Her own demise could just conceivably mark the end of the matter. The Trings' support had been out of friendship.

It was odd about Cynthia choosing to maintain her attitude over the lease — first conceived, presumably, as a delaying tactic. She had relented a little, of course, mentioning the end of term. Should he have pressed the matter harder last night? Definitely not: majestic forbearance had been the right attitude. He had set the thing up for Quaint to have another shot: let him do the haggling over the small change with the nice lady.

This time he avoided his own reflected gaze as he considered this not wholly worthy circumvention: he waited for the vitamin C tablet to dissolve.

He had found Cynthia Tring something of an enigma. Both Quaint and Pitty had predicted as much in their different ways. She had been widowed five years earlier, Pitty said. Her husband had been a promising entrepreneur. There had been no children. He had died young leaving her practically penniless. She had remarried just over a year before. She had met her second husband through taking freelance typing — supplementing her salary from her job with Pitty's old firm.

Tring was a scholar, and still actively so: research into the lives of saints apparently. His wife had been captivated by his intellect, or so Pitty insisted, while admitting the alliance was an odd one. Treasure had certainly found it so.

He shrugged, and went on shaving.

He realized now that Lady Brasset's intention had bothered him more than he had been ready to admit. Was he right, still, in playing it strictly by the rules? If the Sandy Lane development were stopped through the whim of an old lady—a dead old lady—he might have to face some uncomfortable moments with the Emir if the old man heard the story.

He stepped into the shower. He shivered slightly under the cold spray—though 'cold' was not wholly accurate. Less warm than luke-warm was good enough for toning up the physique in November, consonant still with inducing a credible sense of stoic well-being.

Of course he was right about the honest approach, and there was quite a lot going for it. Pitty had said on their way back from the Trings that the local conservationists had refused to waste time on the Round House: far too much better stuff about—and in danger. No doubt his first look would assuage his own fears.

He still wondered what Louella had unearthed in the diaries—and the letter she had prized so much. The library opened at 10.00. He intended being there then. He would declare his interest to Sims the librarian. According to Pitty, the chap would be for anyone who opposed poor Louella, almost as a matter of principle. She could have been as misguided in her judgement of the documents as she had been about the building itself: there was a thought.

The nagging pity was that wheels had been set in motion at the DoE. But for that, there'd have been no problem: a stony-hearted conclusion, but true.

So it was up to him, with a conviction yet unjustified but strongly latent, to apply enough cold water to dampen officialdom's interest. Symbolically he adjusted the shower controls.

The brisk walk from the Beachcomber to the Round House had established one thing. The elimination of Three Winds and its attached neighbour, South View, would be no loss to the nation. The joined houses were starkly evident from the road. Without their windows they might have been mistaken for an undemolished coastal defence position.

The rain had stopped but there was dampness in the air and under foot. There was daylight of a sort, but the sky was heavily overcast, with a chill wind blowing from the east.

The sea, visible from Treasure's room, was out of sight at road level. He could hear it pounding behind an irregular bastion of huge broken concrete blocks which extended some way down the beach: high tide wasn't for two hours. Seawell Developments had a better arrangement planned for preventing the road being engulfed at every spring tide. He had examined the model at lunch the day before.

He strode up the rising approach to the Round House. For the first fifty yards no building was visible. The drive was straight to that point, flanked by thickets of cupressus. Then the way divided in two around a sprawling barrier of bushes—more topped Lawsonias tangled with laurel, giant privet, stunted pines and trespassing bramble. The ground flattened here so it was not until he rounded this artless and hardly tended windbreak that he came, at last, on the object of his visit.

The house was set well back across a wide oval of gravelled drive. Thus the visitor was treated on the instant to an angled but full view of the south aspect.

Treasure's first impression was one of profound relief. If the unattractive pile before him had started life as something better, he was sorry for the fact. He wished good luck to anyone concerned to get the place listed. Too many much worthier façades had literally bitten the dust for this one to rate protection—even with present-day enlightened attitudes. It was a sad sight. And if, underneath, there was a gem waiting to be rediscovered, the rescue costs would surely be relatively enormous. Nor did he feel his initial judgement was partial or philistine—only realistic.

He moved along the outer edge of the drive with a lighter heart. Nothing Seawell planned could fail to improve on this ugly blot on the environment. It was now safe to indulge in dispassionate dissection.

The upper half of the two-storeyed building sat on the lower like a sinking second tier on a gigantic, un-iced wedding cake. The upper storey had a round tiled roof rising to a squat chimney at the apex. Its walls were brick, pierced by wide-framed sash windows, three of which were visible from where Treasure was standing. The middle one of these openings had another smaller window above it.

The ground floor offered nothing so bland. It too affected roundness but only crudely. The walls were a patchwork of sections in an almost perverse variety of materials—some pebbled, some brick, some cement and concrete—cobbled together with irregular shaped windows at unlikely intervals.

A grand panelled front door, seemly enough under a well projected cornice and oval fanlight, had been made to lose all pretension to elegance by its surrounds. Abutting on its flanking half-pilasters were wall sections of concrete breeze blocks; they were whitewashed—an exercise in apologetics that had not been repeated for several seasons.

On the nearest part of the building a lean-to-shaped addition thrust out like some massive, low, medieval buttress, except it too was fashioned in cement blocks, this time wholly undisguised. From this obtrusion sprang a tall asbestos smoke-stack with a coolie-hat cover at the top: the remains of a bird's nest hung out from the westward side.

'Not even round, is it? Crooked, really. Gosh, you are beautiful.'

Treasure turned at the voice to find Tracy Mane standing beside him to windward. He smirked, disarmed by her presence and the compliment. 'You're up early. How did you know . . . ?'

'Saw you pass our place in your Aquascutum sheepskin.' She was hugging herself in a dark blue duffel coat. The wind was whipping long wisps of jet-black hair about her face.

'According to Lady Brasset, the ground floor wasn't round when it was built. Cruciform, actually. You can work it out probably,' said Treasure. 'She'd seen what she thought was the original plan . . .'

'In an illustrated book by . . . Sloane?'

'Soane.'

'Yes. She said so on the phone. Built like a Greek cross. Is that what you mean? The north and south ends were rounded.'

'Apsidal.' She frowned at the term. 'Bowed, if you prefer,' he added.

'I'll believe you. The top floor's like it was from the start. Downstairs, the four empty triangular bits between the sort of wings—they were filled in, built over in the war.' She was leading the way to the front door. 'Want to see inside? I don't have a key but . . .'

'I do. Courtesy of Mrs Tring.'

'There are no classes on Saturdays.' She was applying her appraising look again. 'Bet you and Cynthia clicked.'

'I found her charming,' he answered coolly.

'And the rest! God knows what she sees in the Canon.'

'In that you are without doubt perfectly and perceptibly accurate.'

'Sorry, sorry, sorry. Hey, if you're wondering what that is, it was the boiler house.' She pointed towards the lean-to. 'Not in use. Obsolescent.'

After entering the house, they crossed a semi-circular, interior colonnade that served as a hall. It showed blind arches on the outer wall and open ones opposite, none stemming from columns. Groups of four slim moulded shafts sprung from the floor, and without punctuation later divided gracefully into pairs to form ogee arches. The effect was pleasing so far as it went. The colonnade was blocked at differing distances, but at both ends, by cheap partitioning.

Moving on around a pretty spiral staircase, they went through what had evidently been a screen of two more arches—the left-hand one bricked up, the right housing a door. Descending two steps, they came upon the main area of the building.

It was like a small, abandoned and ill-used church built on a north-south axis, and insensitively adapted as a complex of offices.

On either side were well-proportioned, rectangular 'transepts' evidently intended to be viewed through trios of drop arches with shafting similar to those passed earlier.

Beyond and across the square central space was the north end, rising up two wide steps to the same level as the entrance area. Here nothing should have been allowed to impede view or movement: the whole was meant to compose a broad bay, lit by what must have once been eight fine venetian windows.

Turning about, Treasure stooped in order to look backward through the open screen door and beyond the staircase to the main entrance. In this way one could still—if only just—appreciate the way it was framed inside a small coffered alcove. Natural light was shed upon this from above through some hidden niche opening, opposite.

'Soane called it a plan for a hunting cabin,' said the banker quietly. 'I suppose it would have adapted well enough for a modest-sized ladies' academy.'

'Place used to be full of desks in the old days,' Tracy volunteered. 'Some cabin though. Would that mean they'd never expect to sleep in it? The hunters, I mean. There aren't any bedrooms. Upstairs is one big room, except for the landing. Underneath there's a tiny basement. Otherwise it used to be just this.' She spread her arms out. 'Without the built-on bits you haven't seen.'

'Don't want to, either.' He eyed the frame doors that led to 'the built-on bits'.

'I suppose there was only one washroom before the Navy put in loos and a big kitchen and . . .'

'And wrecked the place.'

'Up there—' she nodded towards the north end, visible through the glazed upper half of a cement block wall perched along the upper step—'that's apsidal?'

'Sort of. There must have been two more windows than there are now. Closed them in because of draughts, I expect.'

'It was called the eating-room when it was one piece. That's what Lady Brasset said. I had to measure it while she was on the phone.'

'I see,' he replied absently. He was assessing the extent of the desecration—the doors in the walls of the transepts, the broken friezes, the blocked archways, the extensions and divisions made from wood and glass partitioning, others from more permanent materials.

It must once have been a handsome interior.

'Probably made a perfect secretarial college the way the Navy left it.' He sighed loudly. 'At least nobody found a way of completely wrecking the view of that entrance from here.'

'It is nice.' She paused. 'Don't think I've ever noticed it before.'

'Illustrates a trick of Soane's. Used light like a painter. To alter perspective. Dimension even.'

'So it is by Soane?'

'A Soane design, yes. Executed with enormous sensitivity. Understanding of his style. That's what I'd say. The decorations, the mouldings, that medallioned cornice over there, what's left of it, all very Soane-like. But if it was Butterfield, it was Butterfield under duress. Credit to the chap's good manners, perhaps. Contracted to carry through someone else's design. So—' Treasure shrugged—'would have stuck in his throat, I reckon. But he did a faithful job. You see, he was a Gothicist in the fourteenth-century manner. A muscular designer, not a romantic. Ever been to All Saint's, Margaret Street, in London?' She shook her head. 'No, I suppose you wouldn't have. Keble College, Oxford?'

'Yes,' she answered promptly, hoping the experience would make up for what he had made sound like a grave religious shortcoming. It did.

'Then could you credit this interior, or what's left of the original, was by the same architect?'

'Not really. No,' she affirmed defiantly. She had been to a college ball at Keble and had the dimmest memory of the buildings.

'I mean, even if he was copying Soane's plan . . . Mmm. Very little is known about Butterfield's early life. He trained in Worcester. Long way from here.'

'That doesn't mean . . .' She attempted to sound sage.

'No, it doesn't. But this is nothing like anything I've seen of his. You'd have thought such a strong personality would have shown through in some way. You see, he liked to build cheap. This isn't cheap. Once he designed a sort

of prototype church that could be built anywhere for
£250. That was pretty cheap, even for the eighteen-fifties.
Wire-cut bricks where you'd expect stone. Rough cut
timber for rafters. He often used multi-coloured brick
courses for contrast. Cheap again, but that was his style.
I'm boring you.'

'No you're not.'

'Where d'you do your work here, for heaven's sake?'

'Upstairs. There are only four of us—plus Cynthia. It's
easier to heat up there. She's sold the furniture and stuff
she used to have down here. Want to see?'

The treads of the staircase were stone with moulded
soffits, the balustrading wrought iron. At the top was a
small circular landing.

'Damn, the light switches are downstairs.' She turned
to descend again.

'Don't bother. Not worth it. We can see well enough.'

He had already entered the one room and was
admiring the open rafters. The next thing he noticed was
the roughness of the timber in those rafters, the simple
logic in the way they slotted into the top of the brick
chimney that rose from the fireplace in the centre of the
room. And every fourth brick course was black.

Above each window, flat-topped from the outside, was
an English Gothic arch in painted wood. The walls were
plastered but not embellished by decoration like those
below. He wondered why they hadn't been left as raw
brickwork like the attractive chimney.

He moved around the armless, swivel chairs and the
tidy desks that supported covered typewriters. There was
one larger desk facing the others, its working surface
covered with a muddle of papers.

'Cynthia sets a terrible example. She's a good teacher,
though,' offered Tracy.

He pushed up the window he'd been making for: it
looked out on to the garden. Ignoring the hodge-podge of

roofing immediately beneath, he stared down at the well-proportioned flagged terrace, the circular iron-bound pool beyond it — what was called a moon pool, he remembered — and the long, narrow lily tank below and beyond that again.

All had been totally neglected. The big tanks were dried up and rusted. At least from this height he could admire the artistry involved in the original layout.

There were steps from the terrace on both sides of the moon pool. The ones on the right narrowed half way down to accommodate a subsidiary flight which disappeared under the shallow iron basin. There was probably an implement store beneath, and a place, too, for the gadgetry that once controlled the fountains. Treasure liked postulating such arrangements.

He still had his head out of the window when he realized his earlier mistake. It had been an easy one to make, especially in poor light: an old trick, and it still caught the unwary.

After all, most architects would have chosen brick for the exterior on this job: Soane himself probably, and he was no Scrooge when it came to spending his clients' money.

Of course, it explained why there was no brickwork showing inside — except on the chimney.

There was no brick cladding. The house was timber-framed and what he had earlier recognized as brick was in fact tiling.

'Know what a mathematical tile is?' He called to Tracy. 'No? Well, come and see some.' He smoothed the outside wall with his hand as she joined him at the window. 'Used in many parts of Sussex up to the mid-nineteenth century. Plenty of old buildings in Lewes, for instance, still covered in them, just like this one. They're tiles you nail from the back on to wooden frames. They lie quite flat, not like ordinary cladding tiles. With lime putty between the courses it's hard to tell the difference from brickwork. This is quite a late use of them.'

'So what's the point?'

'They look like expensive brick. All headers — that means the narrow end of the brick. In fact they make a very cheap way of covering a building, or used to, especially round or curved buildings. It's why you see so many bow fronts in old Sussex. Kent, too. Cheap and aesthetically attractive.'

'Cheap enough for your Mr Butterfield?'

Treasure grimaced. 'Exactly his style. Like the rest of this floor. It'd be an intelligent guess to say up here we have Butterfield getting his own back. Below he was pleasing Marshford. Very likely used up most of the cash available in the process. Here we may have Butterfield doing his own thing. Low cost. Very nice. Honour satisfied.'

'Which means Lady Brasset was right.'

He pulled the window shut behind them. 'It means she could have been, and I'm not sure she knew the reason why. She picked Butterfield for his initials, not his style. There's a logic to it all, though. She said later on Marshford used high-toned architects, but without ever paying the rate for the job.'

'But here he got the best of both worlds?'

'Something like that. The unknown Butterfield, if it was him, doing, on the face of it, a Soane hunting cabin, overall quite cheaply.'

'Which would have pleased Marshford?'

'Immensely, I should think. With Butterfield regaining his *amour-propre* on this floor.' Again he examined the well-made room. 'At this point in his life, Marshford was probably most concerned to get a building that pleased him, and one guaranteed not to fall down. He'd figure a design he'd seen by Soane would fill the bill. He wasn't bothered to brag about having Soane work for him. That

sort of idea came later. May well have been sparked right
here, though. I mean using the top names and advertising
it.'

'Like Charles Barry designed Tophaven church.
There's a plaque saying so. *And* he wrote *Peter Pan*,'
exclaimed the budding actress.

'No he didn't. That was James Barrie,' Treasure
declared firmly. 'Different spelling and much later. I
think it's time for breakfast, don't you?'

'Mmm. And I do adore cultured men.'

'Meaning, in this case, reasonably informed ones.
Develops with middle age. Off you go.'

She led the way down the stairs and out of the house.

'Does all this mean the building deserves listing after
all?'

'Not in my judgement. To start with, the Butterfield
bit is still fanciful supposition. Then the ground floor
looks too far gone to be repaired. It'd need virtually
rebuilding. And finally the place is interesting but not
sufficiently exceptional.'

'And you're the big white chief of the developers,' she
added coyly.

He shook his head as he pulled the front door shut.
'Doesn't come into it. There's an inspector from the DoE
due next week. I'm pretty certain he'll take the same
view.' Even so, he wished he were as sure as he sounded.

'Listen to the advancing army.' It was Tracy who
voiced their common thought. The noise was coming
from the far side of the house. 'Actually, it's the bulldozer
thing they're using on the old houses at the back.'

Treasure stopped to listen. 'But not on a Saturday.
And not this early.'

'That's what it is, though. We've got quite used to it.'

The clanking noise was definitely getting louder and
closer. 'You mean it's the machine they've used for
knocking down the houses?'

'That's right.'

He turned about and began hurrying around the house. The girl fell in beside him.

What had once been the well-tended gardens of the Round House—several acres falling away to the north—were now scarcely distinguishable from the field they bordered to the east.

Here and there clumps of trees, patches of overgrown bushes and the remains of an Italianate garden beyond the pools, all bore witness to past glories. Treasure had noted all this earlier. What now captured his whole attention was a large, yellow, tracked vehicle in the middle distance, advancing at centre left. A huge serrated grab-bucket was set menacingly on the end of its folded mechanical boom.

'That's not a bulldozer. It's known as a tracked JCB. But you're right about what it can do. Better stay here.' He strode across the crumbled terrace. Tracy, ignoring instructions, followed.

At that moment the big machine altered direction dramatically, swinging violently to the banker's right across the garden instead of continuing forward towards the house.

It now became clear also to the watchers that the monster's course to this point had been wildly erratic—and not because it had come upon any obstruction it could not as easily have gone over as around. Simply the swathe of flattened scrub traced a route as crooked as a dodgem car's at a fun-fair.

The distance between the Round House and the partially demolished row of houses beyond the garden was not much over a hundred and fifty yards. The JCB had come from there, but it was still fifty paces from where Treasure and the girl were standing when it turned again, this time through a hundred and eighty degrees. It was now making for the wall bordering

Lancelot Elderberry's house next door.

The driver could be seen squashed inside the tiny cab. A stout figure, he was dressed in a padded work jacket, a muffler covering a good part of his face, and a cap pulled well down over his forehead.

He seemed totally absorbed in guiding the machine, and while the course he had driven seemed idiotic, his own actions indicated no lack of familiarity with the controls. On the contrary, one could have guessed he was enjoying himself—showing off his expertise with this elephantine toy.

Certain the man had not yet spotted him, Treasure hurried from the terrace, around the circular pool, down the steps and along the fifteen-yard length of the lily tank, unaware Tracy was close behind. He veered left at the end which, with a few more strides, put him in the wake of the machine.

The JCB was turned about again: now it came back along the path it had already used, but its speed had been increased.

For what felt a dangerous few seconds, Treasure stood directly in the machine's path. He waved his arms and shouted above the clatter at the top of his voice: Tracy did the same. It was then the driver saw them.

Instead of stopping, the man swung the contrivance to the left, away from the house. He brandished a clenched fist at the two, furiously motioning them to clear off.

'What's he doing?' Tracy shouted.

'I think he means to make a very large hole in the Round House. I don't know how to stop him, but I'm going to try,' roared the banker. 'Back to the terrace.' He ordered, moving fast.

'Shall I send for the cops?'

'No.' He had his reasons. Even so, it was a decision he knew he might find it impossible to justify later—unless he could stop this idiot.

The machine was swivelled around once more. This time the driver's intentions were eminently predictable, like the reason for the increased speed. He had aligned his mount with the centre of the house. Now he threw levers that not only began his forward progress, but also stirred the sleeping giant maw at the front.

Slowly the bucket arms of the JCB began unbending. As the massive elbowed sleeves extended, the chromed shafts beneath them stood revealed, glistening even in the still poor light.

The grab had jolted from its locked travelling position. It reached and dipped over the uneven ground like the head of some prehistoric gargantuan reptile.

Now there was no deference paid to any obstacle. The route was obviously to be straight along the lily tank, up over the moon pool, and on to the terrace and house.

Already the caterpillar tracks were straddling both sides of the tank at the far end.

'Is that boiler house open?'

The girl nodded. 'Think so.'

'See if there's anything in it like a crowbar or bigger.'

'Aye, aye, sir.'

It all depended on which way the driver swerved to avoid running him down—assuming he swerved at all, but Treasure thought he would.

The banker walked deliberately from the centre of the terrace towards the advancing JCB. Then, after a few paces, he turned slightly left. He was holding up both arms, motioning to the man to go back, if without any hope of compliance.

Treasure continued to the edge of the moon pool, got into it, then sat down near the left edge, legs crossed, arms grasped behind his head in approved demonstrator style.

He was indicating as clearly as he could that this was where he intended to stay—a human object less criminal to circumnavigate than to challenge.

Already the grab-bucket was dipping over the far edge of the pool when the driver made his decision. Confident of his machine, satisfied the narrow tank he had traversed had crushed under him without incident, he turned the JCB twenty degrees to his left.

He noted the effortless response. He had allowed for the tilt while the left track searched for a hold on the steps up to the terrace.

Too late, but still without apprehension, he saw the gap that must be bridged because the steps divided, the near half running out of sight beneath him.

He was prepared for the collapse of the moon pool on that side — but not for the disintegration of the support over the storehouse concealed below.

Treasure had counted on it. He threw himself to his left, out of the pool.

The huge machine had one-sidedly plummeted ten feet before its operator's efforts to swing it to the right could take effect. Using the purchase from the extended grab arm was also a ruse attempted too late.

To Treasure's intense satisfaction the JCB was, momentarily at least, immobilized. One track was burrowing beneath the ground, the other rotating uselessly in the air. The machine's extended member was bending every mechanical sinew to lift its torso out of danger — but without result, while the track below ground stubbornly continued to counteract the effort with more burrowing.

Clouds of dust enveloped the scene. Debris flew in all directions.

'Any good? Weighs a ton.' Tracy had reappeared, dragging a three-foot-long, rusted steel plate with a raised ridge down the centre. 'Part of the boiler,' she added breathlessly.

'Get it on my shoulder.' There was no time for

commending initiative. He knelt down. A moment later he was staggering the few yards to the struggling Leviathan.

He found he was chest high to the rear, lower end of the right-hand track.

The driver, expert enough on conventional terrain, had so far failed to master his predicament: he was still in the cab trying.

Treasure fed the steel plate at an angle into the place where track and driving wheels meshed. He had no idea whether it would stop the mechanism, and he jumped back sharply before there was time to find out.

If the effect of digesting a steel plate was not terminal to the machine, it was sufficiently unnerving for the driver.

The raucous screeching of angry metals, the staccato clatter of non-meshing cogwheels, the din of some unidentifiable part, previously noiseless but now protesting misuse, plus the certainty of malicious human intervention—it was all too much for the beleaguered operator. He stopped the engine just as Tracy's secret weapon was spewed out by the mechanism to crash harmlessly to the ground.

The banker, seizing the chance, climbed up the machine and wrenched open the cabin door. The driver struck down at him with a clenched bare fist but missed. Treasure grasped the extended arm and pulled.

The other man was caught off balance and came head first out of the cab. He ended sprawled across the dormant right track of his vehicle, a position he then had difficulty altering. One foot was still stuck in the cab.

The man's cap was askew. His muffler had unwound. He lifted up his head. 'Treasure,' he uttered painfully. 'For God's sake, you've got to get me out of here. Fast.'

'Quaint! You bloody fool,' exclaimed the banker.

'My hero!' cried the exultant, exhausted Tracy as she threw her arms around the Vice-Chairman of Grenwood, Phipps.

CHAPTER 7

'More coffee, Ali?' Since their host, Tony Quaint, seemed to have lost his manners along with his reason, it was Treasure who made the offer.

It was little more than half an hour since the end of the Round House incident. The three men were consuming coffee and toast in the breakfast-room at Quaint's home — a small manor house in a hamlet near the London road beyond Petworth. The fast drive inland from Tophaven had taken twenty minutes. Treasure and Quaint had hardly spoken during the trip.

Treasure had made the snap decision to fetch the Rolls and spirit Quaint away from the scene of his misdemeanour before anyone else appeared. Tracy was still with them.

Quaint had hurt his back when he had been pitched out of the JCB. He couldn't drive his own car which had been parked much too conspicuously at the demolition site. Tracy had driven it on Treasure's instructions, following behind them.

The car was better out of Tophaven, but, not to mince matters, so was Tracy — at least until the banker had forged some publicly acceptable explanation for what had happened.

Quaint's home being so unexpectedly close had simplified things. Finding Sheikh Mhad Alid ben Haban had spent the night there had come as no special surprise.

Tracy was breakfasting in the kitchen with Mrs Quaint, a quiet, collected sort of woman. She hadn't fussed unnecessarily over her husband's back which, in any case, appeared to be mending. She hadn't asked questions either. After producing the hot coffee she had tactfully shunted Tracy offstage.

Quaint was angry as well as humiliated. He was taking it out on others. 'I don't care if it's Saturday. *I* work Saturdays. You can do the same. You're supposed to be management, aren't you? You can handle a JCB, can't you?' he bellowed into the telephone his wife had placed on the table beside him.

The unfortunate subordinate on the other end of the line was being allowed only the briefest of interrupted responses. 'Vandals, I keep telling you . . . Started up a JCB. Ran riot all over the site . . . Of course they got it going easy enough. You don't need a key for a JCB. Anyone can start one. *I* can start one.' Quaint noted Treasure's glance of caution. 'Well, probably I could. Anyway, drive over there. Get the thing out of the hole they've left it in . . . No, not a very big hole.' He scowled at the coffee-pot. 'Put it back where it belongs . . . Yes, of course immobilize it. Don't want it happening again . . . *If* anyone asks tell 'em we've been vandalized. Enquiries being made . . . There wasn't any damage to the building . . . Leave the tenant to me. It's a Mrs Tring. I'll . . .' Again he caught a glance from Treasure. '. . . We'll be in touch with her. Now get cracking.' He slammed down the phone. 'So that fixes that. Oh God! My back.' He straightened painfully.

'We'll be in the clear. Home and . . . er . . . home and away. Yes?'

'Home and dry, Ali,' Treasure corrected, wondering why he was giving lessons in idiomatic English at a time like this. 'The point is it should never have happened. It was hare-brained.'

'When I telephoned Tony, after you telephoned me about the Lady Brasset, he said not hare-brained.' Ali looked accusingly at Quaint. 'He said it was our best chance if everything else is failed. Not my idea. Tony is altogether responsible. I said to ask you, Mark.'

The sallow-faced little Arab affected righteous innocence. He tried not to look Quaint in the eye—nor to think of what his brother, the Emir, would say if he ever heard.

'It was our best chance.' Quaint didn't trouble defending or denying. 'It wasn't us who forgot to get the certificate of immunity.' He stared pointedly from one man to the other. 'Pah! Another ten minutes—five—I'd have had that place in ruins.'

'Along with our reputations,' said Treasure bluntly.

'Not at all. All right. I didn't bother clearing the idea with you for obvious reasons. We're not so fastidious about things in the building trade. Can't afford to be these days.'

'No one can afford acts of blatant stupidity.'

'But it would have looked exactly as intended. A teenage tearaway run riot with our machine.'

'One who knew how to operate a JCB.'

'Plenty of kids do, especially the way I was making it look. And those things are never immobilized. They sit about on building sites all over the country—evenings, weekends. No one would have been any the wiser, except we'd have lost one unlisted building surplus to requirements. It wouldn't have been there next week for some interfering bureaucrat to preserve for the bloody nation. And Seawell does own the freehold.' Quaint slurped back a whole cup of coffee. 'And I didn't know the Brasset woman was dead. I went . . .' He stopped speaking, painfully straightened his back, then remained silent but glowering.

'And you really believe you'd never have been twigged?'

'Please, what is twigged?' Ali had his pen poised.

'Found out,' Treasure explained automatically.

'Rumbled,' said Quaint at the same moment. Then he

went on. 'Of course we'd never have been rumbled. There was no one about. Early morning. Sheltered site. No close neighbours except that writer chap the girl mentioned. She says he sleeps through anything.'

'You weren't to know that.'

'Risk worth taking. Anyway, he'd be used to demolition noises by now. I tell you there'd have been no one to prove a damn thing if you and the girl hadn't come out of nowhere. How was I supposed to know you were down here already? Later this morning, you told Ali.'

'I changed my mind.'

'Anyway, you're supposed to be on our side. And that goes for the girl too, if she's got any sense.'

'She's very nice, the girl. She's your girl, Mark?' Ali nodded approvingly.

'No, she is not my girl. And I came down primarily to see a promise was kept. A promise made to the late Lady Brasset by my company, and later by Seawell. That was yesterday afternoon. I'd hoped I could count on your word, Ali.'

'I'm very sorry,' mumbled the Sheikh, staring into his empty cup. 'Very sorry, also, for Lady Brasset.'

'Miss Mane is the daugher of one of the freeholders, who should have nothing to lose or gain now, whatever happens to the Round House, Ali. That's assuming Seawell keeps its other promise.'

'We're ready to pay all. Everybody. The conveyances are processed. They get cheques in the post Monday, if you think that's right, Mark. Banker's drafts better, perhaps?' Ali's statement was delivered eagerly.

Treasure nodded. 'And in a few days it's ninety-nine per cent certain the DoE will agree the Round House doesn't rate listing.'

'You can't be certain,' grumbled Quaint.

'Pretty certain they won't stop it coming down. I've been over the place. I was doing it while you were getting ready to masquerade as a vandal. Lucky you didn't demolish me with the house.'

'If you'd put a light on upstairs . . .'

'Well, I didn't. And if you're suggesting that would have stopped you coming, why didn't you go back when you did see me?'

'You asked me that in the car.'

'And you never gave me an answer.'

'I was in terrible pain in the car . . .'

'Well, you're not now.'

'I am, actually. Anyway, I carried on because I thought you'd have the sense to know it was me. Know what I was doing. Push off and let me do it.'

'With another witness there?'

'The girl? Your little friend?'

Treasure paused, then decided to ignore the innuendo. 'If you'd had that place in ruins, as you say, Seawell would certainly have been blamed. It would all have been too convenient. In the end you might easily have been sued by the leaseholder.'

'For pennies?'

'Who might very well have pressed the DoE or the local authority to make Ali rebuild the place. What Lady Brasset took to be the Soane plan really does exist, you know.'

'There's a lot of supposition in the Brasset theory.'

'All right. But what if your corporate vandalism had meant no planning permission for the marina? I assume you still hope to build that next?'

'They would do that? The Department of the Environment?'

'They could, Ali, and very possibly would. Government ministries don't like being made fools of.' He turned again to Quaint. 'And I couldn't have left you to wreck the building in any circumstances since I couldn't know it was you in that cab.'

'Would it have made any difference?'

'Not much. I'd have been marginally less worried about being run down if I'd known it was you and not some thug you'd hired.'

'I could have been killed going down that hole.'

'Which makes two of us. OK, the worst has been avoided. I'm sure no one saw or heard us, and that includes Elderberry. The story is, we spotted a vandal and chased him away before he did too much damage.'

Ali smiled knowingly. 'You pay the girl, no?'

'No, I don't pay the girl. Miss Mane is not that sort of girl. There are other sorts,' said Treasure testily.

The Arab was about to question what he took to be a refutation of a fundamental fact of Western European life, as he knew it: then he thought better not.

'Tracy Mane will go along with us, don't worry,' the banker continued. 'Whatever happens, Ali, you weren't there.'

'He wasn't,' Quaint put in.

'I meant, he had nothing to do with this morning. Obviously he was involved in the plan, or he wouldn't have been here last night. Thank heaven you had the sense to leave him here.'

'He overslept.'

Ali nodded sheepishly.

'I was going to suggest you had another go at Mrs Tring over the lease.' Treasure addressed Quaint again. 'As things are, I'll try doing it myself. I met her last evening. She seems an eminently sensible woman.'

'And sexy with it. Putty in your hands, no doubt. Ouch!' Quaint had embellished the comment with an energetic gesture which turned into a painful one.

'Please, you do this for us, Mark? This is the lady who also does not accept payment?'

'So it seems, Ali.'

The young Sheikh shook his head ruefully: what was

the world coming to?'

'It doesn't go absolutely flat. This seat,' complained Tracy.

'Because this is a conveyance, not a boudoir. You're meant to be looking out of the window, not staring at the roof. More interesting.' Treasure turned the car out of the Quaints' long driveway and headed towards Tophaven.

'Not much going for it as a passion wagon.' She operated the lever that brought her seat-back into the upright position. 'Now I feel like the Queen on a triumphal tour of the South Downs.'

'Well, you don't look like her. Pay attention. I want you to forget you saw Mr Quaint driving the JCB. The whole thing was an unfortunate mistake. No real harm done . . .'

'Except to Mr Quaint.' She giggled.

'Exactly. But if it gets out there'll be no end of fuss. To no purpose.'

'OK. And Daddy gets the house money on Tuesday at the latest?'

'As will all the other freeholders.'

'You scratch my back, I'll scratch yours.'

'I don't require my back scratching, thank you very much.'

'You can do mine any time.' She turned away from him, dropping the duffel coat off her shoulders. She leant back so that her hair dangled in his lap.

'You're looking at the roof again, and distracting the driver. Probably an offence in law. Sit straight and do up your seat-belt.'

'Mmm. So masterful.' But she did as she was told.

'Getting the money for your house isn't dependent on your keeping quiet about Quaint.'

'You mean you want me to do something else for that? Goody!'

'I mean I'm appealing to your better nature over the whole episode.'

'*Pro bono publico*, and all that jazz.'

'Yes.'

She hesitated. 'Does it matter I told Mrs Quaint?'

'She doesn't count.'

'You can say that again. Talk about the downtrodden wife. Why do women like that stick it?'

'Bad as that?'

'Worse. We had little heart to hearts in the kitchen. He hardly tells her a thing, or only half of what's going on. Leaves her to draw the wrong conclusions. He went to see Lady Brasset after he got home yesterday. Tarted himself up first.'

'When?'

'Around six. She thought he was off to see a new girl-friend. Then he asked her to look up Louella's address in the phone book. She knew it, though. And she told him all about Louella. They used to be in a car pool together. One for transporting old people.'

'You got the idea Quaint has girl-friends his wife knows about?'

'Loads. Makes no secret of it, or what they cost him. But he keeps his wife on the breadline. Insists they're nearly bankrupt. You know she was the boss's spinster daughter? Only child and reached the desperate age—for someone who cares about that kind of thing. She couldn't exactly have been a looker either. Must have married her for her loot. She inherited the lot. He's spent it *and* run the company up the creek. Looks bad, I'd say.'

Dun & Bradstreet had something to learn from Tracy Mane.

'He couldn't have seen Lady Brasset . . .' Treasure let the words dwindle into thoughts.

'No. He was back by seven when the Desert Prince arrived. He wasn't expected. The prince, that is. Not by Mrs Quaint. He and Mr Quaint went out to dinner and came back late. The prince . . .'

'Actually, he's a sheikh, not that it matters.'

'Hard cheese. Still not my type. All right, the sheikh was pickled when they got home. Not used to booze he told Mrs Quaint. Suppose they planned knocking over the Round House, ahead of Louella getting it put in the stately homes category?'

'Something like that.' He might have assumed that would have been Quaint's automatic reaction as soon as he heard about Lady Brasset. He should have allowed that Ali would have phoned Quaint the moment he got the news—at about 4.30 the previous afternoon. The visit to Louella was an unexpected twist. It triggered a new line of thought not concerned exclusively with Quaint.

'What time did Lady Brasset call the Round House from London yesterday?' he asked.

'Let's see. Cynthia was out for a bit. It was just before she got back. Around five, I'd say. Ten to, perhaps.'

'But you took the call?'

'Yes. Classes finish at four-thirty. I'd stayed on to see Cynthia. I knew she was coming back. Then Lancelot Elderberry came over to look at a typewriter he's buying when term's over.'

Treasure glanced sharply at the girl. 'Elderberry was there? And you told him what Lady Brasset was ringing about?'

'Mmm. He helped me with the measurements she needed.'

'And that was the first Elderberry knew . . .'

'About Louella's sleuthing? I should think so. He and I paced out bits of the ground floor while she waited on the phone. She wanted to know if the measurements matched with the plan she'd seen in the Soane book. Cynthia came back just as she rang off.'

'And did the measurements match?'

'No. The Round House was a bit bigger. The original bits, I mean.' Tracy settled into her seat. 'This car is so cool.'

'Sorry, I'll put the heating up.'

She shook her head and grinned. 'Cool glamorous not cool cold. Like the driver. Do we absolutely have to go to Tophaven?'

'Yes, and you're incorrigible. Kindly respect the fact that I'm an older man who's lived a very sheltered life. Cool can never mean glamorous, though. And poking out your tongue won't change the fact.'

'Don't believe the sheltered life, and I bet you're under forty.'

'Bit over, as it happens.' He was just forty-two, and it irritated him that he was increasingly unready to be accurate in the matter. 'When did the others at that meeting know what Lady Brasset was up to?'

She frowned, more because the subject bored her than because she had difficulty supplying an answer. 'I told Daddy first. I expect Lancelot told the Daws. Mr Daws rang Daddy asking him if he'd organize a meeting. Poor Daddy. Everybody goes to him for free advice. Especially ex-service people.'

'That's a great credit to him.'

'Suppose it is, really. Some write him about their personal problems. Or telephone. Sometimes from miles away. Men who've served under him, mostly. Mr Daws didn't, of course. He isn't ex-service. Just picks Daddy's brains. Anyhow, this time Daddy put his foot down. Said the freeholders should consult with their lawyer. That's Denis Pitty.'

'So someone rang him?'

'Daddy again. Got him to join the others for dinner at seven. At the Beachcomber. Mr Daws had to stand everybody a free meal. Couldn't get out of it. The meeting was his idea. Serve him right.'

'I see. Tell me, what was Mrs Tring's reaction to Lady Brasset's call?'

'Oh, she knew already about why Louella had gone to London. Not about her seeing you . . .'

'No, that was last-minute, I think, after she'd learned the planning permission was through. So Mrs Tring knew Lady Brasset had dug up evidence . . .'

'In the Marshford Papers? In the library? Yes. Louella came over to the Round House to tell her Thursday evening.'

'You were there then, too?'

'No. Cynthia told me a bit about it in the morning. I was in before the others. That's why I told Daddy. At lunch-time.'

'I see.' He didn't indicate his earlier misunderstanding—or his present surprise. 'You go home for lunch?'

'Usually. Daddy's by himself.'

'D'you suppose Mrs Tring told anyone else?'

'About Louella's dreadful disclosures? She may have. Her husband probably. Does it matter?'

'No,' he answered, without being sure he meant it. 'Just idle curiosity.'

But why had Lady Brasset been so much less circumspect than she had implied to Grenwood and himself? Perhaps, at the end, she had abandoned concern at being thwarted by the Tophaven Council. Certainly it had been Seawell and Roxton International that had been worrying her when she came to Grenwood, Phipps for protection against the rapacious instincts of property developers.

Still, he found the dead woman's behaviour inconsistent unless . . .

'Are you really taking me straight home?'

They were passing through the industrial estate that ringed the outskirts of the town.

'Since you insist.'

'Grr!'

He glanced at the time. 'We can go on afterwards, if you like.'

'Where?' Her eyes opened wide.

'The library.'

She fell back in the seat, pouting. 'Thank you, but I couldn't stand the excitement.'

CHAPTER 8

'I wasn't prying, Mr Treasure, I assure you.'

'On the contrary, Mr Sims. I should have assumed you were showing a wholly professional attitude.'

'That was it. That was it entirely. Well, almost. But Lady Brasset. She quite spurned assistance from the staff. One hesitates. Such a tragic accident. But she was . . . how can I put it? . . . She was almost perversely suspicious. Oh dear. I really shouldn't say such things now.'

Treasure nodded understandingly. Physically, and in mental attitude, Sims was a male replica of Mrs Daws, twenty or so years on. He was a worrier, the melancholic lines set deep into his brow. The remorse about speaking ill of the dead was genuine enough.

They were seated side by side at a reading desk in the reference room. There was no one else present. No one had been excluded: as usual, there were no other takers.

The Marshford Papers were arranged on the desk. Treasure had spent half an hour with the material before Sims had been able to join him. The sole assistant librarian had been late for work.

'So instead of sharing in her research project, you were duplicating it?'

'You could say that. Yes.'

'You didn't know what she was looking for, of course.'

'A re-awakened interest in some aspect of the town's history, I thought. As Chief Librarian—' now that the other one had turned up—'one feels a working knowledge of archive material in active use . . .'

He droned on in a subdued tone. It was difficult to catch all the words, but even the cadence sounded unconvincing.

'There was no hint from Lady Brasset as to her special interest?' Treasure had interrupted at random. He knew the answer, of course. 'You were perhaps trying to assess the irritant quotient to the Council of whatever it was she was trying to uncover.'

Sims turned a blotchy pink. 'That wasn't . . .'

'You have my sympathy, believe me. I've learned the lady had a certain reputation as an interfering busybody. A meddler. It's easy to credit. I spent an hour with her yesterday afternoon. Nice old thing, but I imagine also formidable in battle.'

There was relief on the other's face. The hesitancy of manner began to fade: the voice gathered a bit of resonance. 'It was the new library, you see. Everything's approved. The money. The site. The plans. She might have been finding a way to block it. It could be ready in a year. I'd so looked forward. You understand, Mr Treasure? Sydney Marshford built this terrible place. What if there was something in these wretched Papers . . . ?'

'To stop you getting a new library? Yes, I do see. There isn't, though?'

'It appears not. But the thought's been haunting me. You've no idea. I'm getting on, but I'm far from past it. My wife died some years ago. There's only my married daughter. The new place, it'll be an interest. A challenge.'

Even so, woolly mittens not steel gauntlets seemed most appropriate for Sims.

'Difficult to imagine what a past benefactor could have arranged. To stop things.'

'You'd be surprised, Mr Treasure. He set up enduring considerations. Considerations and penalties.'

'I'm sorry?' Treasure shook his head.

'For instance. Certain services and practices were prescribed for the church he built. The vicar gets an extra annual benefaction if he . . . if he steadfastly observes them.'

'No doubt the money involved was appropriated by the Church Commissioners in 1948, when everything went into the common pot.'

'No, Mr Treasure. Never. It was too carefully protected in law. Policed, administered by paid trustees. And it's indexed, you might say.' A sort of smile briefly illuminated the naturally drawn countenance. 'It's not a fixed sum of money.' He coughed gently. 'They none of them were. It's half the income from the trust fund for the previous year. A handsome consideration, and subject to a minimum.'

'You mean if the income isn't up to scratch, the trustees make up from capital?'

'I believe that's how it works.' Sims nodded uncertainly. 'Mr Marshford was very High Church. A Tractarian. He's still ordering the services, you might say, even though the living's reverted to the Diocese.'

'You mean the Bishop appoints the incumbent?'

'Since the death of Randolph Marshford. Up to then the family held the living.'

'You said "none of them" were fixed sums of money. Did you mean there are other lingering benefactions?'

'Oh yes. There's the Chairman of the Council.'

'He gets something?' There was no suppressing the surprise.

'So long as the six main streets in the town are lit artificially during the hours of darkness. Of course, they always would have been in modern times. It was to do with protecting ladies. Many of the benefactions were. Sydney Marshford had nine surviving daughters. All spinsters. At the beginning he also owned the gas company.' There was resignation not cynicism in the tone.

'Who else gets a hand-out?'

'A benefaction,' Sims corrected solemnly. 'The station-master. He's called manager now, of course. For keeping the ladies' waiting-room heated in the winter months. We still do have a ladies' waiting-room. Also the town clerk if at least five ladies are employed at the town hall.'

'Probably a high number for a small town in . . .'

'1869. Exactly, Mr Treasure. Now they have more women there than men.' He gave a slight cough. 'I myself receive one of the smaller honoraria.'

'Fixed sum?'

'No, like the others. It's really very small.' Even so he didn't trouble to volunteer how small. 'For arranging a ladies' invitation lecture here annually. The speaker has to be a writer. Of non-fiction.'

'On an improving subject, no doubt.'

'The exact words, as it happens. There's no problem in finding suitable lecturers. The attendance, though, is often quite small.' He sighed. 'Then there's the editor of the *Tophaven Weekly Gazette*.'

'Another beneficiary?'

'For publishing twelve articles a year by women writers. Again, there's a prescribed list of educational subjects.'

'Are there any more worthy recipients?'

'There used to be. The times have defeated the intention in some instances. There's no longer a visiting doctor at the workhouse . . .'

'Because there's no longer a workhouse? No doubt he had to give extra attention to female inmates.'

'Exactly.' Sims swallowed. 'Pregnant ones on Thursday afternoons. The head teacher at the church school used to get an extra payment, but that's closed now.'

'But surviving recipients are getting away . . . I mean enjoying their benefits without anyone objecting? The station manager, for instance. He's employed by British Rail. You're employed by the Council. The editor of the paper by its proprietors, and so on. The Chairman of the Council, surely that's an elected, unpaid office . . .'

'Oh, no one can possibly object, Mr Treasure, nor deprive the recipients. It's accepted the benefits detract nothing from anyone's professional or . . . er . . . amateur status.' He paused before adding meekly. 'We have always had a winter lecture programme here at the library.'

'I expect the trust deeds were carefully drafted.'

'Very carefully. Mr Denis Pitty remarked on it to me only last year. Mr Pitty is solicitor to the Marshford Trusts. Also, I believe, a trustee. A most competent lawyer.'

'Yes. I know him.' Treasure smiled. 'You mentioned penalties . . .'

'A figure of speech. Sydney Marshford offered benefits so people would perform certain duties after he was gone.'

'So the penalties were the loss of the income if they didn't perform?'

'More than that, Mr Treasure.' Now he was searching for words again as he had been at the beginning. 'It's difficult to explain. Through his er . . . kindness to certain influential or key members of the community, he created an unofficial body of . . . of opinion formers naturally inclined to sympathize with his known

attitudes . . . to support them . . . and any that might
come to light. It's stupid, I know, but I had it in my head
that Lady Brasset, who was known to be against the new
town hall, might . . . well . . .'

'Come up with something in the Marshford Papers that
would make the opinion formers feel they shouldn't be
going ahead with your library. Or find a penalty for their
doing so.'

'That's right. I really haven't been able to sleep.'

'But you've found nothing in the papers? Frankly it's
difficult to imagine what . . .'

'There could have been difficulties over the land this
library stands on. The lease hasn't expired yet. Not like
the town hall.'

'What sort of difficulties?'

He looked baffled. 'None, I suppose — except in my
imagination. You see, Sydney Marshford gave the town
hall and the library to the town, but he only leased the
land. The town was to get the freeholds when the leases
expired.'

'Odd arrangement. And they expired at different
times?'

'Yes. Two years ago in the case of the town hall. The
Council was able to sell the land for private development.
It fetched a good deal. The money went some way to
paying for the new town hall, although not as far as was
expected. It's been built on derelict land, at the back of
the town. The new library is to go next door. The lease
here expires next year.'

'But none of what you call Marshford's penalties
applied to the lease?'

'On the contrary.' Sims looked deadly serious. 'Both
buildings had to be in use for the purpose they were built
to perform when the leases expired. That was to
encourage the development of the town centre around the
two buildings in the last century.'

'Otherwise the leases wouldn't have reverted to the town?'

'Exactly, Mr Treasure. They would have remained with the charity that acquired them, after the death of Sydney Marshford's last surviving daughter.'

Treasure looked about the room with exaggerated emphasis. 'It seems to me we still have a library here.'

'I know. I know. There's nothing to fear except . . . except some loophole might have existed. Something overlooked . . .'

'Which Lady Brasset could have found. Mmm, I can see why you were worried.'

Even so, if there were such a possibility, why had Sims left it over the years for an outsider to reveal? Presumably he had always had the Papers at his disposal? There was a simple explanation, of course. The man was a fool — an educated one, too, but they were always the worst kind.

'She was so firmly against the new town hall.' Sims seemed to be musing now almost to himself. 'Unnecessary expense, she said. It did cost rather more than was budgeted.'

'And you figured Lady Brasset was looking for reasons to keep this place going?'

'Until the last minute, when I found I was wrong. In fairness, she had never actually spoken out against the new library.'

'But she did about the town hall?'

'Frequently. I simply assumed.' He shook his head dismally. 'She was so secretive about her purposes. But the last words she was ever to say to me were ones of encouragement about the new library. She was lighting a cigarette in the hallway downstairs. She always did so as she left. A quick drag before driving, she used to say. Never smoked in the car. "We must all put our weight behind hurrying the new library along," she said to me. Her very words. She then made some pertinent points about computer indexing. Her parting message, as it were.'

It was a touching account, allowing for a measure of sentimental licence.

'Anyway, her interest was in saving the Round House,' Treasure offered brightly.

'So I understand.' Sims let his hands drop on to the papers before him. 'I could have helped, perhaps. If only she'd asked instead of misleading me. The photocopies she took on Thursday had nothing to do with the Round House.'

'I don't think she wanted anyone to know why she was going to London.'

'Hmm. It was common enough knowledge yesterday.'

'You heard it yourself?'

'I think it was my assistant who mentioned it.'

The banker was mildly irritated at the man's vagueness.

'Lady Brasset mentioned some diary entries with the dates. I made a note of them at the time. Looked them out before you came up. They're in the 1836 and 1838 volumes. I'd like to copy them.'

'Of course.'

'They make it pretty clear Marshford was instructing his architect to use a plan from a pattern book by John Soane—or rather Sir J.S., though there can't be much doubt it was Soane. There's a copy letter somewhere Lady Brasset said threw more light on the business. Helped to identify the other architect.'

'Indeed?' It was only a polite acknowledgement.

'Yes. She actually hand-copied Marshford's own copy but thought she might have left it here by mistake. I've not been able to find her copy or the original.'

'All letters to Sydney Marshford and copies of his own letters are in these linen-bound folders. They're also identified by year.'

'I know. The year was 1839. This is the one.' Treasure pulled forward one of the folders and opened it. 'Not much in it.'

'It was early days. At that time Marshford was quite selective about what he kept . . .'

'And very unhelpful when it comes to names. He just uses initials and a string of contractions. A sort of private shorthand.'

'At the beginning, yes. That would be before he employed clerks for the donkey work.'

'He does it in the diaries too. I suppose he kept them simply for his own pleasure.' The banker shrugged impatiently. 'Anyway, I can't find this letter. You haven't got it?'

Sims exhibited something near to wonderment. 'Everything is here.' He spread his hands as though about to pronounce a blessing on the memorabilia of Sydney Marshford, Esquire. 'Normally readers are obliged to return archive material to the librarian at the end of every day. Because there was so much in this case, with Lady Brasset coming daily to use it, I arranged for it to be left here. The room is locked every night. There are very few readers. None yesterday. For my own part, I've appropriated nothing.'

'She could have put the letter back in the wrong folder I suppose. I've looked in a few. You'd think her own copy would stick out like a sore thumb, too. I haven't come across it.'

'She might have taken her copy and the original away with her. The original by mistake, of course. She could then have mislaid them elsewhere.'

'She mentioned the possibility herself. Tell me, d'you ever remember seeing a Marshford copy letter addressed to a W.B?' Treasure briefly described the contents.

Sims shook his head slowly. 'As I told you, I spent many hours with the Papers. I recall reference in the diaries to the house to be built on the shore. Its purpose, an academy for young ladies. I have no recollection of the letter.'

'Pity. It's important, you see. There are only three references to this W.B. Two are in the diaries. Both a bit vague. The letter was Lady Brasset's *pièce de résistance*. According to her, it was much more explicit.'

'Furthering her theory, if I understand you, that the Round House is a building with an important provenance.' Sims very nearly committed a wry smile. 'Forgive me, Mr Treasure. In view of your connections, are you anxious to expose such a document. Even to credit it exists?'

'If it exists, I want to see it. So, I suspect will the DoE.' He ignored the deeper implication. 'Are you suggesting it doesn't exist? That Lady Brasset invented it? She said she must have left both documents here, or taken her copy with her and lost it.'

The librarian swallowed as though to suppress embarrassment — or it could have been something close to indignation.

'Only you and I have had access to the Papers since Lady Brasset left here on Thursday, Mr Treasure. I'm quite sure you haven't appropriated the letters. You may take my word for it, I haven't. We can make a thorough search, of course.' He hesitated. 'If you ask me, though, Lady Brasset may have composed the letter to add credence to a thinly substantiated theory. I'm sorry to make so bold a suggestion.'

The last fact was evident enough. The room was scarcely overheated, but Sims was sweating profusely.

CHAPTER 9

'Truly, the house is quite untouched. The damage is all in the garden.' Treasure was speaking into the pay-phone in the hall of the Beachcomber. The hotel didn't run to room phones—even in the bridal suite. 'I'm so sorry not to have reached you before this. I did try several times . . .'

'I was out early, Mark, and Algy's been in the greenhouse all morning.' Cynthia Tring continued in the calm tone she had adopted nearly from the start of the conversation. After Treasure had affirmed the building was safe, her reaction to his admittedly sketchy account of the dawn assault on her property had bordered on indifference.

'Garden's a bit of a mess in places.' Perhaps he had made too light of what had happened. At least he hadn't had to lie. Describing the driver of the JCB as a raving idiot had exactly covered his opinion of Anthony Quaint. 'Roxton's, the contractors, will be fully insured.' Not that there was any likelihood of their putting in a claim. He hadn't relished the job of explaining things to the Trings, but having agreed to do so, it was proving easier than he'd expected. 'I thought, perhaps in the circumstances, a financial settlement. I mean a sum of money rather than . . .'

He was stopped by the husky chuckle from the other end. 'What a splendid ambassador you are, my dear.' She had sensed his discomfort. 'We'll see. Since we're closing the college . . .'

'That's really what I meant. Seems rather pointless putting the garden to rights.'

'I agree,' she cut in. 'And you think it was mindless vandalism? I mean, it could have been more deliberate,' she continued ruminatively but with hovering conviction. 'I suppose if someone — the owner of one of the other properties . . .'

'I doubt it,' he interrupted with a justified assurance he could hardly explain. 'Anyway, that's the kind of possibility better not discussed on the phone, don't you think?'

A less oblique reply had been impossible with one of those other owners standing a yard away.

Mostyn Daws was palpably feigning concentration on the single sheet of paper lying before him on the reception desk. He had been doing so since just after Treasure had begun the telephone conversation several minutes earlier.

The transparent plastic dome attached to the wall above the phone was presumably intended to insulate users from outside noises. The banker was sure the thing was acting as a strictly local amplifier. Mrs Daws had unintentionally confirmed this suspicion by pointedly taking herself out of range at the start of the call, and with undisguised bashfulness. Her own preoccupation with a large ledger had seemed wholly genuine.

'Then you must come to lunch at one o'clock,' Cynthia had answered promptly.

'I didn't mean . . .'

'I know you didn't, and the food won't be up to much. Better than the Beachcomber, though. I suspect anything might be.'

'I'm sure of that.' He was sorry only the outgoing part of the conversation was being made covertly available to the hotel's proprietor. 'Thank you, I'd be delighted. See you at one.'

The visit would allow him to quash any extra suspicions about the assault on the Round House — also to re-introduce the question of the lease. If Cynthia was so relaxed about the early morning outrage, something might have happened to make her less obdurate about giving up the lease before the end of term. She had slept on the matter. Could it be she was now seeing her declared attitude as pointlessly obdurate—even perverse? The four students could easily be taught from some other base for a few weeks. He intended to suggest some rooms at the Beachcomber. After all, there was still the incentive of a payment for the Trings.

'Won't be in to lunch, squire?' Daws's question had a rhetorical ring—careless in the circumstances.

'I'll let you know,' Treasure answered, boot-faced. 'But I'd like to keep my room for tonight.' It seemed there was less chance of anyone actually taking the Round House apart while he was about.

'Ah yes . . . Yes, I think that can be arranged.' Daws made a pretence of studying the reservation sheet, a habit he would probably maintain till the day not far hence when he vacated his manifestly seldom patronized establishment. 'Yes, that's fine.' He looked up. 'Delighted you're extending your sojourn with us.' The comment could scarcely have been more unctuous if Treasure had asked the rate for permanent residence. Then the expression changed. 'No cheque in the post, I'm afraid, squire.'

'Cheque?' Treasure at first affected incomprehension. 'You mean from Seawell? I imagine that would go to your lawyer, Denis Pitty.'

'Rang him first thing. He went through the mail specially. Office isn't officially open Saturdays. Very good of him. No cheque, though.'

'Then you have to wait a bit longer.' Really, it was nothing to do with him. 'I expect Pitty will chase them on Monday.'

Daws made a pained grimace that brought his wrinkling brow chinwards and stretched the edges of his mouth nearly to his ears—as though he had bitten on a raw onion. 'Seen the Round House yet?' he enquired.

The question was a clear enough reminder that Treasure could hardly be absolved from connection with the Sandy Lane development.

'A quick look, yes. Bit of trouble with vandals in the garden, it seems.'

'Oh yes? Lot of that about these days.'

Was it possible the episode earlier had gone unnoted by the local residents? If Daws didn't know about it then presumably nobody did.

'Thought I'd stroll up there now,' Treasure added casually.

'Proper dog's dinner of a place, if you ask me.' Daws looked about his deserted premises prior to a confidential offering. No hibernating guest appeared suddenly to spoil the strong sense of privacy. Only Mrs Daws glanced up, too late to savour the charade. 'No disrespect, you understand, but I used to think some of Lady B's ideas were just plain nuts. Bonkers. Fertile imagination, you might say, eh?' He nodded, knowingly tapping the side of his head with an extended forefinger.

Treasure didn't linger. The fellow's action and comments actually showed appalling insensitivity. Yet his beliefs were those of a certainly nosey, and probably fairly acute, long-term observer. If you accepted them, they gave support for growing unease in at least one connection.

To forget a gas burner was one thing: to invent a letter was quite another.

Taking a view from the upper storey of the Round House, a report that an anarchist had run riot in the garden with an army tank would have seemed entirely credible.

The JCB had been removed. In the process, Quaint's obedient minion had enlarged considerably the damage done to the terrace area. He must have been obliged to go onwards and upwards before going back into what was left of the lily tank.

The house was still inviolate. A double furrow in the wet ground led directly back to the official demolition area. In several places it ran over the crisscross of earlier tracks. To the uninformed, this would make a useful contrast with the evidence of the erratic, irresponsible outward foray.

This observation digested, Treasure left the house again. He walked around to the terrace, meaning to examine the damage more closely, but was soon deflected by his main preoccupation.

He turned to face the house, hands thrust deep into the pockets of his coat. It was at times like this he still sorely missed the pipe he was dutifully abjuring.

Was the place what Lady Brasset had insisted? On the whole his two inspections suggested she might have been completely right. Another hour with the Marshford Papers, after Sims left him, had unfortunately produced no more enlightenment — despite the references provided by the lady herself.

The librarian's copious notes in painstaking copperplate had been equally unfruitful. Curiously, neither of the eager devillers had seen, or else troubled to note, a diary reference to the lease. He had scribbled down the reference: the Trings might be interested.

A dog's dinner of a place, Daws had said. Treasure wondered: would he have been wiser to let Quaint knock it over? He had sounded off imperiously about the rule of law to Quaint and Ali at breakfast. But could he contemplate with equanimity possibly months of haggling with the authorities, first about the provenance of the building, and then about its importance to posterity?

His pragmatic view was that the Round House should not be allowed to hinder or to obstruct permanently a perfectly sound development: the place was just not good enough. It was an interesting, badly mauled curiosity. No one living cared about it. No one would miss it. So, off with its head?

'Would you be Mr Treasure, sir?'

He was a very small man, capless, but otherwise identifiable by his costume as a postman. He looked cheerful, healthy and about fifty. There was a bundle of letters in his hand done up with cord.

'That's right, but those can't be for me surely?'

'No, sir. Mostly for the Round House and Commander Mane, these are. Should have had one for you, though. In a manner of speaking, that is. I take it you are the gentleman her Ladyship was with yesterday in London.'

'Lady Brasset, you mean? Yes, but . . .'

'I heard Mr Daws talking about you just now. He was saying to Mr Elderberry you'd be up here. That's why I come round looking for you, begging your pardon.'

'I still don't see . . .'

'I do a bit of gardening for her Ladyship. Her death. What a terrible sad thing it is, sir.'

'Awful. Let me see? You'll be Mr Jacks.'

'That's right, sir. Eddy Jacks. Perhaps her Ladyship mentioned me?'

'Actually, it was Mr Stock, the policeman.'

'Ah, old Cliff, was it?' He drew closer. It seemed to be a day for secrets. 'She rang me, see? At the cottage. Yesterday afternoon.'

'Your cottage?'

'No, hers. I don't have a place of my own. I'm a lodger. In a council house.' Jacks paused as though it was the last not the first point that carried the most significance.

But it was not the postman's housing arrangements that intrigued. 'You talked to Lady Brasset on her own telephone? At what time?'

'Five o'clock, or just after. In the garage I was, mending that hedge-cutter. Dratted thing. Bit hard of hearing her Ladyship's got. Nothing serious, you understand?' He paused again. 'And that's the daftest thing I'll say this year, her being dead now. Anyhow, she'd had this extension bell put in the garden.'

'And a telephone?'

Jacks shook his head in mild surprise. 'No. She could walk all right. Phone's in the cottage.'

'In the kitchen?' Treasure didn't recall seeing it.'

'Front hall.'

'But did you go in the kitchen?'

'No, I didn't. My key's to the front door. There's a spare one as well. Under a flower-pot. Everybody knows. I told her that's asking for trouble. Burglars. Never been bothered, though. Anyway, I got my own. She knew I was coming yesterday. If the phone rings a long time when she's out it's usually her wanting me to do something. That's why I answered.'

'And did you notice . . . ?'

'She said to look in her sheepskin coat. Right-hand pocket.' The postman was determined to tell his story his way. 'As like as not I'd find a piece of folded notepaper there. Copy of a letter. From the library. She thought she'd lost it, or left it somewhere, in the library or here, at the Round House. She'd rung everywhere about it. Then, last thing, after seeing you it was, she thought she remembered — clear as anything — she'd put it in that coat pocket.'

'And it was there?'

'No. Only a packet of cigarettes. Empty. I couldn't tell her. She'd rung off. Phone-box, you see? It took me a bit of time searching. She probably ran out of coins, or she was in a hurry.'

'Yes, I see. Did you smell . . ?'

'If it had been there I was to put it straight in an envelope and post it to you, sir, marked confidential. I took down the name and address. It was so it would catch the last post yesterday. Important she said you got it pronto. In the haste, of course, I'd forgotten. Yesterday was Friday. You probably don't see your office post till Mondays.'

'No, I don't. But if there wasn't . . ?'

'It's been worrying me, you see. Her last wish. And I hadn't done it. Bit of luck hearing you was here, sir. I'd have written otherwise, I expect.' There seemed some doubt — self-doubt in the last expression. 'So long as you know I did my best.' Would the garrulous little man fall silent at last? No. 'You'll keep it to yourself, sir?'

'About the letter? Yes, if you like. And you didn't smell gas in the cottage?'

'Didn't smell nothing. If only I had, I'd . . .'

'Surprising, really.' Treasure firmly halted the new flow. 'I mean, with that kind of build-up you'd have thought the whole place . . . Have you told the police?'

The other man looked sheepish. 'No call for that, sir. None as I can see. Bearing in mind I wasn't there. In a manner of speaking.'

'How d'you mean, you weren't there? You've just said . . .'

'I done my duty by her Ladyship telling you, sir. About the letter, I mean. So far as others is concerned, it's none of their business, is it?' He hesitated. 'My afternoon for her Ladyship, it's Saturdays. Yesterday was Friday. I work all Fridays,' he finished slowly and pointedly.

Treasure gradually got the point. 'You mean you're supposed to be delivering mail on Fridays, not doing jobbing gardening?'

'Collecting and sorting. That's right, sir. It got done all right yesterday,' he added defensively. He had dropped the conspiratorial undertone. 'One of my mates and me. We double up sometimes in the afternoons. More in summer than winter, usually.'

'But you did yesterday, which meant you could do an extra half day for Lady Brasset.' Treasure looked at his watch. 'I'm afraid I must get on.' He began walking towards the front of the house. Jacks fell in beside him.

'It was the hedge-cutter, sir. Broke down on me last week *after* it was in for repair. And with the job half done. Two weeks they had it, and the privet overdue for the last cut then.' He frowned his disgust with 'them'. 'Her Ladyship said she'd take it back. Quicker if I do it, I said. It was the mild October we had. Nothing stopped growing, you see, sir. So I stripped it down myself on the bench. It's right as rain now. I can finish the cutting this afternoon. Been paid in advance for the week. Not that I wouldn't do it anyway. Fine lady she was. Real lady.'

Treasure frowned. 'I see the problem, but if you were in the cottage yesterday, I really think you have to tell the authorities.'

'And be up in the coroner's court? There'll be an inquest all right. Reports in the paper. My superior sees it. So I'll be disciplined. Worse perhaps. It's my job I've got to think of Mr Treasure. Been in it since the Navy. It's not that I've got anything to say. I heard the phone. Went in. Answered it. I looked in the coat pocket—that was in the hall cupboard—and came out again.' He stretched his chin by way of punctuation. 'There's others who was there without jobs at stake. Let them do the reporting. Won't bring her Ladyship back, of course.'

'There were other people at the cottage?' The two had stopped beside the little post-office van parked at the side of the drive.

'Two I saw from the garage. They didn't see me. Both stayed long enough to have gone in at the front. There was someone else I didn't see. Thought it was her Ladyship come home and then go off again. I saw the car. It was like hers. Not sure about the colour, come to think.'

'Who were the other two people?'

Jacks looked uncomfortable. 'Thats for them to say, sir,

isn't it? They weren't burglars, I can tell you that.'

'You knew them?'

The postman nodded. 'Friends of her Ladyship. Most likely they knew where that key was. Can't say about the third. Didn't stay long, whoever it was.'

'Look, I'm sorry, but I still think you have to report this, especially if no one else comes forward.' If there was even a possibility that someone else had entered the house . . .

'I only told you on account of her Ladyship and the letter, sir.' It was the tone of the genuinely aggrieved.

'OK. I won't tell anyone, and there's no need for you to mention to anyone you've told me. But in the circumstances you could be in a lot of trouble for not reporting what happened. Ask anyone whose opinion you trust. In fact, I think you should see a lawyer.'

'I don't have the money for that, sir.' The statement was matter of fact and begged nothing.

'Do you happen to know Mr Denis Pitty?'   .

Jacks looked up sharply, then nodded.

'Good. If you'd like to see him, let me know his fee later and I'll reimburse you. He may suggest you make a statement to him and sign it. That won't put you in the clear, but if he can't persuade you to come forward either, at least there'll be something on the record. Will you see him — or someone else? As I say, I'll pay the costs.'

'Can I think about it, sir?'

'Sure. The other thing you could do, of course, is approach the other two visitors to the cottage. You could wait a bit, I suppose, to see if they're coming forward on their own. Did either of them arrive after you took the call from Lady Brasset?'

'One did. And the third who I never saw.'

'Well if the last one you saw says he went in, didn't smell gas, and has told the police, then your testimony would probably be superfluous. May not be good law, but it's obvious common sense.'

'That'd be all right then, sir?'

'Sort of. I'd still be happier if . . . Tell me, what time did this chap show up?'

'About twenty past five, sir. Might have been a bit later.'

'And he didn't see you?'

'No, sir.'

At least Treasure had established the sex of the person. 'Why not if you could see him?'

'I'd switched both porch lights on earlier. For her Ladyship. For when she got back. With them on you wouldn't notice the light in the garage. Not if you was visiting at the front.'

Treasure remembered the side door to the little brick garage. It had been glazed at the top: a small square of glass, blown out by the explosion when he had seen it. The work bench would be at the far end of the garage with the internal light there too, probably. So someone working there at night could easily step back and see through the upper part of the door without necessarily being seen himself from the outside—particularly if he didn't want to be seen.

'All right, Mr Jacks. You'd better tell me what you decide to do later. I'll be at the Beachcomber till this time tomorrow.' He gave the postman a visiting card. 'Phone me in London if you miss me here.' Despite the man's irritating recalcitrance, he felt in a way responsible for his dilemma. 'Thank you for telling me about Lady Brasset and the letter.'

'So long as I did the right thing there, sir. Thank you very much, sir.' He retreated towards the door of the Round House, pulling the cord from his clutch of letters.

As Treasure hurried away, something made him glance back. He thought he had seen someone out of the corner of his eye: possibly Jacks coming after him? But the postman had gone in the opposite direction. It was of no consequence: a trick of the light, perhaps.

The person who had earlier arrived to speak to him had retreated further out of sight behind the high rhododendron on the far left of the drive.

At first it had been inappropriate to interrupt the conversation with Jacks. Then too much had been heard for the fact to be acknowledged — or the consequences of the revelations to be ignored.

As soon as the postman had driven off, the figure stole back another way, across the garden.

CHAPTER 10

'Well met, Mr Treasure!' exclaimed a breathless Lancelot Elderberry. He cannoned out from behind a gatepost at South View where he had evidently been lurking — but not for very long. He was clad in a loud check cloak with a black felt hat, the brim dashingly turned up on one side.

' 'Morning to you,' replied Treasure with extra ebullience because he couldn't, on the instant, remember the fellow's name.

'Been to the Round House again, I see.' Elderberry tried to fall into step with the banker. After a succession of little hops and one long skip, he gave up. 'I'd have been a fright in the army,' he chortled, shuffling along matching three of his steps with the other's two. 'In any case the uniform wouldn't have suited. I did my bit, though. In the war, I mean. The last one.' There was more chortling. 'I was attached to the Ministry of Information. Rather loosely. That was a lark.'

'And how, Mr Elderberry —' he'd just remembered it — 'do you know I've been twice to the Round House?'

The question was put lightly, but he needed to know the answer.

'Aha! A little birdie told me.'

Treasure didn't show his displeasure. So Tracy had . . .

'No, nothing so exciting,' Elderberry continued, unaware he had nearly ruined a reputation and a warming relationship. 'Saw you leave there in your beautiful Roly-Poly when I was getting up. How silent it is. I didn't hear it arrive.'

'Hope I didn't wake you.'

'Goodness, no. But isn't the house a perfect fright? I knew you'd think so as soon as you saw it.' He didn't pause for agreement. 'They've started work on the garden, I see. Had a little look after breakfast. Huge great machine. Seemed to be digging drains. Grumbling about all over the place. It went away as I arrived. D'you think I frightened it? Gave me an idea, as a matter of fact.' He took a deep breath through his mouth. 'Nothing from Seawell Developments for the freeholders this morning.'

So that was the purpose of this chance encounter.

'Mr Daws mentioned it,' Treasure responded noncommittally.

'Denis Pitty isn't wildly helpful. Wait and see seems to be his motto. Would you think the spirit of dear Louella is steering the Seawell ship away from us deserving poor, marooned upon this pesky shore?' Elderberry glared at the broken concrete across the potholed road.

'Cheer up. They've bought the Round House since they learned about Lady Brasset's intervention. Intended intervention.'

'I've given that close thought in the silence of the night. It could have been something your friends did on the spur of the moment, which they're now regretting. Which still leaves tiny me and the others in the cold. I have my worst misgivings if I wake at three in the morning.'

'Same for everybody. It's to do with the basal metabolic

rate,' Treasure declared briskly.

'Well, that's a blessing.' Elderberry glanced behind them. Treasure resigned himself to the feeling that more confidences were on the way. 'A word in your ear, dear sir. Shall we cross?'

They had nearly reached the hotel drive. Elderberry steered the banker to the seaward side of the road.

'It'll have to be a quick word. I'm running late.'

'What I thought,' continued Elderberry as they mounted the steps on to the municipal promenade, 'what I thought when I saw that great machine lolloping across the garden was.' He strung out the last letter allowing it to end as a diminishing hiss. 'What—' here there was a dramatic pause followed double presto by—'what if it had run amok and knocked down the house?'

'There'd have been a hell of a din and a worse row later.'

'A *fait accompli* nevertheless. Don't you agree? Of course you do. You can't preserve a load of rubble.'

'And you can't go knocking down . . .'

'You can't but I can. Do hear me out. It's outrageous, but, you see, I know this absolutely charming boy.' He looked from side to side, not for eavesdroppers but as though acknowledging the adulation of a crowd. 'He'll do simply anything for me. *And* he drives one of those machines—like the one in the garden. Works on motorways. He's a big strong boy. So, I mean, what could be simpler? I'm sure he'll know how to start that monster. He could come tonight and . . . and poof!' He stopped, made a circle in the air with his arms. Hurrying to draw abreast again he murmured, 'You wouldn't need to know a thing about it.'

'Except you've just told me.' In a way he wished . . . 'Look, Mr Elderberry, I know you mean well . . .'

'So where's the harm? Your Seawell people own the building, for heaven's sake.'

'The harm is it's illegal, immoral and transparent. Apart from other considerations there's a lease.'

'Oh, bother Cynthia Tring and her wretched lease. *She's* not on the breadline.'

'Neither are you, by the look of it.'

'I am, as it happens, skint. The market for my work is drying up. So am I drying up. I can't write pornography, and nothing else sells. Morality's not involved. I'm no good at it.' He stared petulantly at the outgoing tide. 'The money for South View is the only thing between me and steep decline into penury, accelerated by urgent current obligations.'

'But I'm sure you'll get your money. Equally, I tell you any fool scheme like the one you've suggested will land you in jug. They've had some trouble on the site already. Anyone starting more is bound to get nabbed.'

He didn't intend to enlarge on what he meant by trouble unless pressed.

'All right.' The other sniffed. 'Never knew big business was so lily white. It was only a brilliantly creative idea I was trying out, if that's the way you want it. I . . .' Suddenly he halted, swallowed, then continued urgently, 'We must go back. You were in a hurry.'

Elderberry turned about and moved off at a considerably faster pace. It was clear speed had now become a mutual objective.

'I think someone's waving at you,' remarked Treasure innocently. Glancing back, he had noticed an extremely tall, thin young man bearing down on them, and making signs.

'Take no notice. Total stranger. Probably begging,' cautioned Elderberry, head down into the wind and now moving as fast as his short legs would carry him.

'Lancelot! Lancelot!' cried the alleged stranger, now only a few paces behind.

'Go away, horrid boy. We have nothing to give you.'

Elderberry had gone red in the face. 'Never buy from street traders, Mr Treasure. Especially at the seaside.'

'Lancelot, it's me.' The gangling, pale youth with yellow hair was now leaping sideways abreast of the two. It seemed sensible he should do something energetic to keep his circulation going. The cotton shirt and trousers looked scant protection against the elements. 'They've said they'll pay more, Lancelot. I've got to take it, haven't I then?' The accent was East London.

'Oh, it's you, Bobby,' said Elderberry, affecting total surprise. 'It's Bobby. I'm helping him through a difficult patch.' This came as an aside in Treasure's ear. 'One does one's best for the lame ducks, especially in these hard times. Not now, Bobby,' he shouted at the youth. 'I'm busy with someone important. Important,' he emphasized, even more loudly. 'I'll see you later.'

'No you won't, Lancelot. You're always saying that. He's always saying that.' Treasure was now being addressed directly between the gazelle-like leaps. 'He doesn't answer the door, and he hangs up the phone. I've got to know, Lancelot. The offer's on the level. From the magazine. It's enough to get me to L.A. with a stake. That's all I need, see?' Again he was addressing Treasure. 'It's just for the winter, see? It's me chest. Suffer terrible I do. And it's a good magazine. Good money.'

This was too much for Elderberry. 'Good magazine! Good money! It's an obscene, garbage-sifting rag,' he expostulated, pretences evaporating as his temper soared. He didn't decrease the pace which was now headlong. 'I'll sue, you know. I'll sue and I'll win. Them and you. See if I don't, you . . . you Judas. You can't flout the law in this country and expect to get away with it, you know,' shouted the paragon who a few minutes before had been planning a nocturnal demolition of someone else's quite sizeable property.

'Lancelot, don't be like that.' The youth was now in

front of them jumping backwards with remarkable dexterity. 'You said you'd lend it me. You said last month.'

Some passers by were staring at the ill-assorted trio: Elderberry alone was a sufficiently bizarre companion.

'I really must leave you now, I'm afraid,' said Treasure with a generous infusion of sadness supporting the necessity. He was prepared to outdistance the already overstretched Elderberry even if this meant breaking into a sprint. They had nearly reached the end of the Esplanade. 'Lunch date, you understand. See you later, Mr Elderberry, I expect. Goodbye, Mr . . . hmm . . . Good luck.' He waved as he hurried down the steps, leaving the winded Elderberry with his mouth open. The youth was prancing round the unfortunate author like an undernourished cannibal sizing up his first square meal in a long time.

Esta Daws stumbled on the pavement. She was near the library.

'You all right, love?' A woman older than she, but pushing a pram, stopped to enquire. The woman had a kind, happy face: all contentment and solicitousness for others — and why not? It was beautiful — the baby in the pram.

'Yes . . . yes, thanks. Caught my heel, that's all.' She hurried away along the High Street, bumping into someone; not caring.

It was still quite crowded for late on a Saturday morning, with everybody in a hurry. The shops closed at one. She hadn't done the bit of shopping she'd said she came out for. She hadn't even changed the books.

She stopped, pretending to look in a window. It was an electrical store, but nothing registered. Her eyes were welled up with tears. The glasses wouldn't disguise her distress: that was why the woman had asked if she was all right, not because she'd tripped. She fumbled in her bag for a hanky.

Oh God, why couldn't it have come right? They'd sacrificed everything: Mostyn's job, her money, the bit they'd saved together—then just about every penny he'd put away. That was the unfair part. She never should have let him do that.

And it had all gone in that lousy, stinking, chance-of-a-lifetime hotel. It was why they'd put off having children: then and again every year after. It was never the right moment. She had understood at the time—and all the other times, before and since. You couldn't run a hotel practically single-handed with a baby to cope with as well, Mostyn said. Like they didn't need children to limit their mobility when he'd been moving up in the pet food firm, Mostyn said. There had been something else before that.

The offer from Seawell had been salvation: a real chance to start again. They weren't getting as much as Mostyn had hoped at the start. It was enough, though.

Mr Pitty had bargained hard for everybody. There was strength in numbers, he'd said, with him working for all the freeholders. She'd been sure that was right. Mr Pitty was honest, and he was used to property dealing: talked the language. It wasn't his fault it was all going wrong at the last minute.

She went on staring at the big refrigerator in the centre of the window. The word 'bargain' stood out on the huge showcard. Now it looked as if there would be no bargain made for them: no sale: no starting again—not if he was right, unless . . .

She'd had to tell him what she thought. It had been there all the time as a suspicion at the back of her mind. Now she couldn't ignore it.

He hadn't wanted to talk: said she was letting her imagination get the better of her. She wasn't involved.

Anyway, she should stop worrying, everything would be all right. But he hadn't *looked* confident.

'Your handbag's open, miss.' It was the young man who spoke. The girl he had his arm around couldn't have been more than twenty, bit younger than he was. They were standing beside her, looking in the window. 'You OK, then?'

Did she look that terrible? This time she just nodded, giving them a quick smile of thanks before moving away. She couldn't risk speaking in case she burst into tears.

It wasn't right he had made the sacrifice for the two of them: taken all the risk. She shouldn't have said how much it all meant to her. It was her fault they'd talked about nothing else for weeks. Now he didn't want her disappointed. He'd find a way, he'd said. That was before the meeting yesterday. He hadn't believed the meeting had solved anything.

It was awful how wrong people were about him. You had to get under how he seemed on the surface. Deep down he was different. You had to know him to understand him—and to love him as dearly as she did.

Matilde Stock, wife to Police Constable Clifford Stock, shut the back door behind her. She hung her coat on one of the pegs, took off the dirty pinafore, dropped it in the laundry basket, and tied a clean apron around her ample waist. Next she shot a glance at the three saucepans bubbling on the electric cooker.

'I switched on when you said, love. The oxtail smells a treat,' said her husband. He was sitting at the table in the kitchen of the modern, semi-detached village police house. He had been reading the *Daily Mail*.

'So, we eat soon.' Matilda beamed. 'It's good I went. Like you said, not so much damage, except the kitchen. But the dust everywhere. *Tiens.*' The last word came out like the cluck of a mother hen.

Mrs Stock was short, plump, jolly and very Belgian. In the nearly forty years of their marriage she had altered hardly at all—to the enduring satisfaction of her devoted spouse. She had lost none of her insatiable capacity for hard work, nor her delight in home cooking.

Lance-Corporal Stock, then a Military Policeman, had observed the same fine qualities in Matilde's mother all those years ago in her native Liége. He had been billeted with the family. He still remembered those four months. They were the luckiest in his life—and the best fed. He had wooed and won Matilde, mostly while her mother had been cooking. He had known only one cook better than Matilde: her mother.

'Labour of love, Tilly. You won't get paid for this morning, I'm afraid.'

'*Ça ne fait rien,*' she muttered into the oven where she was arranging bread. Her deep voice and rough accent never did much for the delicate nuances latent in spoken French. This didn't bother her husband: he hardly knew a word of the language.

He folded up the paper. 'You're a good old girl.'

'Not so much with your old,' she called back happily. She drained the potatoes and banged the lid back on the saucepan. Next she began stabbing at the larger lumps of meat with a cooking fork. She was a vigorous operator in the kitchen. 'I can do this much for a grand lady. *Quelle affaire, hein?* Such a fine home. Now people coming for the funeral can see for dust.'

'You mean, couldn't have seen for dust before, love. Won't be anyone at the cottage, I shouldn't think. Not that one or two couldn't stay there, I suppose. It'll be back to normal today, almost. They'll paint it Monday, I expect.'

'So, Richard the son. He won't come?'

'From Australia? He might do. Came for his Dad's funeral. It's a tidy way, though. I'll fetch the beer.' He got up and opened the larder cupboard. 'Gas Board's doing a good job, I'll give 'em that. They had all the glass back in the windows when I was there first thing. They'll charge, of course. Doesn't look like it was their responsibility, the explosion, I mean. Is their inspector bloke still there?'

She nodded, taking the two warmed soup plates from the oven. 'Mr Pitty, too. Such a looker, that one.' She sighed. 'Real Errol Flynn.' Matilde's loyalties died hard.

'Errol Flynn was dark,' said her husband impassively. 'Did they ask about the cooker? Seems they had someone there Wednesday mending the pilot lights.'

She looked up sternly from ladling steaming pieces of oxtail on to the plates. 'Ah! How should I know if the pilot lights worked on Thursday? That man, the inspector, was asking. Did I make a cup of tea when I was there? Ça alors. I was there to work, I said, not to make tea.' She went back to the ladling. 'We had coffee, her Ladyship and me, if she was there. Instant. The water we boil in the electric kettle.'

'But she wasn't there Thursday morning, was she, love?'

'Not for any of my mornings for two weeks. Always off to the library when I arrive. They said she had the soft spot for the librarian. Mr . . . Mr Sims.' She rocked her head, smiling with a touch of devilry.

'Then *they* are barmy, including Eddy Jacks, because he's one of them. Ought to know better. Just literary friends, her Ladyship and Mr Sims,' snorted Stock.

'I think it's only in joke.'

'That's as may be.' He changed the subject. 'You didn't happen to use the cooker on Thursday, love?' He understood why they'd especially want to know if the pilot lights had gone on the blink again.

'No, I did not.' She placed the heaped plates on the table. 'Not because her Ladyship said not to have coffee. Always, for me, she says such things must be like

Shakespeare, er . . . take it or leave it.'

He looked puzzled for a moment. 'You mean, as you like it, don't you, Tilly?' He wasn't an authority, but it was the one he'd learned at school.

'There's a difference? *Bon appétit*.' They both raised their glasses of light ale. 'The letter, though. It's a mystery, that one.'

'What letter?'

'I didn't tell you? When I go to the front hall first thing, there, on the mat, was a letter. I swear.'

'The post?'

'No, no. Not the post. Before the post comes. It comes by hand. Yesterday perhaps. A blue envelope. I think I know the writing. But no. Or I can't remember. So. I put it on the silver tray on the little table. Later, it's not there.'

'How d'you mean, love? Someone picked it up?'

She shrugged, a meaty spoonful of oxtail poised between plate and mouth. 'Mr Pitty, he is in the hall ten minutes after. I heard him from the salon. I said, "There's a letter for her Ladyship." "Where," he said. "There," I said.' Her lips closed over the spoon.

'And it wasn't?' her husband asked. She nodded vigorously. 'Someone else picked it up, love.'

'*Pas de personne*. There was no one. The *inspecteur* from the gas and his assistant, they were in the kitchen. Mr Pitty is the only one in the hall.'

He poured them both more beer. 'Well, I'd say it stands to reason Mr Pitty isn't going to pinch Lady Brasset's letters. Anyway, he probably has a perfect right to appropriate mail, he being her executor, like. Funny, though. You sure you couldn't have made a mistake, Tilly?'

'Why should I make a mistake over such a thing? Ah, it's possible. I hope it's not important.' She fetched more potatoes from the cooker. 'Now, I still have all my 'ousework to do yet. Are you going to football, or do I have to have you between my legs all afternoon?'

'Under your feet, you mean, love.' He smiled at her fondly. 'No, it's football for me.' Not that there hadn't been a time . . .

'And you think you'd smell gas in the hall?' asked Treasure into the telephone.

He was seated in the Daws's office behind the reception desk at the Beachcomber. The door was closed. Tracy, who was at the desk outside, had volunteered the use of the private phone. This was the second call he had made. The first, very brief one, had been to Quaint.

'Could smell it in the attic in the circumstances you describe, Mark,' answered Harold Arkworthy, talking from his home in Chipping Campden, Gloucestershire. 'Funny stuff, gas. Insinuates. Like some people. It's an old cottage, you say?'

'Very, but modernized. I mean proper insulation. That kind of thing.'

'Which stops air getting out as well as in, of course,' commented Arkworthy. He was Managing Director of one of the largest cooking appliance makers in Europe. 'Makes it more likely a gas leak would spread round the rooms.'

'Under doors, you mean?'

'All round doors. Through floors. Are there central heating radiators?'

'I think so.'

'Well, there's your most likely conduit. Right through the place. I mean, not knowing the house it's difficult to be certain, but if someone left a burner unlit for . . . how many hours?'

'About eight before someone went in.'

'And the kitchen has a door to the hall. Mmm. I think there'd be something wrong with your nose if you didn't smell gas in the hall. D'you want some sort of technical report done? I'm only a poor bloody accountant, you know.'

'But quite highly placed, and noted for observation, Harold. No thanks. You've confirmed what I thought.'

'Glad to have been of service. What are the bank's customers for if you can't interrupt their gin and tonics every time you smell gas. Where are you, anyway?'

'Tophaven.'

'Good God. Is Molly with you?'

'No. In the States.'

'Ho, ho. So you're shacked up for the weekend in an old world cottage with a platinum blonde and a leaky gas cooker. Very tricky that could be. Hope it's not one of mine. The cooker, I mean. We don't want a double scandal if you blow yourselves up.'

'Very droll. I'm here on business. Some of us have to keep the economy turning. Have another gin, and thanks for the information. See you soon.'

But he had to take some more banter from the other end before he was allowed off the line.

He had avoided reporting Louella's death, even to an old friend. It was unlikely Arkworthy had known her: it would be in the papers next day. He smiled to himself about one thing. The night before he had instinctively noted the name of the gas cooker. It was not a brand made by Harold Arkworthy's companies.

'How much do I owe for the calls?' He had come out of the office.

'On the house,' said Tracy. 'I'm in charge, 'Morning, ladies. Lunch isn't quite ready yet,' she called to two very aged crones who were making slow progress from the residents' lounge towards the dining-room. 'Though it'll probably be over by the time they get there. If they get there,' she added in an undertone. 'What's the time?'

'Twelve-thirty, and I'm not here for lunch,' Treasure

answered. 'Are those ladies guests?'

'Surprising as it may seem, yes. This *is* a hotel, Mr Treasure,' she pronounced loftily. 'They're the last of the permanents. They came with the place and they'll have to be sold with it. Oh, Mr Daws has you crossed off for lunch already. Did you tell him, or Mrs Daws? I think she was looking for you.'

'I told Mr Daws. Indirectly.'

'He's gone for his regular Saturday pint. Pub along the road. Left the memsahib in charge. Then she got taken by an urgent need to change her library books. Rang me to stand in. Lucky I was available. But then, I always am.' She fluttered her eyelids. 'So if you, too, have need for a lovely young body . . .'

'Thank you, I have my own.'

She made a face at him. 'Actually I'm glad to be here. Daddy's a bit miz. There was no . . .'

'Cheque from Seawell this morning,' he cut in with feeling.

'You heard?'

'From several sources.'

'Daddy's sure Louella's scheming has spoiled the deal. Incidentally, he's guessed something was up this morning—in the Round House garden.'

'What did you say?'

'Told him what happened. About the vandal you bravely chased away. Well, drove away.' She smirked. 'Daddy said it was a pity you didn't leave him to it. That he might have knocked the house down.'

Treasure shrugged. 'So he was right on one count. Possibly both.'

'Daddy said he'd set fire to the place himself if he thought he'd get away with it. Didn't mean it really. He's terribly law-abiding. Pretty depressed, though. Pity he never got to see Louella. He did try. Might have got her to drop her beastly crusade.'

'When was this?'

'Yesterday. When he knew what she was up to. He went to see her. In the cottage. But she was still in London.'

'Any idea what time?'

She shook her head. 'I'll ask him, if you like. Is it important?

'Could be.'

CHAPTER 11

'Your cup, Mark?' Cynthia Tring held the bone china pot ready to pour. Treasure was on her right.

They had finished lunch—the Trings, Treasure and Denis Pitty. They were lingering over coffee.

The dining-room was well proportioned. Unlike the drawing-room, though, it was only sparsely furnished.

The four were seated at a small gate-legged table—mahogany and quite old. The chairs, in contrast, were newish reproduction. Indentations in rugs, marks on walls, and a somewhat eccentric arrangement of pictures suggested the former presence of a good deal more equipage. There had probably been a sideboard, a chest of some kind, certainly a heavier table and more chairs. At a guess, the banished pieces were probably in the same class as the surviving breakfast table.

At his time of life, the Canon would not be much given to entertaining. To be realistic, his wife was unlikely to live out an inevitably long widowhood in such a relatively large establishment. It made sense to dispose of unwanted furniture. The antique market was booming. Yet the near-brutal denuding of this room had been overdoing things—unless the Trings were very hard up indeed.

Treasure remembered Lady Brasset's quip about not living like a Cardinal: and Cardinals didn't have wives with tastes for ultra-suede dresses. Cynthia looked very becoming.

'Thank you. Delicious coffee. Like everything else.' He smiled, pushing his cup towards her, and trying to make it clear the hostess was included in the compliment.

'Fortunately, Louella's affairs are in apple-pie order,' offered Pitty, bringing them back to the subject being discussed — in a way, immodestly. Cynthia had earlier announced he had been in charge of all the deceased's business affairs.

Treasure had been mildly surprised and irrationally irked to find the lawyer had also been invited to lunch.

Pitty had evidently not been summoned to arrange a settlement over the damage at the Round House. No one had seemed much interested in the subject. Perhaps it had been correctly assumed it was hardly Treasure's province to haggle over petty claims against Seawell Developments.

'Everything goes to Richard, the son. He's a doctor. Used to be in New South Wales,' said Cynthia.

'South Wales . . . South Wales?' questioned her husband from across the table.

'*New* South Wales, I said, Algy. But he's moved somewhere in the north,' his wife countered with a touch of impatience. 'Denis telephoned him last night.'

Pitty nodded. 'Took the news of his mother's death very stoically. May not be able to come to the funeral.' He glanced at Cynthia.

'Good deal of the estate was entailed for the grandchildren. Remember from the husband's death. Best way,' said the Canon.

'Yes, virtually the lot,' Pitty confirmed promptly.

'Pretty well everything,' Cynthia came in simultaneously.

The Canon shook his head. 'Didn't Louella have money of her own? Intended giving it away in due time to avoid death duties. Hmm.' He sighed. 'In the midst of life. Well, there it is. She liked to play the stock market, d'you see . . .'

'It was only pin money, really.' Pitty was quietly dismissive.

'Did you handle that for her?' Treasure asked, showing a mild professional interest.

'. . . except she had no real head for figures. None at all. Did well at it, though. So she said.' The aged cleric had continued, unaware of the exchange.

'Through a broker.' Pitty nodded. 'Small stuff, though.'

'Made thousands. Tens of thousands, she told me. All thanks to Denis here. She was into commodities, as they say.' The Canon pressed on to the evident if curious discomfort of the lawyer.

'She tended to exaggerate these things, I'm afraid.' It was Cynthia to the rescue. 'I don't mean Denis's flair. I mean money she kept for what she called her gambling.'

'Gambling,' her husband repeated, though whether as affirmation or moral censure it wasn't clear.

'Sweet of you to take Algy to Chichester, Mark,' Cynthia changed the course of the conversation. 'Since he stopped driving it's become quite a job fitting in his travels with mine.'

'Pleasure. I'd intended dropping into the cathedral anyway while I was near.'

'Well, his committee meeting's there too. In the cloisters, actually. I'll tell you my secret parking place. Otherwise you have to park miles from anywhere. I can pick him up later, but it's my turn to do the flowers here in the village church. I've still got to pick them up in Tophaven.'

'Sorry I'm no use,' Pitty said. 'Dashed nuisance. Got a client in half an hour. Saturday afternoon, too.'

'Bully for you,' commented Treasure affably. He

turned to his hostess. 'If I might tell Sheikh Mhad Alid to have his solicitors ring Denis on Monday about the lease . . .'

'Then they can work something out,' she cut in. 'For the end of term.' She was looking at Pitty as she spoke.

So Treasure had won half a cake: Seawell or Roxton were going to have to pay for it: the banker had done his best.

'Monday afternoon would be fine. I'm out in the morning . . . Glad to ring them, if you like? Know the partner involved,' Pitty offered helpfully.

'Of course, you're acting for the freeholders. Tit for tat. Give you the chance to tickle up Seawell about the deserving poor of Sandy Lane. I gather Mr Daws was an early supplicant this morning.' Treasure thought also of the besieged Elderberry.

'Absolutely. Had me going through the bally mail at eight-thirty.'

'You really should charge overtime for Saturday work,' said the hostess, with a wide-eyed glance that lingered on Pitty a fraction longer than seemed appropriate.

For the second time in as many minutes, Treasure was conscious Cynthia and Pitty were by look and innuendo conducting exchanges to which neither he nor the Canon were privy, or meant to be.

'Actually, today's unusual,' the lawyer admitted self-effacingly. 'Even had someone beg an appointment as I was coming out. Comes of living over the shop.'

'Over the shop,' echoed the Canon. 'Who might that have been, Denis?'

'Algy, what an improper question,' his wife scolded.

'No one important, Algy,' the lawyer answered blandly.

Treasure wondered. 'None of you visited Lady Brasset's place yesterday, I suppose?' he inquired on impulse.

There was marked reaction to the question in the sense

that no one immediately replied to it.

Eventually Cynthia drew in a breath as though to speak, but it was Denis Pitty who got in first. 'I was there.'

'We were there together, of course,' said Treasure.

'No, I mean much earlier. Just before lunch. I was driving through the village. Remembered I had some share transfers for Louella to sign. Why d'you ask?'

Treasure shrugged. 'Obviously you didn't smell gas.'

'I didn't go inside. Louella wasn't there.'

'Wasn't there,' the Canon reiterated. 'Cynthia could have told you that when you rang about my will in the morning. She knew Louella was going to London. Could have saved you a journey.'

'Denis just said he was driving through Colston, Algy.' Cynthia spoke abruptly, almost angrily. She was showing the nervousness Treasure had marked at the start of their first meeting. 'So I couldn't have saved him a journey. On the phone we were discussing *our* wills, not Louella's movements.'

'Not Louella's movements. Quite right, Cynthia. Shame I hadn't wandered down,' the Canon ruminated. 'I have a particularly sensitive nose.' The feature in question was certainly prominent and aquiline. 'It was remarked upon even during childhood. I might have detected escaping gas. Your question had special relevance to us, Treasure?'

'Not really,' the banker lied. It had been an ill-judged and unsubtle attempt to find out if Eddy Jacks had taken his advice and seen Pitty: much better to have asked the lawyer privately, though it was difficult to broach the subject directly without breaking a confidence. 'It occurred to me someone might have been there during the day. As the Canon suggests, gas does hang about the air.'

'I didn't smell gas,' Pitty commented, 'but I only went to the front of the house. Came away when there was no answer. Thought Louella was probably at that wretched library again.'

'I . . . I wasn't there. At the cottage,' broke in Cynthia. The words came out more as a declaration than as a mere statement.

'Buildings are often now preserved for fear of what may replace them,' Canon Tring pronounced, staring at the road ahead. He was gripping an old leather attaché case in his lap.

'What a very profound observation,' said Treasure, and meant it. He slowed the Rolls to a stop at the T-junction.

'Very. Regrettably not mine. Sir Hugh Casson. Sound architect and a first-rate President of the Royal Academy.'

'Agreed.' The banker swung the car left on to the A27. 'Are you wondering whether the Seawell building in Sandy Lane will be an unworthy replacement for what's there at the moment?'

'You couldn't do worse than that ghastly hotel, for instance.'

'I really meant the Round House.'

'The Round House. There you have the advantage. I don't know what the developers have in mind to replace it.' The Canon looked sharply at his companion. 'I'd feel confident of your opinion.'

'Which could be unduly prejudiced.'

'Unduly prejudiced? Not unless my judgement of your character is sadly awry.'

'Thank you. The new building I'd describe as seemly.'

'Seemly. Meaning better than inoffensive? Well, that's something.'

'Oh, much better. Aesthetically, stylistically, it owes more to, say, Lutyens than Corbusier. On balance, I think the community and posterity will gain from the change. Of course, one doesn't know how the Round House would look put back to its original shape.'

'Assuming anyone would pay for the experiment. I remember it before the war.' The Canon grunted between phrases. 'Well before the war. Relatively unremarkable.'

'Lady Brasset . . .'

'Was a Colonial at heart. Venerated anything built before the Civil War. The American one.'

'She was on the way to proving it was a joint Soane and Butterfield creation.'

'Bit fanciful. Soane was dead. My generation never really cared for Butterfield. Nothing wrong with his churchmanship.' He paused. 'He did Balliol College Chapel in the 'fifties. Eighteen-fifties. They remodelled it again less than a hundred years later.' He nodded as though doubly to remark such swift, decisive action. 'Hmm. I recall recognizing his iron screen for the chapel. On top of a lorry it was, going to an Oxford scrap yard in 1940. They'd thrown it out, you see.'

'Helping the war effort.'

'War effort? You could say that. Oh, no doubt. Like the Round House. Navy took that, for the women. The WRNS. Marshford would have approved. Besotted by the fair sex.'

'Plagued by it too, I gather. All those daughters. Who was Miss Darlington, the one who started the ladies' academy?'

The Canon looked momentarily surprised. 'She was Sydney Marshford's mistress for donkey's years,' he announced in a matter-of-fact tone. 'Should have married her when his first wife died, but by then he judged she was too old to produce a son. There'd been a daughter by mistake, years before. Didn't augur well.'

'What happened to her?'

'The child? Fostered off with suitable provision. Never,

of course, owned as progeny. Miss Darlington returned after her confinement to run the academy. Marshford's second wife bore him a son—or somebody's son. Threw everything into reverse. His will and so on, and all those mostly feminist endowments he couldn't undo.'

'You mean he lived to regret his generosity?'

'Rather to realize he'd overdone it. The public benefactions for females in general were meant only to provide a cloak of objectivity. In case his private and particular ones ever came in for scrutiny.'

'Were there so many of those?'

'I think not. And there's the point.'

'He overkilled.'

'Overkilled? Is that the going expression? The endowments of all kinds led to great legal wranglings with the son, when he came of age.'

'With his half-sisters?'

'Half-sisters, official and unofficial. Always girls, it seems, except for that one son. Terrible hypocrite, Marshford. In mitigation, he did make provision for all members of his brood.' He paused. 'Sometimes in circuitous ways.'

'Like Miss Darlington. The reason I asked about her, there was something in the diaries I read this morning. Meant to mention it at lunch. It was in the 1868 diary . . .'

'That was the year of the second marriage.'

'So I gathered. Rather later than the period Lady Brasset was researching, I imagine.'

'I imagine. A good woman, Louella, but lacking in scholarly application.'

Treasure smiled at the gratuitous comment. 'Anyway, if Miss Darlington was the man's mistress it's not surprising there was to be a freehold reversion in her favour when "labour's done". I believe that was the phrase.'

'Very apposite,' the Canon remarked drily.

'And after a "seemly interval",' the banker continued. 'That's also his phrase, and not so carefully circumspect when you think about it.'

'The interval would refer to the time since she stopped working, not since she ceased labouring with his child. Otherwise you're right. It would have been a careless entry. The diaries generally do nothing to diminish his moral reputation. That's why they're so deadly dull. The property she was given was the small house originally leased to her in the town, in her capacity as academy principal.'

'The diary didn't say. It couldn't have been the Round House?'

'The Round House? Unlikely. That lease was hers from the start, theoretically in lieu of fees.'

'It was a longish lease in that case. And an odd length. It's the one that expires next month.'

'Next month. Marshford was an odd person. The lease was to provide income for Miss Darlington. It was left unsaid it was long enough to do the same for her secret offspring. And succeeding generations, I suppose. Though not in perpetuity.'

'That might have signalled something improper?'

'Marshford would have argued so.'

'And it could have been given as a freehold in the first place.'

'In the first place. Precisely. Saved a lot of bother. As it was, though, the proprieties were not put at risk. Miss Darlington and her child enjoyed the benefit of whatever income could be derived for the time being. If Marshford's legitimate lineage had not been so profligate, they, in turn, would now he coming into the unencumbered freehold.'

'Which one of them sold to an insurance company. You're singularly well informed about Miss Darlington. I assume your family bought the Round House lease from her, or her daughter? Is it an eccentric sort of document?'

'To be sure, I've never read it,' the gaunt-headed clergyman declared without regret. 'I doubt my father did either. Meat for lawyers, I should say. You turn right here.'

Treasure did as he was told, though the route seemed to be taking them further away from the cathedral whose spire had been tantalizingly close for some time. It was the fault of the one-way system. The Canon's directions had promised well since they had left the City ring-road — cannily provided for those who, after motoring round several times without finding ingress, give up and go away. They were threading through a maze of Tudor loops and Georgian right-angles inside the City.

'As for the acquiring of the lease, it's always been in the family,' he continued. 'Louella didn't know this. None of her business. Cynthia wouldn't have told her either. Miss Darlington . . . she was my great-grandmother. Sorry, turn left here.'

The instruction was too late — or should have been. Treasure swung the Rolls hard left before realizing the error. The Canon had directed him the wrong way up a one-way street. He braked hard in time to avoid the boy on the bicycle, but not soon enough to prevent the same lad from taking his own avoiding action, causing consternation, but no injury, when he mounted the pavement. Pedestrians scattered like chaff.

Treasure had left the car to placate the people involved — and a few who weren't. It was on his return he discovered the only person seriously discommoded was the Canon himself.

For a moment the banker believed Miss Darlington's great-grandson might actually have expired. He was sitting bolt upright, but due, possibly, only to the support of the seat-belt and headrest. His stretched skin was deathly pale. There was no indication he was breathing.

'Canon, you all right?'

The lips parted a fraction. 'All right. Be so good. Pills. Right-hand pocket.' The eyes remained unblinking.

Treasure quickly dipped into the raincoat pocket: empty. The jacket underneath was more productive. The silver pill box contained a single tiny white tablet. He pressed this find into the Canon's mouth.

'Hits you between the eyes,' murmured the suddenly reanimated cleric a few moments later.

'What does?'

'TNT. What I've just swallowed. A sovereign aid in angina.'

'Also for blowing up bridges in larger quantities.' Treasure was unnerved but did his best not to show it. 'I'm sorry. That was my fault. Near-accidents can't be good for bad hearts.'

'Not at all.' The Canon was now taking extra deep breaths: there was still no colour in his face. 'Misdirected you. Pain's nearly gone. Nothing serious.'

Treasure was roughly familiar with the difference between a bout of angina pectoris and a coronary thrombosis. He was unqualified to judge which he had just witnessed but he had a notion with angina the pain should have been totally banished by the medication.

'We could pop into the local hospital.'

'Not necessary. Nor the morgue either.' The sunken eyes twinkled with the quip. 'How many pills left in that box?'

'None.'

'Bother. If it wouldn't be too much trouble, I think I'd best go home. Give my meeting a miss. I can take a taxi from . . .'

'You'll do nothing of the kind. I'll drive you. There's bound to be a chemist open. We can pick up more explosives . . .'

But the Canon insisted he had plentiful supplies of medicaments at home. After only a mild protest he agreed to be driven there in the Rolls. He slept most of the way.

'What a very smooth and quiet motor this is,' he remarked as they stopped in front of his door. 'I'm much obliged to you.'

'Not at all. What's next? D'you need any shunting up the steps? Shall I fetch Cynthia?'

'Cynthia? She'll be in Tophaven or at the church. Quite unnecessary, I do assure you. What would be helpful—another of those trinitrate tablets under the tongue before I start moving about. If you'd be so kind? Big bottle on the table in the dressing-room where I sleep. That's through the big bedroom. Door in front of you at the top of the stairs.' He handed Treasure a small bunch of keys. 'The Yale does the front door.'

As he mounted the stairs inside, Treasure debated whether it would be more sensible to stay until Cynthia returned, or to fetch her as soon as he had the old man settled. That problem, at least, was quickly solved.

He opened the door facing him. There was a gasp of surprise from the direction of the double bed. Cynthia Tring was in it—and Denis Pitty was in it with her.

CHAPTER 12

Treasure pressed the 10p coin into the slot. 'Miss Gaunt? It's Mark Treasure. Sorry to disturb your Saturday afternoon.'

'You're not, Mr Treasure. You're in a call-box. Give me the number and I'll ring you back immediately.'

As usual she ordered the priorities correctly, and without prompting.

He pictured her in what he always assumed was her tiny, neat Islington flat. Now she was probably setting aside a letter she was writing to her brother in Canada, gently lifting the sleeping cat from her lap, and next — not the smallest bit ruffled by his intrusion — taking up the notebook and pencil easily to hand, dutifully to record whatever was required.

In fact Miss Gaunt was in the middle of painting her quite large kitchen. She had earlier made the regular monthly cheap rate call to brother Edward in Toronto: they took it in turns to pay. As she dialled the number Treasure had given her, she scrambled desperately to find any bit of paper to go with the nearly dried-up ballpoint-pen which, at the highly inconvenient moment her employer had chosen to call, was the only writing implement in sight.

It was a case of reality falling short of theoretical perception, but without endangering immutable legend.

Nor would Treasure's image of the implacable Miss Gaunt have encompassed her just having unceremoniously bundled the tiresome Aquinas, her tabby, all protesting, on to the tiny balcony. This had been to stop him any more brushing against the fresh paintwork and pots.

'You are still at Tophaven, Mr Treasure.' So much was evident. She re-opened the conversation in the level, patient tone he associated with her office persona.

She had had to look up the Tophaven area code to be certain of getting it right, though memory could have served.

'Yes, on the outskirts, at the moment.' The telephone-box he was using overlooked a country crossroads a few hundred yards on from Lady Brasset's cottage. 'I'll stay over tonight. Same hotel,' he went on, providing the answer she needed to the question she had avoided putting directly. Miss Gaunt considered it her business to know where her boss was at all times, but only if he chose to make it so. 'Got a bit involved. Poor Lady Brasset was killed in an accident last night.'

'I'm sorry. Motor-car?'

'No, gas explosion. Nasty business. At her house outside the town.' He might have added, 'in a quiet country area'. No car had passed since he had pulled up on the greensward beside the crossroads.

As he spoke, a yellow and chrome racing bicycle coasted by. It turned downhill towards Tophaven, the rider in black sports gear — track suit, gloves, canvas shoes and woollen Balaclava. The motor-cycle goggles seemed to be overdoing things, like the elaborate hand signal on the totally deserted crossing.

There were no buildings in full view; just a few rooftops visible over the hedgerows and between the trees. Colston village had petered out a quarter of a mile back. Although Treasure knew the official Tophaven town boundary was just down the hill, the immediate area was so unspoiledly rural he wondered how Telecom justified keeping a call-box here.

Pitty had explained Colston was just a back way to Chichester: even this seemed to be a well-kept secret.

'Should I tell Lord Grenwood? You mentioned they were old friends.'

'Not necessary,' he replied promptly. Better Grenwood should learn through the obituary columns of *The Times* that an alleged secret old flame had been extinguished for ever. To be alerted by phone on a Saturday might be inappropriate, especially if Lady Grenwood had answered — or so her husband might have thought.

'I can tell him on Monday, if it isn't in the paper. They weren't close.' Through a window of the box he watched two small boys and a shaggy brown mongrel inspect the Rolls from different angles. The dog had hair over its eyes as well as everything else. It was probably distantly related to an Old English Sheepdog.

'The reason I'm ringing. Did we get anything yesterday from the Investment Department on that insurance company, the er . . .'

'The Rackburn & Claremont? Yes, they came back quickly with most of what you wanted. But you'd left early for Tophaven.' There was no hint of censure, only the establishment of credit where it was due to the Investment Department. It happened that Miss Gaunt's closest office friend was secretary to the manager.

'Good. Remember any of it?'

'The salient features, I believe.'

'Private company?'

'Yes. Not actively trading. Registered offices in Bedford Row.'

'Probably solicitor's chambers.'

'I thought that too. The last filed balance sheet is two years old.'

'I see. Capital?'

'Reorganized three years ago. Ten thousand 10p ordinary shares, only ten per cent subscribed.'

'Assets?'

'Nominal, including the property portfolio you asked about.'

'Did they say when the property was last valued?'

'At the time the share capital was altered.'

'Fine. List of shareholders?'

'Forty-nine per cent held by . . . could it be HBAM Research and Development AG? I think I have the initials right. It's a Swiss company.'

Treasure thought for a moment. 'Yes, you've got them right.'

'Good. The remaining shares are held by National Bank Nominees.'

'Directors?'

'Two. Oh, they have one share each. One is Swiss. I

think his name was Hoch. The other was Sydney Smith. I
remember because I have his letters. I mean *the* Sydney
Smith. The nineteenth-century one.'

'Good for you. That was all I asked for, I think. They
did well in the time.' He wished now he'd asked for a good
deal more, but it had only been out of curiosity.

The grapevine of commercial intelligence services
available to merchant bankers is powerful, accurate, swift
working and grinds exceeding small when required. If he
had wanted the name or names of shareholders
represented by National Bank Nominees, these could no
doubt be provided, but not today.

The small boys, aware his eye was upon them, were
now carefully examining the dashboard of the Rolls
through the windows. They were standing on tiptoe,
hands ostentatiously clasped tight behind backs to show
they weren't touching anything. The mongrel, not nearly
so fastidious, having inspected each wheel in turn, had
urinated generously on one of the pair at the front,
reserving a token libation which he had just expended on
the other. His territorial claims established, he was now
advancing amiably upon the phone-box.

'One other thing,' continued Miss Gaunt. She too was
involved in animal studies. Aquinas was at the window
opening and shutting his mouth, indicating bleats. These
were mimed because in feline lore his mistress could
perfectly well see his demand to be allowed in: there was
no point in wasting energy shouting about it. Dogs are
seldom so provident of effort. 'Sydney Aquinas, I mean
Smith, Sydney Smith,' Miss Gaunt pulled herself
together. 'His address is in Tophaven.'

'Indeed? That's very interesting.' The grinding had
gone quite small.

He turned the Rolls down the sloping drive of Lady
Brasset's home.

The drive was longer and steeper than it had seemed the night before, bending left after leaving the garage to the right. The property was well shielded from the road by neatly boxed cupressus which certainly wouldn't have taken kindly to trimming in November. Healthy specimen shrubs, some evergreen, flanked the drive on the left, opposite the house. The giant privets Jacks had mentioned would be on the other boundaries.

After his embarrassed departure from the Trings, Treasure had decided to look in on Jacks as soon as he had called Miss Gaunt.

In retrospect, the episode at the Canon's house had ended as less of a disaster than might have been expected. The old man had remained unaware of what had happened. Treasure had extended the time of pill-fetching and of conducting the clergyman into the drawing-room. Pitty had joined them there almost immediately, proving the adage, Treasure had concluded drily to himself, that smart dressers are often perforce the fastest ones as well.

Cynthia had appeared shortly afterwards in a brown leather coat over what she had been wearing at lunch. She could afford to be more ruffled than Pitty. Her nervous excitement was easily explained as part of the convincing concern she was showing over her husband.

Her car had failed to start, she had explained to the Canon. Denis had stayed on, trying to fix it. They had both been in the garage at the rear of the house when the Rolls had returned, which is why they hadn't heard it. Denis had driven his car there too, away from the front where it had been during lunch. There had been something about using jump leads from his battery to hers — an apposite invention, indeed.

It had all sounded plausible enough, unless you happened to know it was lies.

In a way, Treasure had resented becoming part of a

conspiracy without the option. He felt, too, that Cynthia had overdone the explanations. He had been glad to leave. The Canon had become quite lively again. The woman's parting attitude had spelled gratitude without any suggestion of shame. It was as though the circumstances of Treasure's return with the Canon had been exactly as Cynthia had related. If anything, there had been a touch of bravura in the final undeviating farewell stare.

Pitty had followed Treasure out to the car. He had thanked him profusely, and then made the astonishing assertion that all was not what it might have seemed: that he could explain everything. He had pressed the banker to join him for a drink at his apartment later in the day.

Treasure was still grudgingly admiring the gall of the man when he was abruptly brought back to the present. As he rounded the bend to the flat area of the drive in front of the cottage, he nearly rammed a very small Fiat car. It was parked dead ahead of him with no regard for safety or the convenience of others. He swerved and braked hard for the second time that afternoon. There would have been room enough for two quite large cars abreast if the Fiat hadn't been straddling the centre.

'Silly me!' Lancelot Elderberry emerged hurriedly and confusedly at first from the front porch, as Treasure got out of his car. The mortification in the words of the still cloaked and hatted novelist was emphasized because they had to carry over the buzz from a petrol-driven implement operating nearby.

'Bit tight,' said Treasure testily, indicating how little room he'd had to park in.

'Sober as a judge, I assure you,' answered the other, dropping a raised limp palm, but aware the quip had failed. 'So sorry. I'll be off in a flash. And you don't need to turn or back to get out, you know. Just carry straight on. There's another gate.'

It was a pretty little house which Treasure was now seeing for the first time in daylight. A thatched roof over white-painted brick gave it a kind of picture-postcard attraction. From where he was standing only the newly glazed kitchen window witnessed the event of the night before.

'I know. I was here last night.' Treasure smiled. It was difficult to be angry with Elderberry. 'Got rid of your friend? Bobby, wasn't it?'

'Tch! Such a caution. Put him on the train to London. A dear boy, really, but being manipulated. There's no other word for it. I'm trying to protect him. There's talent there. Writing talent. Not a gift to waste, d'you see . . .'

'You said he was a lame duck.'

'That too.' Elderberry shook his head indicating the depth of his burden.

'And the obscene magazine?'

'No place for a sensitive bloom. I promised his parents. Charming people. From the north. Originally.' He made a circle with one podgy hand in an action vaguely directional. 'Well now,' he went on. Endowing the wayward Bobby with a parental and geographical provenance was clearly intended to make an end to him as a subject. 'Warm for November, don't you think? I just dropped in to return a book dear Louella had lent me. There's no one in.'

'Did you expect anyone?'

'Aren't they supposed to be mending the place?'

'I think they've done it. You didn't use the spare key?'

'No, it's . . . I mean, I looked about to see if there was one. Under a mat or somewhere.'

'There certainly was one, I'm told. Everyone seems to have known about it. Perhaps the police took it.'

'Very likely. I've just arrived,' Elderberry volunteered almost defensively.

Treasure was surprised at the statement: nothing so

conspicuous as a bottle-green Fiat had passed the crossroads in the previous ten minutes. The only wheeled conveyance that had gone by at all had been the bicycle. Perhaps Elderberry had come by an indirect route from the town.

'You've got rid of the book?'

'Pushed it through the letter-box. A slim volume of Swinburne. Quite valuable and part of a set. The executors might have wondered where it was. Afraid I've had it rather a long time. I've left a note with it. Nice doggy,' he finished without enthusiasm.

The mongrel had reappeared. It was sitting at Treasure's feet, panting. He had patted it on the head when leaving the phone-box to which it had earlier applied nominal anointment. Now it was staring up at him through strands of matted brown fur half accusingly, half pleading for further kind attentions.

At the approach from the other man the dog shuffled behind Treasure's legs for protection.

'All right. Rotten doggy. They sense it, you know,' declared Elderberry. 'I've never felt the same about dumb creatures since I rescued a bee from a swimming pool.' He pursed his lips and drew in a deep breath, sharply through the nose. 'It stung me.'

'I'm here to see the gardener,' said Treasure. Explanations seemed somehow to be in order. 'He may have a key.' It was a point Elderberry could have checked for himself before consigning valuable books to letter-boxes. The noise of the machine was ample evidence of Jacks's presence.

'No matter. My mission is accomplished. Conscience salved. Or is it ever? Heigh ho. Back to the grindstone. Perhaps I shall see you later.'

Elderberry squeezed himself into the tiny car, which took a sustained lurch to starboard. He crouched over the steering-wheel, hat brim pressed on the windscreen.

There was a painful crashing of gears before the vehicle proceeded — backwards for nearly a foot: then it stalled. The rear bumper finished about an inch short of the Rolls's nearside.

'Now we're away,' Elderberry offered confidently through the open window, as though the first effort had been for practice. The engine came to life again. 'Love your Roly-Poly,' was his parting sally as he disappeared up the drive in a cloud of foul-smelling vapour.

The dog came out from behind Treasure, wagged its tail, and turned purposefully to head back across the front of the cottage. It waited at the corner by the garage, looked back at Treasure, let out a single sharp bark, then vanished.

As the noise of the Fiat faded, the banker realized the drone of what he assumed had been the hedge-cutter had stopped altogether.

He followed the dog, who he found waiting impatiently at a wicket gate that barred the far end of the flagged path between the garage and the house.

The side door to the garage was open. A bunch of keys hung from the lock. Treasure stepped inside, closing the door behind him. Lady Brasset's Metro left little spare room around the workbench, but without a car there was space enough — and for manoeuvring the lawn-mower stored at the side.

As he had expected, even with the car *in situ*, anyone at the bench could look back through the glazed panel in the door and at least fleetingly see a car going past to the front door. It would not be possible to see anyone get out there — for instance, Elderberry earlier. It happened that at the moment, from where Treasure was standing, there was a perfect view of the driver's door of the Rolls, but he would never have parked there if it hadn't been for the obstruction.

A grubby instruction book on a hedge-trimmer lay on

the workbench. The rough outline of the implement itself was traced by a scatter of screws, spanners, screw drivers and discarded, worn looking parts. The vice attached to the bench was opened to its maximum width. Jacks was not a tidy worker, though he could not be faulted for failing to accept a challenge. Treasure remembered the manufacturers of the trimmer had gone out of business a dozen years before.

The banker tried the light over the bench, then let himself back into the narrow way between the buildings. The dog, still waiting at the gate and appearing perfectly at home, bounded across the terrace and the large irregular-shaped lawn as soon as Treasure released him.

The grass was flanked mostly by flowering shrubs. There was a rose-bed still very much in bloom on the west side, and a small herbaceous border at the bottom, to the south, with nothing showing now save for black, frosted dahlias.

Beyond the borders, the boundaries of the garden were clear enough—marked by tall, unexciting privet for the most part badly in need of trimming.

You could see where Jacks was at work. The western boundary hedge, to the right, had been box trimmed to two-thirds of its length. A squat pine tree punctuated the view at that point: beyond, the hedging continued unkempt. It was around the pine the dog had scrambled.

Treasure strolled across the lawn. He intended asking the postman what he'd decided to do. If the man had already been to see Pitty, as the banker suspected, there seemed no reason for not saying so, particularly in view of who was paying.

The dog reappeared before Treasure reached the pine tree, tail down, its movements cowed and frenetic. First it made towards Treasure, then wheeled about, ducked back under the tree, only to appear again a moment later. Once more it turned back.

'Mr Jacks! You about?' Treasure called. He followed a grass path that after skirting the back of the rose-bed wound around behind some bushes and the pine. He could see where it rejoined the main lawn, just before the herbaceous border, further down the garden.

As he rounded the tree, the first thing he came upon was the hedge-trimmer lying on the ground, its blades pointing directly towards him. Beyond was an upset stepladder, and under that, his right hand grasping the handle of the trimmer, was the motionless body of Eddy Jacks.

The blood had stopped oozing from the jagged gash in the throat. The face was very white.

Quickly Treasure established the man was dead. By comparison with that dreadful fact, the wad of twenty-pound notes protruding from the trouser pocket made little impact at the time.

CHAPTER 13

'Can you say exactly what time you arrived, sir?'

The young policewoman was standing with Treasure in the drive of the cottage. The patrol car she had come in half an hour before, with her male colleague, was parked beside the Rolls.

An ambulance had backed in close to the garage. The doctor's Range-Rover had arrived by the other gate. The police photographer had sensibly left his Cortina in the road.

WPC Clark was short, dark, pretty and entirely unaddicted to the sight of mutilated dead bodies. Both she and Treasure had been happy to remove themselves from the centre of enquiry and action at the end of the garden.

'Five past three, I should think. Give or take a minute.'

'But you didn't go straight to the scene of the accident?'

'No. I talked to Mr Lancelot Elderberry who was here.'

The girl smiled. 'That's Mr Elderberry of South View, Sandy Lane?'

'Yes. I can't believe there's another one. He'd been delivering a book. We chatted for a bit. Then I looked in at the garage.' He saw the questioning lift of the nicely arched eyebrows. 'Pure curiosity, I'm afraid. Door was open. I knew it'd been reglazed this morning. Wondered about other damage. The Gas Board did a smart job patching up.'

'After the explosion last night, sir? We heard about it when we came on this morning. It's ever so sad about Lady Brasset. And now this.' She looked down again at her notebook which she had rested on the bonnet of the police car. 'And the hedge-cutter was going all the time?'

'Mmm. Until it ran out of fuel. As I said, I assumed Mr Jacks was busy trimming. The doctor says he died before I got here, though, probably between two-fifteen and two-forty-five. Something to do with his body temperature.'

'Yes, sir. When you found the body what exactly did you do?'

That word again: he wondered how less exact people would be without the asking. 'I felt his brow. Searched for a heartbeat, a pulse. Pushed the ladder off the body. Oh, and I tried to get the hedge-cutter from his grasp. Don't know why. Reflex reaction, I expect.' Like glancing away for a moment to stem that fit of nausea, but hē wasn't going to be that exact.

'Then, sir?'

'Then I ran to the house, grabbed those keys on the way, got inside, and dialled 999. Oh, I also rang Lady Brasset's doctor. His number's on a card by the phone. There was a chance he'd be closer than the hospital. He was, of course.'

'Did you think Mr Jacks might be alive?'

'Frankly, no. But he was a long way off stone cold. Except, of course, he'd lost a lot of blood. Covered in it, as you know. So was everything else.' He shrugged. 'I suppose I was hoping for a miracle.'

WPC Clark appeared to note the last point as seriously as an earnest evangelist—or perhaps she was still on the point before.

'Then you got here,' he added, smiling.

'At three-seventeen, sir. Yes. Can you tell us the object of your visit, sir?' The switch to the optional and the plural indicated—even demurely—this wasn't just Miss Clark being nosey. He assumed it was Miss: there were no rings.

'I dropped in to see Mr Jacks. Thought he'd be here. Wondering if he'd come across a letter Lady Brasset had lost. I'd been visiting Canon Tring and his wife, here in the village.' It was all true, not the whole story, but as much as he intended to volunteer for the moment.

'Well, thank you very much, sir. They'll be in touch if there's an inquest.'

'And there will be,' said a voice behind them. It was the doctor. He was a big, cheerful man wearing thick, rimless spectacles, a skiing jacket open over an ancient sweater, and carrying a black, oblong medical bag.

'Glad you called me. Nothing I could do. But he is one of my patients. Or was.' He made a resigned grimace. 'Local coroner, stickler for death from misadventure with dangerous power tools. Especially cutlery. That's why our vigilant constabulary took pictures. He'll go for broke on that hedge-cutter. Quite right too, I suppose. Wouldn't have passed British Standards twenty years ago. No automatic cut-off *and* a lock-on trigger. Take your head off, and then some. Public needs telling about obsolete devices. That one came out of the old Brasset house.'

He adjusted his glasses. 'Well, Miss Clark? Made you a

sergeant yet, have they? Saw you go a delicate shade of green when I was trying to put the neck together.'

He blew his nose on a red check handkerchief, then turned to Treasure. 'He was clutching that cutter in what's called a cadaveric spasm. Means instant rigidity. Don't often see it. Not that sort anyway, Miss Clark.' He watched her blush. 'Last act before death. *Before* death. Can't happen after. Grip like iron. No wonder you couldn't open it.

'You're London, then? By the way, I think the Canon will survive. Got to look in again later. Flaming nuisance for you to come down for Jacks's inquest. Coroner may accept a statement, that is if WPC Clark sets it out nicely. Do your best, honey.'

He looked closely at his watch. 'Well, I'm off. Got a very old one down the road just about ready to croak. Private patient too. Still, can't grumble. Kept her going so far in spite of the progress of modern medicine. Talk about a big day for the Great Reaper. Thank God old Jacks was a bachelor. No prostrate widow to comfort with intravenous Valium.' He waved a hand at the Rolls. 'That's a nice jalopy. Cheerio, then. Keep taking the tablets.'

The doctor hurried away towards his car with short steps and a boxer's gait, shoulders working. Then he stopped and turned about.

'Suppose you don't know where Eddy Jacks got all that loot from? No? Thought not?' He'd anticipated Treasure's denial from the preliminary shake of the head. 'Take care,' he called.

The Range-Rover backed sharply up the drive and nearly mowed down Constable Stock who was rounding the bend on a bicycle.

'Regular caution, our doctor,' said the policeman, alighting beside the two. 'Great talker,' he added. ' 'Afternoon, Mr Treasure. Hello, Mary. Keeping busy, are you? I just heard the news. Thought I'd best come down. Poor Eddy. Accident then?'

Treasure left it to the girl to reply.

'Seems the stepladder toppled when he was doing the hedge. He fell back without stopping the cutter. Lacerated his throat. Bled to death.'

'Oh my lord! And you found the body, sir? 'Afternoon, Ralph.' The question was rhetorical and Stock had turned his attention to the other uniformed policeman who was approaching the group, carrying the hedge-cutter. 'Anything I can do?'

'Not really, Cliff,' answered WPC Clark's colleague, who was a sergeant. 'Taking this with us.' He raised the cutter. 'Nothing wrong with the ladder. That's back in the garage. They're taking the body down to the hospital. There'll be a PM.'

'Cause of death plain enough from what I hear.'

'Always a chance it was a heart attack. They'll want to be sure. Tricky case for the insurance, that's if Lady Brasset was insured for third party.'

'Accidents to employees,' put in the policewoman soberly. 'But since her Ladyship was dead . . .'

'Responsibility devolves to heirs and assigns, as like as not,' observed Stock with the assurance born of frequent attendance at magistrates' courts.

'I wouldn't be certain about the insurance liability,' said Treasure in an automatic, defensive reaction: he was on the board of one of the larger insurance companies. 'I gather Mr Jacks was unmarried. There may be no dependants.'

The sergeant gave a wry smile. 'What's the betting there'll be a long-lost dependant fourth cousin showing up somewhere if there's insurance money ready for claiming? What beats me is the five hundred quid Eddy had in his pocket. Five hundred! Eddy Jacks!'

'In cash, was it?' asked Stock.

'Well, it wasn't in cigarette coupons. All in twenties. Nice clean ones.'

'Eddy had a flutter on the horses pretty often,' the village policeman said thoughtfully.

'That's what the doctor said. Used the betting shop on the Esplanade. Have to check there, Mary. And his bank, if he had one. Could be he's cashed some National Savings Certificates. That'll be the post office. But five hundred nicker? The Superintendent will need to know where it came from. Likes everything neat, our Super does.'

The last remark had been addressed to Treasure, who had been dividing his attention between the speaker and the sight of the ambulance men loading the blanketed body.

'Well, thank you for your help, sir,' the sergeant concluded. 'We'll be on our way now. Next stop Eddy Jacks's landlady. House and garage secured, Mary?'

'Yes, Sergeant, and I've got his keys. Goodbye, Mr Treasure, Mr Stock.' The girl smiled and got into the driving seat of the patrol car.

'Marvellous workers, those lasses. Always cheerful that one, too,' said Constable Stock after the other vehicles had left. 'Sad business this, sir, coming on top of her Ladyship. Like a jinx. Hope there isn't another one. They do say deaths can come in threes.'

'Only in predictable thrillers,' Treasure joked.

Stocks nodded, propping his bicycle against the cottage wall. 'Well, I'd better check everything is locked up and they haven't left anything down the garden.'

'I'll come with you.'

'We saw you passing on the way to the Canon's earlier, sir. Very distinctive motor-car, that. I hear the Canon's poorly.'

Few local events seemed to escape the constable's attention. 'Yes. Your talkative doctor's looking after him.'

'Did Mrs Tring get her letter back, d'you know, sir?'

'Which letter?'

'Ah. It was one my wife found on the hall floor when she got here this morning, addressed to her Ladyship and hand delivered. Must have been there last night, but nobody saw it to pick it up.'

'It was from Mrs Tring, you say?'

'My missus says. Definite, she is. Bothering her all day. Knew the writing and couldn't place it. Remembered after our meal, midday.'

'And it was delivered yesterday?'

'That's right, sir. It's not likely Mrs Tring would be dropping it in after she knew her Ladyship was dead.'

'So what happened to this letter?'

'That's the mystery, sir, still. The missus thought Mr Pitty had picked it up, but he said not.'

'He was there this morning.'

'Oh, he was there all right. We wondered if Mrs Tring had popped over and taken it herself. That's what Mr Pitty thought. Front door was wide open a good part of the morning. She could have picked it up without anyone noticing.'

'Maybe she did. She didn't mention it at lunch. No reason why she should, I suppose,' though there was one he could think of.

'I'll ask her, sir. Just to please my wife, really. She feels responsible, see? With workmen about the place. Well, you never know, do you? And it might have had something valuable in it.' The constable paused. 'Now that's a funny thing, sir.'

They had walked through the garden and were standing on the far side of the small pine tree, close to where Treasure had found the body.

'Well, it's got to be funnier than the last time I was here, I can tell you.'

'Sorry, sir. I meant it's odd old Eddy was cutting from the bottom.'

Treasure looked both ways along the hedge. To the right several yards of it had been trimmed and boxed to a height of around eight feet. Immediately in front of them began the section which had been largely untouched. Only a short stretch of this had been clipped and, as the policeman had indicated, only at the side and to head height.

'He'd done quite a bit over all,' said the banker, looking to the right.

'Ah, that was last Saturday. Those clippings are a week old. They don't dry out this time of year. Done before the cutter packed up on him. I know. I was round the other side, on the footpath. There's a public right of way there. Short cut for me to my football. Last Saturday I could hear Eddy cussing because the cutter wasn't working. Gave him a shout to mind his language. Only joking, really. He'd cut this much already.'

'Did you see him today?'

'Hear him you mean, sir. It's tidy thick, this hedge. No. Football was early today. Afternoon light's drawing in, see? I got a lift in a friend's car. Didn't come this way.'

'But you think he'd have started cutting at the top? Is that the technique? The professional way?'

The policeman smiled. 'Wouldn't know about the professional way, sir. Neither would Eddy, he being a postman, not a proper gardener. Cutting hedges is boring whichever way you do 'em. Me, I chop and change when I'm doing ours. Start at the top one side, bottom on the other.'

'It seems Mr Jacks started at the bottom today.'

'That's as may be, sir, but I understand he fell off the ladder.'

'It was on top of him when I found him.'

'That's what I mean, sir. Eddy wasn't very tall, but

even he wouldn't have needed steps to cut that height.' He nodded at the cuttings which on close examination were slightly fresher-looking than the others.

'Perhaps he was just going up the ladder?'

'Not with the cutter working, sir. Not likely.'

'Well, perhaps he'd just climbed up, started the cutter and the ladder collapsed on him at that moment.'

Stock was studying the ground. 'That'll be it, sir.' There was a pause. 'I expect.' He looked up at Treasure. 'With the ladder on top of him at the end, that's what it's got to be, really.' Still he sounded doubtful.

At five o'clock Treasure was striding briskly along the beach. He had started from outside the Beachcomber and was now nearing the pier.

The incoming tide was still a good distance out. The big pebbles higher up the strand were barricaded off by a thick and pungent line of seaweed and jetsam. He was walking on smooth sand and enjoying the feel of it: he even liked the smell of decaying seawrack.

The light was fading but the wind had dropped. More rain was threatened in the sky, but for the moment it was dry and surprisingly warm.

He wished he still had the dog with him. It was part of the seaside fantasy to have a dog at your heels as you struck out over a deserted beach in winter—even a dog that was called Dung because it enjoyed rolling in cowpats. According to PC Stock, Dung belonged on the Fairfax farm, was a noted ratter, and scrounger from local outworkers. Probably Jacks had shared Saturday tea biscuits with him.

He looked up at the braced ironwork on the underside of the pier, the pigeon-breasted latticework that guarded its promenade above, the wide roundel that bulged out half way along the pier's length, the other even bigger one at the end. It was there the tiered pavilions stood, darkened now and lifeless, but home in summer for a surviving troupe of what John Betjeman called 'lesser Co-Optimists'. You could easily evoke the sound of the music: double-four tempo.

Treasure turned about. He had come to the beach for exercise and to think—not to ruminate on childhood memories of Weston-super-Mare.

One thing he was sure about: there was more than a coincidental link between those two deaths. Could he prove the link was more than circumstantial?

Jacks had been into the cottage at five without smelling gas—a time when a reasonable authority considered it would have been nearly impossible to ignore the gas if it had been escaping since before eight.

There had been at least three visitors to the cottage seen by Jacks, two identified as friends of Louella's—people who could have let themselves in with the spare key. So either could have smelled the gas depending on the time of their visits.

Treasure assumed the third caller had been Tony Quaint in a borrowed car—his wife's?—or a fourth, who Jacks hadn't seen. What if the unpredictable Quaint, obsessed with promoting the Sandy Lane scheme, whose wife had 'told him all about Louella', had come upon the key and let himself into the place—perhaps to write a note? What if Quaint had smelled gas and done nothing about it. Worse, what if Quaint . . . ?

The other two known callers might have had just as much at stake as Quaint. And who were they? Commander Mane was presumably one, though Treasure still needed to know what time he had been there. Pitty might be a non-starter. The only visit he admitted to could have been before Jacks arrived.

If neither Mane nor Pitty had been the people spotted by Jacks, there were still numbers of Lady Brasset's 'friends' involved as pending beneficiaries from Seawell who might have called. Which of them who, given the option and the notion, wouldn't have switched off a gas tap? Which of them, in the same circumstances, would have switched one on?

Any number of people could have come and gone by the other gate without Jacks knowing. But if such people heard later Jacks had been there and was naming names, would they assume they hadn't been seen?

The idea that Lady Brasset had met her death through someone else's design had rooted in Treasure's mind after he heard the postman's statement. It had taken growth when he had come upon Jacks's body, but it might still have withered except for the uncomfortable observation of Constable Stock.

The explosion plan had been far from foolproof, but if it succeeded it had the merit of producing the perfect murder.

Certainly a murderer would have had to go to the cottage to switch on the gas, but he could well have done so certain he wouldn't be seen, or confident that if he was seen his presence wouldn't be considered unusual. On the whole Treasure favoured the approach by stealth. In either case the perpetrator of Louella's death could count on accident as the verdict.

What then if a murderer learned Jacks had entered the house at five and not noticed escaping gas? What if the same person learned the postman might be naming him — or her — as a caller? What if a murderer knew Jacks had divulged his information to Treasure — withholding names only — and that Treasure had pressed him to inform the police? In that circumstance would another swift, credible-seeming accident eliminating Jacks be enough to close the affair?

Of course, it was far more likely any supposed murderer had gone ahead without knowing Jacks had had a confidant. But even assuming he knew about Treasure, would the risk have still seemed reasonable to this audacious character? The chilling answer seemed to be 'just possibly'.

With Jacks out of the way, it would be up to Treasure first to fulminate any suspicion, then to offer uncorroborated hearsay as evidence of a preposterous double killing.

Most people wouldn't care to become involved on such a basis—especially important people. There'd be the consideration of unpleasant publicity; the possibility of the whole thing being a ghastly mistake; the risk of looking plain foolish. And all three thoughts had been through Treasure's mind: perhaps a murderer had been counting on it.

Even so, there had to be corroboration of a kind. Jacks had told someone else, perhaps more than one other. Had one confidant tried to shut him up with money? Had another taken his life? Neither would be bursting to provide confirmation: one, Treasure considered grimly, might be watching events, wondering whether to kill him too.

The sound of running right behind him made him spin round.

'Damn. I wanted to surprise you.'

It was Tracy Mane, barefoot and breathless, a comely waif in her duffel coat and a sandal in each waving hand.

'You did surprise me,' he answered gruffly. She had scared him out of his preoccupied wits.

'Shall I do my Isadora Duncan on the beach? It's very good.' She danced around him twice.

'It depends what you believe Isadora Duncan did on beaches,' he replied, less ruffled.

'Whatever you have in mind, sir.' She grasped the hem of the open coat and dropped an elaborate curtsey.

He looked about self-consciously. An elderly couple were regarding them from the promenade. 'Get up, you're making a spectacle of us.' He was glad it was nearly dark.

'Goody!' She locked both her arms around one of his and fell in step with his long stride.

'Won't your feet catch cold?'

'Not if you take me somewhere warm and dry.'

'I'm not taking you anywhere. You're a hussy and a baggage.'

'And you're such a dish, and pompous, and so very hard to get.'

'And the last is the only valid reason for the attraction, if any actually exists, which I doubt. If it does, I can promise you the reason will endure.'

'See what I mean?' She stuck her nose in the air. ' "And the last is the only valid reason for the attraction, if any actually exists", pom, pom, pom.' It was an excellent parody, complete with an exaggerated mime of Treasure's characteristic straight-backed, long-pacing progress. She held on to him more tightly. 'I'd do anything for you.'

'Then you can tell me what sort of car your father runs.'

'Why, d'you want to borrow it? It's a Metro. He's terribly pleased with it. Washes it every Saturday. Why do you really want to know?'

'I'm doing a survey for British Leyland. Remember you told me he went to see Lady Brasset on Friday? D'you know what time?'

'Mmm. I asked him. He can't remember. Not exactly. It was after tea. Why all the questions?'

'Pure curiosity.' He paused. 'Promise me something?'

'Anything.'

'It's not that sort of a promise, but it's serious. I don't think Mrs Quaint should have told you her husband went to see Lady Brasset last evening. He wouldn't like it.'

'You mean he'd beat her up if he knew she'd told me?'

'Of course not. He's not that type.'

'Wanta bet?'

'Anyway . . .'

'Anyway, I won't mention it to anyone. Why's it such a dark secret?'

'It isn't. It's just that . . .'

'He'd beat her. OK.'

He changed the subject. 'Did you hear about the other accident at the Brasset cottage?'

'No? Someone hurt?'

'Eddy Jacks, the postman. Killed himself working one of those hedge-cutter things.'

'Oh no! Poor Mr Jacks. Oh dear. He was such a sweet little man. He was in the hotel at lunch-time. Just after you left. He was looking for Daddy.'

CHAPTER 14

'Fact is Cynthia and I, well . . . we love each other deeply.' And with this halting and strangely unaffecting declaration, Pitty handed Treasure a whisky and soda.

The living-room, like the rest of the apartment was on the second floor of a large, red brick, late Victorian house. On the two floors below were the Tophaven offices of Pitty and Co., Solicitors. There was an attic storey above.

The house was one block inland from the sea, but with nothing but a public garden in front to affect the view. It was at the other end of town to Sandy Lane.

This room, and Treasure guessed the rest of the living area, had been styled by a competent and probably pricey decorator. The ceiling had been lowered, the lighting diffused. There were angled spots on the good pictures—a big Donald Blake landscape over the fireplace, a pair of John Piper etchings on the opposite wall; near the door, a striking Bruno Hollander watercolour of a girl's head.

The furniture was mostly modern. The chairs wide, chunky and in leather—like the long sofa. There were numbers of glass and metal tables, and bookshelves. A fairly discreet bar took up one corner, some dulled steel gadgetry in another was playing a piano recording, though the sound came from all around.

The window wall was now a dramatic gold velvet curtain, in contrast to the others which were painted white: with the drapes pulled back there was probably a good view of the pier.

It was six o'clock and dark outside. The blazing 'log fire' was a gas-operated phoney, but comforting. The whole impression was of a well-heeled bachelor's pad. Treasure had no desire to see the bedroom for fear envy might strike.

'It's none of my business. I didn't come . . .' he began.

'I know you didn't. You carried the thing off so well, though. Saved our bacon, I can tell you. We both feel—that is, Cynthia and I want you to know it's not just an affair. She made a terrible mistake marrying Algy, but there's nothing to be done about it. In the circumstances, nature has to take its course.'

'You mean you're quietly waiting for him to shuffle off this mortal coil so you can marry his wife.' It came out sounding harsher than he'd intended. It hadn't been he who'd raised the subject.

'That's the ticket. Yes,' replied Pitty, persisting with his passé idioms and apparently impervious to slight. 'He's OK for his age, you know? Heart's a bit dicky as you gathered. Not that serious, though. Last for years, probably.' The accompanying expression reflected selfless, stoic resignation.

'Dashed awkward, of course,' continued the lawyer, as

though explaining some unavoidable business clash. He was pouring himself a gin. 'She keeps up the façade pretty well, though, don't you think? I mean you'd never guess she wasn't crazy about . . . well, his mind. That was it at first, you see? Bowled over by the old intellect. I mean, brilliant chap in his day.'

'You and Cynthia have known each other some time?' One had to say something.

'Oh yes. Long before she met Algy, as a matter of fact. She was a secretary at Ribert and Glens up the road. When I was a partner there. Do take a pew.' He motioned Treasure towards an armchair, taking one opposite himself. 'Not that there was anything going on between us then. I was still married at the time, of course.' The tone now was sternly sanctimonious.

Treasure steeled himself to the non sequitur: the man was either stupid *and* naïve or else he assumed other people were. 'Ribert and Glens? Did they act for the insurance company who had the freehold on the Round House?'

'Used to. The Rackburn & Claremont, you mean? They lost the business years ago.'

'When the company changed hands perhaps?'

'About then . . . yes . . . I should think so.' Pitty was suddenly hesitant and began choosing his words more carefully. Treasure's disclosed familiarity with the insurance company seemed to have sounded some kind of alert.

'They didn't come to you? Was it about the time you set up on your own?'

'Might have been. Conflict of interest, though. Algy Tring was what you might call a founder client of mine.' One wondered whether the status had deserved the consequence. 'He came over, like a lot of my old clients at Ribert's. Plenty of partners there, of course. Small conflicts of interest don't matter then. Often saves the customers money to use the same solicitors if relations are friendly. Awkward in a very small outfit.'

Treasure nodded. 'Of course, Canon Tring was—still is—the Round House leaseholder. Loyal of you to choose keeping his business instead of taking on an insurance company.' He was unashamedly fishing with flattery.

'The Rackburn is a small show, I believe,' said Pitty, again on his guard. 'Insurance companies tend to share out their legal work, you know. Conveyancing, and so on. That way they're in touch with more solicitors across the country.'

'Which opens more sources of business for them. It's two way.' Treasure hardly needed lessons in that field. But he also knew the Rackburn had effectively ceased trading. 'I suppose some lawyer made a reasonable turn on the Round House deal yesterday. Not to mention the newish owners of the Rackburn & Claremont. I gather, incidentally, one of the directors lives here in Tophaven.'

'Indeed? Yes, I think I knew that.'

'Name of Sydney Smith.'

'Mmm. Lots of those around. Whisky?'

Treasure declined. The first drink had been a stiff one and he was still nursing half of it. 'Might I use this phone to confirm my dinner reservation for tonight? Norfolk Arms in Arundel. I have the number here.'

'Be my guest. Dining with a client in Brighton myself. Otherwise I'd have suggested we got together,' Pitty claimed jovially. He went to the bar to replenish his own drink while Treasure made the call.

'. . . and you'll ring me back right away? Thank you.' The banker replaced the receiver as Pitty returned to his seat. 'Line to the restaurant engaged.' He took a sip of his whisky. 'Returning to the lease business, I know Seawell will be grateful for anything you can do to push that one along. Mrs Tring—Cynthia—seems to have softened a lot over the termination. Every day counts, I gather. The compensation they have in mind is sensible. By the way, might I see the lease?'

Pitty was in the act of swallowing a large draught of gin and tonic. After the question he was convulsed by a fierce fit of coughing and spluttering. The banker made to get up and offer help. Pitty waved him back to his chair, forcing brief smiles between the paroxysms. 'Sorry'—more convulsions. 'Swallowed a nut'—heavy intake of breath. 'Wrong way'—apologetic grimace, followed by several painful-looking gulps and then more coughing.

Treasure had watched similar reactions to surprise situations acted out on the stage without ever finding them entirely credible. Now he wasn't sure whether he had provoked just such a consequence in real life, or whether Pitty's choking had been coincidence.

The lawyer wiped his brow. 'Phew! I do apologize. You were saying?'

'I mentioned to the Canon I'd be interested to see the Round House lease. He said you had it. I gather it's the original head lease composed by Sydney Marshford himself, or under his careful direction.'

'Of course, if you'd like to see it. I could send you a copy.' The other paused. 'Can probably find it now. Must be somewhere downstairs . . .'

It was one of those offers where the speaker by his tone was begging a reprieve—a 'please don't bother now' or a 'some other time will do' response.

Treasure was not inclined to be lenient. In the first place he had ceased entirely to trust Pitty's declared motives. As much to the point, he'd done the fellow an enormous favour earlier in the day: he deserved his pound of flesh. Finally, the whole purpose of the visit had been to see that lease.

'If it wouldn't be too much trouble?'

'Not at all.' Pitty got up. 'Shouldn't take a moment.

Help yourself to a snort when required.' He hurried out of the room.

A few seconds later the telephone rang. At first Treasure ignored it, assuming it would also be ringing wherever his host had gone. Then he remembered he was waiting for the Arundel call.

'Hello. Tophaven 273 . . .' he was about to add his name but never had the chance.

'Pitty? This is Richard Brasset. I can hardly hear you. Damn awful line again. Shout if you can hear me.'

'Quite clearly, but . . .' Treasure hollered. He could hear the caller reasonably well though there was a good deal of crackling.

'Good, I just caught that. Let me do the talking. I can't make it to England for ten days. You'll have to have the funeral without me. At least gives you time to figure what you've done with my mother's money. Did you hear?'

'Yes, but I really must . . .'

'It's two in the morning here. I've been four hours working on that mishmash of figures you telexed. They don't make sense, Pitty. I'm not a fool . . .'

'Dr Brasset, this isn't Pitty.'

'What? It's no use, I can't hear you, but get this. I kept warning my mother about you. She wouldn't listen, but you won't be pulling wool over my eyes. I want financial reports that add up. Especially covering my father's trust fund. That capital is sacrosanct by law. You ought to know that. It was intact nine months ago at the last balance. I warn you, if I'm not satisfied I'll call for an independent audit. Probably will anyway. Think on that. And another thing, you telex me how that Gas Board explains my mother's death. I want their written report. Did you tell them she was on a strict diet? No cooked breakfast? No eggs? Couldn't have blown herself up with a cooker she wasn't using. There had to be a gas leak, Pitty. It's their responsibility. There'll be damages.'

'Dr Brasset,' Treasure cried determinedly. 'For the last time, this isn't Pitty. Is not Pitty,' he repeated. 'Am putting the phone down.' He was just about to do so when the lawyer returned.

'For me, is it?' Pitty enquired lightly.

Treasure handed him the instrument. 'Awfully sorry, it's Richard Brasset. Terrible line his end. He wouldn't understand he wasn't talking to you. I'll be outside.' He walked straight from the room.

A few minutes later Pitty called his guest back from the landing hall. 'Sorry about that. Expect you gathered he's Louella's son. Cantankerous cove.' The bonhomie was overdone.

'He seemed a bit upset, yes. Didn't catch much of what he was saying.' Evasion seemed the most tactful route.

'Same last night,' Pitty went on earnestly. 'Runs a practice in some outback place. Very noble and all that, and pretty indispensable by all accounts. Appalling telephone link, though. Was it bad both ways with you?' There was hope in the tone.

'Mmm. Something about sending reports. By telex.'

'Yes. Thank heaven someone there has a telex. Had my secretary in this morning bunging off some figures. On the Brasset Trust. Very complicated. Sounds as if they got mixed up in the sending.'

'Oh, and I gathered he couldn't get here for the funeral.'

Pitty nodded, then lifted his eyebrows. 'Doesn't come to his mother's funeral, but can't wait to get chapter and verse on his inheritance. Odd chap, and inclined to be difficult.'

'I see. Certainly sounded terse. Said something about a gas leak. That his mother was on a diet. Wouldn't have used the cooker.' He shrugged. 'It was a bit garbled.' There, he had virtually passed on the gist of what he'd heard without giving offence.

'Absolute supposition, of course,' said Pitty loftily. 'The gas wallahs proved there was no leak. Louella could have come off her diet since she last wrote to Richard. Know what women are with diets. Table was laid. We both saw the egg pan.'

'Might be worth a word to the police, I suppose. D'you think Dr Brasset's going to raise it if you don't?'

They were both seated again. Pitty stared at the ceiling. 'Yup. You're right,' he said. 'No end of fuss if he started tub-thumping about it when the inquest's over.'

'Is the inquest likely to be before he gets here?'

'Might be, although it's not the kind that'll hold up the funeral. Have to see about arranging that too. Soon as I've got the death certificate. No close relatives except Richard, of course. So, as Executor . . .' He looked resigned. 'By the way, no luck with that lease, I'm afraid. We're remodelling the first floor. Dashed inconvenient. Moved a great wodge of documents to the branch office while it's going on. That's gone with them. Should have fetched it back already. I'm going to need it anyway. Get it first thing Monday. Send you a copy.'

'I'll be interested to read it. The Marshford Papers deserve a wider public. Sims, the librarian, he's quite an authority.'

'Thanks to Louella. He never showed any interest before she did.'

'He's a Marshford beneficiary.'

Pitty smirked. 'Gets a fiver every year for organizing a lecture. Few others in the town on the same sort of arrangement. Money involved hardly justifies the administration, I can tell you.'

'You handle them all?'

'For a pittance. Thinking of handing the lot back to Ribert's where they came from.'

'Is there anything in the Round House lease itself that accounted for Cynthia's evident diffidence in parting with it?' Treasure was working on the premise that since he was to get a copy the question was hardly improper.

Pitty parted his hands. 'To be honest, I've never read it.'

'Indeed?' Treasured eyed him steadily.

'I'm pretty certain Cynthia just wanted to demonstrate loyalty.' Pitty had reached for his glass and was now studying the ice cubes he was swirling about in it. 'To parents and pupils. Latterly to Louella. Cynthia's very strict on loyalty.'

There was a moment's embarrassed silence. 'But she didn't know about Lady Brasset's crusade until very recently,' said Treasure slowly.

'No, as I said, it was primarily about doing the right thing by the pupils.'

'So no prizes to the Canon for keeping the lease in the family till the bitter end?'

'Shouldn't think so. Do let me get you a drink.'

'I should be off. Just a finger of Scotch. Lots of ice and soda.' He handed his glass to the lawyer, who had got up. 'Just one other thing. D'you think they'll want me for the Jacks inquest?' They had briefly discussed the accident when Treasure had first arrived.

'Yes, but I'll have a word with the Coroner for you,' Pitty answered from the bar. 'He's a chum. Sort of. Solicitor in the town. Tends to do everything by the book though, I'm afraid. As I said, it was bad luck your being first on the scene. Gather from the police it could easily have been Elderberry's doubtful privilege. Did he say what he was doing there?'

'Delivering a book he'd borrowed from Lady Brasset.'

Pitty looked sceptical. 'Had he been inside the cottage, d'you know?'

'He said not. Didn't know where the spare key was.'

'I'm surprised. Under the flower-pot. Everybody else knows. But it wasn't there last night. She may have taken my advice about burglars at last.'

'Jacks had a key. It was on his ring on the garage door. I used it to get in to phone.'

'Elderberry might have used it too if he'd known it was there,' said Pitty thoughtfully.

'I'd have seen, I think. Was there a reason he'd have needed to get in?'

The other paused. 'None, and please forget I implied there might be. It was indiscreet of me.'

'Well, it's of no consequence to me.' Treasure registered more indifference than he felt. 'You're right. I wish he'd found the body. You know Jacks had a lot of money on him?'

'So the police told me. Racing winnings collected this morning, I'd guess. They're checking the betting shops.'

'And you'd seen Jacks today, you said.'

'Yes, poor chap. He was the hopeful I mentioned at lunch. Came in wanting to consult me just as I was leaving for the Trings.'

'But you didn't accommodate him?'

'Certainly not.' This was followed by a shamed expression. 'Wish I had now, of course. Bit much at the time, though. I gave him an appointment for Monday afternoon.'

'Probably nothing very urgent.'

Pitty nodded. 'Said it would keep. Probably wanted to make a will.'

Treasure, playing by instinct, remained silent. Both men glanced at the phone which had started to ring. Pitty took the call: it confirmed the banker's dinner reservation.

A few minutes later Treasure was seeing himself out of the house. There had been another phone call just as he had got up to leave. He had waved a farewell at Pitty who was engaged in a complicated exchange with an evidently muddled and French-speaking caller.

On the first floor the banker noted the evidence of the remodelling. Pitty had left a door open there. At ground-floor level too: outside in the drive there was a builder's skip close to where he had parked the Rolls. It was brimming with discarded impedimenta, pieces of cupboards, bits of carpet and linoleum, bulbous radiators and—a collector's item—a WC pan of generous dimensions in white procelain with a blue flower motif and a solid mahogany seat. He was examining this relic in the light of a nearby street lamp when he noticed it was resting on the remains of a frame door of much later vintage.

The door belonged with some plywood office partitioning buried further down in the skip. Stuck to it was a black on white painted nameplate: 'S.O. Smith. Managing Clerk' it proclaimed.

'Lots of those around,' Pitty had said when Sydney Smith had been mentioned. Surely if his managing clerk had been a Sydney as well as a Smith he'd have admitted as much? Stephen, Stewart, Samuel, Stanley . . . there were endless other possibilities. Miss Gaunt had not mentioned another initial. Directors' names were always given in full on statutory documents. Of course, she had been speaking from memory. She had recalled Sydney Smith easily enough because of the literary connection. Would the initials SOS have been just as memorable? To Miss Gaunt possibly not.

He turned the car left along the seafront, which was almost deserted. A single young couple hurried against the wind into the comparative protection and certain privacy of a promenade shelter on the seaward side. It was still dry, with fleeting glimpses of the moon behind scurrying cloud. He glanced at the clock: 6.40, still loads of time to change and be in Arundel by eight.

So had the postman really intended to consult a lawyer

as suggested? The decision would have been a very swift one. And wouldn't he have mentioned Treasure had sent him?

Was it not much more likely Pitty had been approached so promptly not as a lawyer but as a Friday afternoon visitor to the cottage? Had Jacks simply asked him if he had told the police? Now there was an explanation that fitted the postman's apparently impulsive action — as well as Pitty's fabrication.

And was it so impulsive? Had Jacks seen Mane before he saw Pitty — and then Pitty at the Commander's instigation?

'Ask anyone whose opinion you trust.' Treasure remembered suggesting that as an alternative to seeing a lawyer — and he remembered why. Tracy had said ex-regulars went to her father for advice. Eddy Jacks had been ex-Navy.

So the visit to Mane, innocently reported by Tracy, had possibly been prompted by Treasure. Had the Commander also failed to persuade Jacks to go to the police with his story? Had he also advised consulting a lawyer? — Pitty again?

It was an explanation that fitted events — except that another fitted them just as well.

Treasure had also told Jacks he ought to approach the two friends of Lady Brasset he'd recognized. Until Tracy had said her father drove a Metro the banker had assumed the Commander had been one of those friends. Now it seemed more likely he had been the unidentified caller — something he'd almost certainly have admitted to the postman, volunteering if he'd entered the cottage or smelled gas. It followed the Commander would have pressed Jacks to approach the two others for equally forthright accounts of their visits. That would have been the logical thing.

And Jacks had seen Pitty. One kept coming back to

Pitty—but in what capacity? If he had been a late visitor to the cottage why hadn't he admitted it at lunch—and who was the other one?

The banker parked the car in the Beachcomber forecourt. He sat in it a moment longer, considering the two courses of action open to him.

Either he had to find the two people Jacks had seen or else he had to go to the police with the postman's own story—a story that without corroboration still sounded malicious and thus potentially scandalous. Both ways a lot of Louella Brasset's friends would be involved. He smiled at the memory of her: he owed her the effort. He would find those witnesses himself. Without knowing of Jacks's experience, they could be totally unaware of the relevance of their own recollections.

He got out and locked the Rolls. He needed to question Commander Mane too—and Tony Quaint, once he got the fellow to volunteer he had been at the cottage at all.

There was still the need for circumspection. There was no quick route to his getting to the right people without alerting a possible dangerously wrong one.

Jacks had used the quick route—but Jacks was dead.

CHAPTER 15

The knock at the door came as Treasure was putting on a shirt. He glanced at his watch: it was nearly seven—the time Tracy started her evening shift at the hotel.

'Come in. It's not locked.'

Disappointingly, it was Lancelot Elderberry who appeared around the door, a study in woe. 'Forgive me,' he uttered dramatically as he stumbled into the room. A fist was clenched to his brow.

He was soberly—for him—even sombrely dressed in a

fluffy black jacket, grey trousers, a black tie, and a shirt
that would have been plain white except for the flecks of
yellow thread. He would just have passed muster at a
funeral, allowing for the brown suede shoes. He had
obviously done his best from a wardrobe unmatched to
solemn occasions. What remained of his hair at the front
had been parted just above the left ear. The few longish
strands had been dampened and brushed across the
fleshy, pink pate.

'I'd have come sooner. Truly I would. Left a message I
was to be sent for as soon as you returned. That is, after I
knew . . . Mrs Daws just rang. I'm deeply sorry.'

'What for?' For the moment Treasure was at a loss.
'D'you mean about Mr Jacks?' he then added hurriedly.

Elderberry nodded. 'Leaving you like that. Such a
shock. If it'd been me, I don't believe my system would
have stood it.' He moved his head from side to side, his
neck seemed to get shorter with every twist.

'D'you want a chair?' asked Treasure, more because the
need seemed to be pressing than simply out of good
manners.

'Thanks.' Elderberry sank into the bridal suite's single
easy chair.

'You'll forgive my going on dressing?' The banker
smiled.

'I was in a panic, you see.' The fat man wrapped his
arms around a good deal of his torso. 'You might as well
know the truth. Sheer panic.' He was breathing
heavily—and filling the room with a smell of gin.

'You didn't show it. Did you know Jacks was dead or
something?'

'Panicked about my letter to Louella.' Elderberry
seemed not to have heard the question. 'Your arriving like
that. I thought you might unearth it. I'd been trying to
pick the lock. And all the time that poor sod was lying
there with his head cut off.'

'Not quite. And surely you didn't know that?'

This time contact was established. 'Of course not.'

'How long had you really been there, before I arrived?'

'About five minutes. Does it matter? It was pure selfishness. I'm riddled with it. My father always said so. He was right.' His head had sunk down into his chest. 'Did you know he was Primitive Methodist?'

'Jacks?'

'No, my father. Minister. Said I'd come to no good. If it hadn't been for my mother . . .' His eyes had clouded.

'If you were only there five minutes you couldn't have helped Jacks. He'd been dead for half an hour.'

'That's what the police said. You can't tell, though, can you? And it might have been more than five minutes. "Death be not proud, though some have called thee" something or other.' His voice had rallied for the quotation he'd half forgotten. 'Too proud I was, you see. I nearly went to Jacks for a key. Too proud and appy . . . apprehensive about what he'd think. Could have spun him a tale. Canny for a postman, though.' He heaved a sigh. 'The spare key had gone.'

'The one under the flower-pot?'

Elderberry nodded. 'Relying on that. Gone. What's it matter what poor Jacks would have thought? Others knew at the time. Should have gone straight to Denis Pitty. Asked for the letter outright. Needn't have gone to Louella's at all today.' He looked confused. 'No, that's not right. No business of Pitty's. Should have gone to Louella's. Got there earlier. Asked Jacks for the key. Saved his life, probably . . . Saved you from that terrible ordeal. Never forgive myself. You know that? Never.'

Treasure was now dressed except for his jacket. He pulled out the upright chair and sat in it facing his visitor. 'You were looking for a letter. What letter?'

'The one that awful boy sent Louella. About me.'

'Which awful boy? Bobby, or the one who drives machines, or . . .'

'Another one. Malcolm. Quite wicked, and so ungrateful. All I did was befriend him. Then he wanted money.' This seemed to be the besetting problem with Elderberry's friends. 'I had no money to give him. He threatened to write to people about me. My publishers and others,' he added darkly. 'He did write to Louella. Found out she was a friend.'

'I assume he was alleging . . . misbehaviour of some kind?' Treasure put the question as delicately as he could.

'It was lies. A tissue of lies from beginning to end. God's honour. But what could I do? All I'd done was give him shelter.'

'How old was this Malcolm?'

Elderberry swallowed. 'Getting on for eighteen.'

There was a difficult silence. 'And Lady Brasset?' Treasure asked eventually.

'Absolutely marvellous. She saw him. I don't know what was said—or done. Haven't heard from Malcolm since, except . . .' He stopped.

'Except?'

Elderberry shook his head. 'Not at all. Louella made me promise I wouldn't see him, so I didn't. I wouldn't have anyway, I don't think.' He sighed. 'I was very fond of him. Despite his wickedness.'

'But Lady Brasset kept the letter as—as a token of your good behaviour?'

'She was going to give it to me in a year, to destroy. She believed me but said I had to be protected—from my better nature. She was right, of course.'

'I'm sure.' Treasure looked graver than he felt.

'It was especially embarrassing because Malcolm was only . . .'

'Seventeen,' the banker offered quietly. 'How long ago was this?'

'Last December. Before Christmas.'

'So you'd have been getting the letter soon.'

'Yes. But who knows who'd grab it now Louella's dead?
The people dealing with the estate. Lawyers.
Accountants. Tax inspectors, as like as not. Busybodies.
Muckrakers. I don't mean you, but one has one's enemies.
Even I.'

'And you were trying to force the lock on the cottage
door when I got there.'

The collapsed, adipose Elderberry cut an unconvincing
figure as a lock cracker. 'Yes. With a credit card. Doesn't
work. Not for me anyway.' He stifled a hiccup. wobbling
his whole frame.

'Perhaps it's the wrong sort of lock. Look, finding the
body would have been worse for you than me. You knew
the chap quite well. There's no chance you could have
saved him.' Treasure felt sorry for the dejected, fuddled
figure. He was also inclined to believe the Malcolm story.
'D'you want me to see if I can get that letter for you? I
shan't try to read it.'

'Would you? How?'

'Let's say I'm a disinterested party with entry rights
pending. I'll have a shot.' He figured from something the
lawyer had said that Pitty probably knew about the letter.
It would have been natural enough for Lady Brasset to
have consulted her lawyer over the episode. It may even
have been Pitty who had seen off the importunate
Malcolm with such lasting effect.

'I'd be so grateful. It was in a tin box. Bottom drawer
of her bureau. Pink envelope, resealed and addressed to
me.' Elderberry had cheered up enormously.

'By the way, how many times did you go out yesterday?'
Treasure asked suddenly and with great firmness.

Elderberry looked up sharply. The brusqueness had
put his expression back into mourning. 'F . . . Friday?
Why?'

'Never mind why. Just indulge me, will you? How many times?'

'I . . . I was working all day. I went next door to view a desirable typewriter after tea.' He gave a thin smile. 'Oh, and I came here for the meeting at seven. I was pursued each time. But positively *pursued*.'

'Who by?'

'That scamp Bobby. The one who accosted us. He was camped by my gate — whoops, there's a Freudian. He was there all day.'

'You mean Bobby followed you to the Round House . . .'

'And back home. Then here later. Then he gave up for the day. Such a pesterer. I refused to talk to him — or let him in. He didn't try to get into the hotel.'

Treasure wasn't interested in Elderberry's movements after he had reached the Beachcomber. If anyone at that freeholders meeting had turned on the gas at the cottage he'd done it by seven. Treasure met all of them at the hotel bar later. They had stayed together since seven, and up to the time Mrs Daws had announced Lady Brasset's death — after Elderberry's prophetic outburst.

According to Tracy, Elderberry had learned Louella was in London — and why — at five. If Bobby had been dogging him all day he could hardly have slipped out without being noticed. So whatever the reason for Elderberry's visit to the cottage today, he hadn't been there yesterday — and he had the vexatious Bobby as alibi. Could there be any doubt in the matter? Treasure thought not. He was still a long way from proving that murders had been done. If they had it was conceivable that more than one person had been involved. Somehow, though, he couldn't see the loquacious Elderberry as partner in that sort of criminal conspiracy.

The banker rose, picking up his jacket. 'I'll do what I can about the letter.'

Elderberry struggled to his feet. 'I should go. Can't thank you enough. So sorry . . . about everything.' He moved towards the door, then stopped. 'You've no reason to think there's something fishy about Louella's death? That would mean Jacks was . . . well . . .'

'No reason,' Treasure lied, preferring that to volunteering grounds for litigation. 'Have you?'

'No. Good heavens no.'

'When Mrs Daws came in to tell us there'd been an accident, I remember . . .'

'I asked if Louella was dead? It just came over me, that's all. Second sight. Get it from my mother. Can't explain it.' He hesitated as though he was going to try, thought better of it, and shuffled out.

'My condolences about Eddy Jacks, squire.'

'Thank you. I wasn't related to him, Mr Daws,' replied Treasure blandly from the customer side of the reception desk.

Mrs Daws had scuttled into the rear office as the banker had come down the stairs. The two aged ladies were moving across the hall, this time in line ahead. They were making progress towards the residents' lounge, though not very much. Both were in long dark woollen dresses: one had on a wilted fur cape, the other a grey shawl.

'Oh, very dry, Mr Treasure. Excuse me a minute. Esta!' Daws called over his shoulder to his wife through the open door behind him. 'Tell Tracy, two medium Cyprus sherries in the residents'. No hurry,' he added less loudly, eyeing the old biddies. 'But the Misses Catchready-Taunton are working up terrible thirsts.' He grimaced at Treasure. 'Has to be Saturday. They don't live it up on the other nights. Won't sit in the bar, though. Don't know what they'll do in their next place. No proper lounge *and* two quid a day over what we charge for permanents.

Don't know they're alive. Maybe they aren't.' The smile froze. 'Sorry, squire, bad taste after your horrible experience.'

'I'm not in to dinner, Mr Daws.'

'Ah, so a little bird told me. Dining at a competitive gourmets' delight in Arundel. You got a table in the end?'

'Your wife was good enough to telephone. It's been confirmed. They're pretty busy.'

'Saturday night. Same everywhere.' Daws looked around the deserted hall. Even the Misses Catchready-Taunton had disappeared. 'Norfolk Arms, where you're going, great favourite of Lady Brasset's. For lunch. She didn't go out much in the evening, I understand.' He shook his head. 'Still hard to believe. Her death, I mean. Eddy Jacks, that was a shock too, of course, but always a risk, those power tools. To get blown up, though.' He tutted several times. 'Beats me with that gas on all day why nobody twigged it. Somebody must have called there since breakfast.'

'Somebody who might have gone in the house, you mean?'

'Or up to one of the doors.'

'You think they'd have smelled the gas from outside?'

'Could have. Bet I'd have niffed it.' He tapped his nose with a nicotine-stained finger.

'You weren't there yourself?'

'Me? Not me, squire. What reason would I have for calling on Lady Brasset?'

'Weren't you friends?'

Daws forced a chuckle. 'In a word, no. Acquaintances only. Friends, no. Bit of a snob, her Ladyship, and who could blame her? Mostyn Daws was not one of her intimates.'

Treasure wondered if Eddy Jacks would have agreed. If so, the . . .

'The lady wife, now, that's different,' Daws went on.

'They had literature in common, you see. Members of the Tophaven Readers Guild.' He glanced over Treasure's shoulder. 'Ah, the fleet's in. 'Evening, Commander. Dining aboard?'

Nigel Mane joined them at the desk. 'Not this evening, Mostyn. Dropped in on the chance of seeing Mr Treasure.' He smiled. 'Care for a noggin in the bar?'

'You'll have to excuse me,' said Daws, unnecessarily since he hadn't been included in the invitation. 'Saturday night. Don't know whether we're coming or going.' He glanced about. 'Early yet, of course.'

'One large pink gin, one Scotch, free peanuts, and the barmaid's available after eleven,' said Tracy, bobbing prettily after putting the contents of her tray on the little table.

Treasure and the Commander were seated in the corner furthest away from the dining-room. The bar was otherwise empty.

'Are you sure that's a small Scotch? I'm driving,' said Treasure.

Tracy gave a surreptitious look to both sides. 'Don't worry, guv, we waters all the drinks 'ere,' she whispered, then added louder and without the Cockney accent, 'If you want refills soon, help yourselves and put it on the slate. I'm taking adulterated sherry to the oldest surviving inhabitants. Always keep me chatting about how they were raped in the Indian Mutiny or on Mafeking Night, in Cheltenham or somewhere.'

'You don't say?' countered Treasure. 'And they told me they never leave Tophaven.'

'So *they're* after you, too?' cried Tracy, wide-eyed. 'Don't you be taken in by those sweet-talking frails. They're man-eaters. Both of 'em.' She sidled up close to Treasure, advising — this time in broad Devonshire — 'Take no chances, kind sir. Lock and bolt your door tonight. But not before I'm inside.' She winked and left.

'Glad I made her learn shorthand,' said the Commander philosophically. 'It's a crowded profession. Acting I mean. Can't all be successful like your wife.' He pulled a pipe from his pocket. 'Poor old Jacks. Terrible thing. Nasty shock finding him like that. Can't imagine how he came to do such a bloody fool thing. You know he was twelve years in the Royal Navy? Able Seaman, so not one of your natural leaders. Even so, every trained sailor knows the importance of safety with machines. You'd die a thousand deaths at sea if you don't observe the drills.'

'He was worried,' Treasure offered cautiously.

'Mmm. That's one of the things I wanted to talk about. Told me he'd unburdened on you.'

'And you were the next stop.'

'Used to it. You advised him to talk to someone he trusted.'

'Or a lawyer.'

'He wouldn't have done that. Not first thing. Incidentally, I gave him the same advice, including the tip he should go to the two people he saw at the cottage.'

'There was a third.'

'Oh, as you know, that was me. Told Jacks as much. No secret. He didn't see me. Only the car, which he might have recognized by the number as well as the make.'

'Don't suppose he was paying that much attention.'

'Right. Just anxious no one should know he was there.' The Commander blew down the empty pipe. 'Often thought of becoming a jobbing gardener myself. Strictly cash. No tax. Help my pension no end. Nobody wants me for anything else. Should be a vacancy for a postman now, of course.' He smiled ruefully. 'Know what they'd say if I applied?'

'Too old?'

'Too experienced. Amounts to the same thing. Never

mind. There's hope yet. Chance of a part interest in a little boatyard up the coast. That's once the Seawell money materializes.'

'I see.'

'Pretty important, that. Going to pay for Tracy at this acting place, too. Been sweating a bit since Louella's meddling, I can tell you.'

'Which is why you went to see her.'

'Yes. Tracy said you wanted to know what time I was there. Understood the reason after Jacks came to see me. I've thought about it. Must have been a few minutes after five. Tracy told me what Louella was up to when she came home at lunch-time. Cynthia Tring had told her about it. Worried me all afternoon. I didn't tell anyone else. Didn't see anyone, as it happened. Knew there was no point in trying to see Louella earlier. Thought she might have taken the early train back from London. Gets in at four-thirty. I was wrong.'

'You didn't go into the cottage?'

'Good Lord no. Louella used to be pretty casual about that kind of thing, of course.'

'Key under the mat . . .'

'Flower-pot, actually. Liberty Hall. Not my style, I'm afraid. Liked people to go in if she was late for an appointment. Always out somewhere, Louella. Usually on good works. Still, I'd rather wait in my car than bust into someone else's house. Better still, prefer 'em to be home if they've invited me.'

'You didn't smell gas, of course.'

'No. Wouldn't necessarily have expected to with the kind of insulation she had there. Not from the outside,' he ended pointedly, pushing tobacco into his pipe.

'Jacks thought one of the others might have gone in.'

'So he said.'

'He didn't tell you who they were?'

'Friends of Louella's, that's all. I didn't push him.

Could be almost anyone.'

'But he'd be able to separate the friends from the acquaintances. He worked around the place, after all.'

'Wouldn't count on it. Louella had a wide circle of callers. Lot of them went to her for help in one form or another.'

'I see. The most frequent visitors could have been supplicants rather than close chums.' He pointed to the Commander's nearly empty glass. 'Pink gin, wasn't it?' He looked towards the bar. Mrs Daws had come in quietly and taken Tracy's place there.

'No more for me. I have to be off and I know you've got a date, so let me tell you why I wanted to catch you.' Mane frowned. 'What Jacks said is obviously bothering you. Did the same to me. If Louella left that gas on so it blew her to kingdom come at eight, why didn't Jacks smell it at five?'

'His not smelling the stuff was odd but apparently not impossible.'

'But if it were proved impossible?'

Treasure nodded. 'You want to try finding out?'

Mane looked about him. Apart from Mrs Daws there was now a middle-aged couple standing at the bar—all were out of earshot. '*Have* tried. Went up there about an hour ago.' He looked at his watch. 'Hour and a half, actually. As soon as I heard about Jacks. Thought the police would still be there. They weren't.'

'Constable Stock and I were the last to leave. That was about four-thirty.'

'Hadn't planned anything. Came to me on the instant, though. Why not check out the gas business? Bit cavalier, I know, but there's a responsibility.'

'One that we share,' said Treasure firmly. 'The police ought to be told Jacks's story, except the implications could be pretty serious for someone . . .'

'If that someone had been in and couldn't have avoided

niffing gas—if the gas was on already.' The two men stared at each other silently for a moment before Mane continued. 'That's why I made the experiment. Privately.'

'How did you get in?'

'Easy. The backdoor key to my house fits the front door at the cottage. Always has. That's why I never cared for Louella leaving spare keys about. Always meaning to have my lock changed. Never got around to it. Pointless, too, I suppose. She said she'd never let on we had keys to each other's places. Pretended it would compromise my reputation.' He smiled wanly, then sucked on the unlit pipe. 'Poor Louella. Anyway, I let myself in, turned on four gas rings, full cock . . .'

'Four?' Treasure interrupted.

'Four over quarter of an hour equalling one over an hour. Technically imperfect for a variety of reasons, but good enough for our purposes. More than good enough.'

'How d'you mean?'

'I shut all inside doors, and sat on a chair in the hall. In ten minutes I was getting a strong whiff of gas. In fifteen I turned off the taps and opened the windows. Had to, for safety. Hall was reeking of the stuff.'

Treasure frowned. 'Yesterday's explosion could have opened airways that weren't there before.'

'True, except the force of that explosion went in the opposite direction—out to the garage.'

'So you think . . .'

'I think we can make every sensible allowance and double it. We'll still come back to the fact if Louella left the gas on early morning, Jacks would have smelled it when he went in.'

'What you mean is someone else switched the gas on much later in the day.'

The Commander frowned. 'I wish I knew what I meant. There are quite a lot of alternative explanations, some of them quite innocent. I mean not involving . . .'

'Criminal actions? Like an old-fashioned gas leak?'

'That's one, yes.'

'What d'you want to do about it?'

'To be honest, I'd like to sleep on it.'

'See the police in the morning?'

'If I . . .'

'If we feel the same way. We'll see them together.'

'Agreed,' said the Commander, evidently much relieved.

CHAPTER 16

'Arundel town is stopped in history?' asked Sheikh Mhad Alid tentatively.

'Steeped. Yes,' Treasure corrected without emphasis.

'Especially the castle. Good position defensively. Modernized,' Ali went on, the wrinkled brow indicating deep calculation, or a headache from the night before.

'The seventeenth Duke of Norfolk still lives there,' said Treasure.

'Norfolk is a long way from Arundel, no?'

'It's an old family. Lots of estates and titles all over the place.'

'Nomadic.'

Treasure chuckled. 'You could say that, I suppose.'

'Anyway, the Duke's not open to offers,' put in Quaint. He drained his wine glass, an action Treasure was coming to regard as characteristic.'

'My brother, the Emir, he likes historic castles.'

'Collects them, you mean?' Quaint was helping himself to the claret, beating the attentive wine-waiter to the decanter by a hair's breadth.

'This one was begun in the reign of Edward the

Confessor,' said the banker. 'Circular keep and double bailey. Looks like a small version of Windsor.'

'My brother, he's been to Windsor.'

'Too pricey, even for him, eh?' Quaint joked, too loudly. Alcohol seemed to do wonders for his back — and his lungs.

'The cathedral too. That is old?'

'Not very. Roman Catholic. Late nineteenth-century. Architect Joseph Aloyius Hansom.'

'Like Hansom cab?' asked Quaint, but only because he was trying to disguise a belch. He stared defiantly at a man who looked round from the next table.

'He invented it.'

'What?' Quaint demanded.

'The Hansom cab.'

Ali was writing busily.

'Some dessert? Cheese?' The banker smiled at the others.

'Food's good here,' responded Quaint, who had eaten almost as well as he'd drunk. 'Bit of Stilton to keep the port company, perhaps,' he added, unwaveringly identifying his needs and priorities.

The meal had passed off quietly enough. All three had kept off controversial subjects. No business had been discussed. Now Treasure was ready to introduce something more important than the age of Arundel Castle.

He had been disturbed that Ali was staying another night with Quaint, and had arranged the dinner because of this. In the circumstances he hardly trusted either man not to do something precipitate and probably illegal about the Round House: in concert they were definitely dangerous.

Dinner and a homily at the end had seemed eminently sensible when he had issued the invitation on the telephone in the morning, just before he had met Jacks.

As he expected, Mrs Quaint, although invited, had been unable to join them. The two men had come in the Arab's small Ford.

'You'll be pleased to know I spent an hour or so at the town library, with the Marshford Papers. Very encouraging,' Treasure offered.

'The letter of the Lady Brasset, the one by Mr Marshford about the architects. It has not been found?' Ali asked, looking at Quaint not Treasure as he spoke.

'Not only that. There seems some doubt anyone can prove it ever existed.'

'Cooked up by the old bird. She was playing for time—and effect.' Quaint belched again. 'Whoops.' He smiled expansively.

'She mentioned it to Mrs Tring. Went to the Round House to show it to her, among other things, apparently . . .'

'But it never actually got seen by anyone? Well, well, well,' observed Quaint with heavy cynicism.

'The librarian never saw the original. I couldn't find it in the Marshford Papers. The copy Lady Brasset made . . .'

'Said she made.'

'All right, Tony, said she made, got lost, according to her. She rang her gardener from London. Told him she thought she'd left it in the pocket of a coat. He was to get it and post it to me.' It was the first time Treasure had mentioned anything he had learned from Jacks to anyone except Commander Mane.

Quaint flashed a stern glance at Ali.

'You think there was a letter, Mark?' asked the Arab.

'Window-dressing,' pronounced Quaint, balancing a large piece of cheese on a small bit of biscuit. 'Crafty old bitch. Elaborate a lie enough and you can improve on its credibility. Old trick. Takes an artist, though.' The cheese fell into his lap.

'This gardener. He didn't find the letter?' Ali pressed.

'Of course he didn't,' Quaint asserted while searching in his napkin for bits of cheese. 'There was no letter.'

'He didn't find it, certainly.'

'Stolen, no doubt,' scoffed Quaint. 'That *and* the original. Librarian suborned, gardener too, I expect, by wicked property developers suppressing evidence about the former—former, mark you—alleged elegance of a sat-upon lighthouse. Saying the letter was pinched would have added bags of drama. You can see some fairy from the Department of the Sacred Environment swallowing that one whole.'

'Bit fanciful, I think,' murmured the banker, though the speech had set him wondering for a moment about Sims. 'Still, it makes it all the more important the developers should be white as driven snow.' He gauged it was homily time.

'Oh, point taken, Mark.'

'It will snow for Christmas?' Ali asked earnestly.

'Not necessarily. Bit of Shakespeare. *The Winter's Tale*.' Treasure wished Ali could avoid writing things down at mealtimes. 'By the way, enquiries are going on about who visited Lady Brasset's cottage yesterday.'

'Who by?' enquired the other two in perfect unison.

'Nothing official yet, so far as I know. The gardener was there all afternoon.' He paused for a reaction. There was none. 'He saw people coming and going.'

'D'you know who he saw?' This was Quaint, with studied casualness.

Treasure found the question enlightening. One of the scenarios suggested Quaint should have known exactly who had been seen.

'I'm not sure,' he said truthfully. 'Neither of you there, I suppose?'

'I was not there in any circumstances,' pronounced Ali as if reciting an article of faith.

Quaint took his time over ingesting a generous draught of port. 'I was,' he said. 'And anyone who wants to make a federal case out of it's welcome. I was there on misinformation received.'

Ali looked downcast.

Treasure avoided showing his satisfaction. At least Quaint's admission had come without involving his wife. Tracy's assessment of the man's character could well be right.

'Misinformation?'

'Ali here rang me. Told me about the Brasset woman's visit to you. What she was up to. He also said she'd gone home.'

'A mistake. My English,' the Arab apologized.

'Thought it might be worth a bit of tactful personal intervention,' continued the big man.

Treasure suppressed a vision of Quaint arriving astride his trusty JCB ready tactfully to mow down the cottage with Louella still in it. Aloud he said, 'Clever of you to find the place. Bit hidden away.'

'Got it second time around. Matter of fact, my wife knew it. Gave me directions. Been to meetings there. Used to know Lady Brasset. Involved together in some charity.' He gave the banker a knowing look. 'That was how I got the idea. Thousand quid to the old girl's favourite lost cause. If she'd drop this damn fool scheme to save the Round House.'

For someone who boasted a genteel background—good school, famous regiment and so on—Quaint's view of the motivations and scruples of decent people was perversely malevolent.

'I'd have gone higher, if necessary,' he said, compounding the felony. 'And Ali knew about *that*.' He paused, then lowered his voice. 'The demolition plan was better.'

'But Lady Brasset wasn't at home,' said Treasure,

Lady Brasset doesn't leave on the gas herself.'

'Well, it's going to be bloody difficult to prove anything else. That's all I can say.' Quaint raised his glass unsteadily. 'Whatever the gardener smelled or didn't.'

'But he is also now dead.' Ali looked from one to the other. 'That will make a scandal? I ask Mr Pitty. He says not to worry, but not to shake the ship.'

'Rock the boat,' Treasure amended involuntarily.

'Thank you, Mark. Not to rock the boat in anything to do with the Sandy Lane development. Just so everything goes smooth. No . . . no headlines. He says the DoE won't protect the Round House. We can knock it down soon.'

Denis Pitty had been remarkably helpful considering he was formally retained not by Seawell but by the freeholders and one leaseholder in Sandy Lane. The injunction to Ali about avoiding publicity Treasure also found intriguing.

'I think Pitty has given you sound advice. I hope we're both of us right about the Round House. Tell me, Ali, why is he looking after your interests so carefully?'

'Ah, he is pressing hard for the money for his clients. It is for them.'

Quaint snorted. 'He hasn't done much for them so far. Only lawyers involved worth their fees are the ones who work for the Rackburn & Claremont. Money for old rope, of course.' He blinked. 'Still, it was Pitty who tipped us off there might be trouble yet over the Brasset accident. Not that we've anything to hide. Ali wasn't supposed to let on Pitty had been in touch. You understand, Mark? All in the family, of course,' he added hopefully. For once the man appeared mildly shamefaced.

'I assumed as much,' said Treasure, sure now that Pitty had lied to him about Jacks, but not so certain about the extent. 'So you'll ring the Tophaven police tomorrow?' He waited for Quaint's nod, then went on. 'You weren't at the cottage today, either of you?'

'With my back? Haven't been anywhere till now,' Quaint complained. 'Excuse me a minute.' He got up slowly, then limped off across the restaurant heading for the washroom.

Ali had shaken his head in answer to the question.

'And Tony's been at home all day?' the banker pressed.

'Yes, Mark. Oh, except he went to see an ostler. No an osty . . .'

'An osteopath?'

'That's right. I expect he forgot. For the pain.'

'When?'

'Just after lunch.'

'Did he drive himself?'

'I think so. It wasn't far.'

'How long was he away?'

Ali looked troubled. 'It's important, Mark? I think . . .'

'How long?'

'About an hour.'

Time to have driven to Colston and back.

'There's nothing else you'd like to tell me that's pertinent?' The Arab looked confused. 'I mean anything else that could upset the Emir?' Having scored with his surprise deduction about Pitty earlier, the banker decided to try another. 'For instance, do you know anything about a Swiss company called HBAM Research and Development?'

'It is permitted to know why you ask this, Mark?'

'Sure. It owns forty-nine per cent of the Rackburn & Claremont, which has just come into money from the sale of the Round House. I believe the remaining shares may belong to Denis Pitty. They're listed under bank nominees, but the sole British director seems to be Pitty's managing clerk. The initials HBAM are your own run backwards, Ali, and Pitty seems unduly interested in your welfare. Does that answer your question?'

'It is complicated,' began the Arab. 'I have many

interests, you understand? HBAM is one,' he went on lamely. 'The investment in the insurance company seemed . . . what do you say? . . . prudent?'

'You could say more than that when you know Seawell has to buy its only substantial asset at a very inflated price.' Treasure looked stern. 'What you're paying for the other properties sets the Round House price out of proportion. Lot too generous. I noticed it when I asked for the figures, before we lunched yesterday. I assumed that part of the total site would justify the difference. Now I've seen it I accept the Round House has the most important position. But that doesn't cover a price per acre three times as high as you're paying for the other properties.'

'The Round House, it has historic importance,' offered Ali hopefully.

'Nonsense. You're going to knock it down. Basically, you're buying land. By the way, you'll be in an embarrassing situation if you can't knock it down. Pitty's right not wanting you involved locally.'

'Not rocking the boat?' came the glum and accurate response.

'Anything that gets people enquiring into your relations with Pitty is what he has in mind. Special prices for properties when the buyer is a company controlled by you and the local lawyer. Not cricket, Ali.'

'Not cricket. I understand.'

'Comes in the same category as taking kick-backs — bribes from contractors.'

Ali looked shocked but not baffled. 'I never have . . .'

'I didn't say you had, and I hope you never will.' He paused. 'Does Tony Quaint know about HBAM?'

'A little.' The Arab gave a quick, nervous smile.

'Not about its owning half the insurance company?'

'No.'

'He knows the name of the company?'

'Yes.'

'Because you're doing a consultancy deal with him on the building contract payable through them?' He was prepared to stretch a point, accepting a difference between a consultancy fee and a kick-back.'

'Tony told you that?'

'Let's say I'm partly guessing. You and he are pretty close. Possibly too close. I wouldn't trust him with all your confidences if I were you. And I wouldn't take presents from him—in any form. Is that clear?'

'Yes, Mark.' The sheikh responded like a scolded schoolboy. 'You will tell my brother?'

'That you've gained personally from a Seawell property deal? I don't think so. Seems to me what the company's paying for the whole Sandy Lane site is about right. The other freeholders should be getting more and the insurance company less.' He shrugged. 'But the others seem happy enough with the prices Pitty negotiated for them.'

'We leave things as they are?'

Treasure sniffed. 'In equity, the Rackburn & Claremont ought to make bonus payments to the others.' He lifted a hand to stem the Arab's protest. 'Except there isn't a way to do that without everybody wondering why—including a lot of interested outsiders like tax collectors.' He smiled. 'Complicated if your insurance company had to give all the money back, of course.'

'How could that be?' asked the startled Ali.

'You can't think of any reason?'

'No.'

'None at all?'

'How could there be a reason?'

'Good. Just a passing thought. I assume it was Pitty who put you up to buying a piece of the company?'

'He came to see me in London. He owned the company. HBAM bought forty-nine per cent . . .'

'For rather more than he'd paid for the whole outfit, I expect.' Treasure shook his head. He saw Quaint coming back. 'No, I shan't tell the Emir about this sordid episode. And don't write down sordid,' he added just in time. 'I will tell him I think you're underpaid for the responsibility you carry.'

'So he pays me more?' Ali brightened.

'Which should stop you needing to take advantage of your position in less legitimate ways.' He nodded at Quaint who was sitting down. 'Ali has decided he won't require you to retain that Swiss company as consultants after all.'

'You mean . . .'

'HBAM. So you can revise the Sandy Lane estimates deducting their fee. That goes for future contracts, too. I suggest you forget about HBAM and any — er — personal connections with it.'

'I see.' Quaint glanced at Ali. 'And where does that leave Roxton International?'

'With a valuable contract and a warm commendation from me to the Emir, providing the Tophaven work is up to standard.'

Quaint considered for a moment. 'Fair enough.'

'OK, Mark,' Ali added quietly.

Treasure looked at the time. 'Ali, you've hardly drunk anything. It's still quite early. Why don't you drop Tony at his place, then drive back to London tonight?'

'I was thinking I'd do that.'

'Good.' Treasure called for the bill. He'd accomplished all he'd intended, including pointing Ali towards Town.

The larger issue remained still. He was now sure Lady Brasset *and* Eddy Jacks had been murdered. He was fairly certain, also, he knew the name of the murderer. The problem was proving it.

CHAPTER 17

The Colston road was a roundabout way back to Tophaven. It was a quiet route, though, and he'd needed time to think.

He recognized the doctor's Range-Rover. It pulled out from the Trings' drive just ahead of him as he drove through the village. It was shortly before ten o'clock: not too late for a call. He was genuinely concerned about the Canon.

'Come in, Mark.'

She was wearing a white, fisherman's knit sweater, sleeves pushed back, and a pleated tartan skirt. Her eyes had met his quite steadily. She touched his sleeve lightly as he passed her.

'Saw the doctor's car. Shan't stop. How's Algy?'

She put a finger to her lips, then pointed upstairs. She motioned him towards the drawing-room.

'Not too good. I'm trying to get him to sleep. Do sit down. Scotch, isn't it?'

'Not if you're not.'

'But I am. So it's two Scotches.' She went to the drinks tray. 'He may have had a tiny coronary when he was with you. There's nothing on the ECGs. Doctor's done two, but he doesn't seem satisfied.'

'Algy's had heart attacks before?'

'Mmm. We've yards of ECGs for comparison. He won't have an operation. Age. Can't blame him. Doctor wants him to stay quiet for two days. More tests tomorrow. I suppose you think I'm every kind of bitch,' she added without pausing. She looked up calmly. 'I've put ice in. Soda? Say when.'

'I never make untutored judgements on private lives.

Your husband is devoted to you. Denis Pitty tells me he is too. Must make life difficult.'

'Denis told me you went to see him.' She handed him the glass and sat beside him on the other end of the sofa. There was a log fire burning in front of them: real logs. 'We'll marry, of course. Eventually. At least I think so. It isn't just a casual affair. And I didn't break up his marriage. That was over years ago.'

'But you love him?'

She shrugged, then said slowly, 'That's a very strong emotion. I'm not sure I'm capable of it. Not any more. I like to be needed. For the moment, Algy needs me.'

'And Denis? Isn't he too successful . . .'

'To need a steadying influence? I don't think so. He's inclined to over-reach himself. The business expansion, it isn't really justified. Not yet.'

'The Sandy Lane business should help balance the books.'

'The fees on that aren't very big,' she said carefully.

'But he does own half the Rackburn & Claremont.'

'He told you?'

'No, the owner of the other half did.' He smiled. 'I wonder if it's going to work?'

'I'm sorry?'

'Denis — er — couldn't show me Algy's lease on the Round House. I think it stipulates it reverts to the leaseholder in certain circumstances. At a guess — if the place has remained an educational establishment for young ladies. Am I right?'

She made no answer.

'Which means I am, or as near as no matter. We'll know on Monday, anyway. Seawell's lawyers will be told to demand a copy, or, as I suspect, to read the one they've got.'

'They have one.'

'Professional negligence.'

'Oversights like that are more common in solicitors' offices than anyone would credit. You can almost bank on them in some circumstances. There's nothing in the freehold documents. Nothing to alert anyone.'

'And nobody's bothered to read the lease. Except you, when you worked at Ribert and Glens perhaps.'

'It was after I'd promised to marry Algy. It was a bonus, not an incentive.'

'But you didn't tell Algy?'

'Let's say I wanted it to be a surprise.'

'And not a disappointment if you couldn't prove Marshford's terms had been met.'

'There's no real doubt. Even in the War it was a women's school of a sort.'

'I agree the other half of the scheme must have seemed more problematical.' He was referring to Seawell buying the nearly valueless lease from the insurance company.

'I'm not party to that,' she retorted promptly.

'A passive observer, perhaps.' He paused. 'So, someone told Denis Pitty about the reversion clause. Algy wasn't aware of it. Ribert and Glens had ignored it. On a long shot, Pitty bought the insurance company for a song. It was already a shell. The owners were probably delighted to get rid of it. No doubt he waved a copy of Algy's lease at them. So they at least knew the Round House lease was pretty nearly worthless.'

'I believe he paid a fair price,' said Cynthia, smoothing a strand of hair from her forehead.

'And sold just under half to a Swiss company owned by the head of Seawell, along with a proposition.'

She shrugged. 'That Seawell should buy the Round House freehold from the Rackburn & Claremont, which they very much wanted to do.'

'Except the head of Seawell had no idea their freehold had such a short life.'

'All he or his lawyers had to do was read our lease.'

'I agree. A case of buyer beware. You could have blown the whistle yourself any time, of course . . .'

'Except I had no formal knowledge . . .'

'Nor legal responsibility. I see that. It was a long shot for Pitty. The sale to Seawell had to happen before Christmas. As soon as that lease expires you or the Canon have to claim ownership of the freehold. Meantime, you had to keep the college going at all costs.'

'There's no dishonesty involved,' she stated quietly.

'I told you, I'm not making judgements. The bare fact is Seawell knew nothing about the lease reversion, but they would have if their purchase had been held up another six weeks. Even when planning permission came through, it's possible Seawell might have been slow about buying the buildings. And Pitty could hardly press any harder than he had been without raising suspicions.

'It was Lady Brasset's intervention that forced the issue. Seawell bought the Round House so fast yesterday, I doubt their lawyers had time to go over all the documents, even if they'd intended to. They probably regarded a lease with six weeks to run as hardly worth a glance. Am I boring you?'

She smiled, kicked off her shoes, and drew her legs under her. 'Not at all. I can't wait for the happy ending.'

'I'll bet you can't. On Monday afternoon Pitty will tell the Seawell lawyers Algy will be claiming title to the freehold on the Round House on Christmas Day. I assume he's delaying till the afternoon to make sure the money already paid to the Rackburn & Claremont is properly dispersed to wherever it has to go.'

'Perhaps. If Seawell want to buy our interest they can.'

'You mean there's no harm in the legal balloon going up on Monday. Or are you hoping there won't be a fuss?'

'Who's going to make a fuss? Hardly your sheikh. He owns half the company that bought the freehold yesterday. Now he'll have to authorize buying it again.

It's not likely he'll sue his lawyers for negligence. They'll be insured for that, of course. But he's made himself terribly vulnerable, don't you think?' She stared at Treasure earnestly, then she broke into a smile.

'I think if Pitty proves your claim . . .'

'He will.'

'Then it may be appropriate for the Rackburn & Claremont to make more than a token repayment to Seawell. You see, I'm not sure what view the Law Society will take of his part in this.'

'As a lawyer? So far he's had none.'

'All right. Maybe he'll get away with it. Sheikh Ali is subject to sterner sanctions if the story gets out.'

Ali was to pay dearly for Treasure's recommendation about his salary increase.

She shook her head. 'The insurance company had a perfect right to sell that freehold. They owned it till Christmas. Seawell made the offer in the first place.'

'That's the ingenuous view, yes.' Treasure paused. 'You realize it's still possible you'll find yourself owning a listed ancient monument?'

'Thanks to poor Louella?'

'On the other hand, if it hadn't been for poor Louella . . . How long had you known she was hunting for ways to get the Round House protected?'

'Not till Thursday evening. She said it was to be her Christmas present to me.'

'She didn't know about the lease reversion?'

'Hardly. She thought if she got the building listed it would keep it out of the Sandy Lane development. Also that the sweet little insurance company would give us a nice long new lease at a nice low rent because nobody else would want the place. She had it all worked out.'

'And she hadn't mentioned any of it to you?'

'Louella was a loner when it came to confounding the bureaucrats.'

'I believe she thought the college was important to you . . . er . . .'

'Financially?' She finished the sentence for him without embarrassment. 'In other circumstances she could have been right. We're pretty hard up, and it happens Algy's never made any money.'

'So if it weren't for Denis Pitty . . .'

'Denis *and* the reversion, I might have been glad to go on running the school. God, what a prospect.' She shuddered. 'Like to get us another drink?' She gave him her glass. Her hand lingered on his a fraction longer than necessary. 'I suppose I shouldn't worry. I still seem to have a modicum of sex appeal. It's just that . . . well, after my first husband died . . .'

'While still quite young, I understand.' He fetched the drinks.

'Suicide,' she said without emotion. 'Threw himself under a train while the balance of his mind was disturbed. But not by me.' She swallowed more of the new drink than was either decorous or judicious.

'I'm sure not.'

'I wasn't at the time. Shatters one's confidence a thing like that. There was no reason, you see. So—' she sighed—'we lived in the Midlands. I came here to recuperate. Got a job. Met Algy. He was marvellous. So understanding, and he needed me. We needed each other. It made all the difference at the time. But it wasn't the panacea, our marriage. As you saw when you . . . when you dropped in on Denis and me this afternoon. I'm truly sorry about that.'

'None of my business. And I must go.'

'Please don't.' This time she purposely put a hand on his and left it there for several seconds, drawing it back slowly. 'I wanted you for a friend, and I spoiled it.' She dropped her gaze from his, stared into her drink, and then drank the rest of it. Treasure had barely touched his second whisky. 'My first husband, then this charade with Algy and . . . and I wish I were more certain about Denis. Life hasn't been easy.' She looked up again. This time there were tears welling in her eyes. 'What I most fear, I suppose, is loneliness, and . . . and rejection.'

The performance was completely out of character. It was even less convincing than one of Tracy's intendedly overplayed caricatures.

'You'll miss Lady Brasset, I expect.'

'Louella? Yes.' The sharpened tone in the voice made it clear Treasure had not come up with the hoped-for response. 'We weren't that close. She was older.'

'But she must have had your interests very much at heart.'

'A dear person. Yes.'

'Did she show you the letter she copied in the library?'

Treasure's obsession with fact, and his disinclination to enter into the emotional spirit of things was clearly irksome to the attractive woman on the other end of the sofa.

'What letter?'

'That's a good question. Lady Brasset described it to me in some detail. I haven't put my hand on the original yet, in the library where it ought to be. As for this copy, it's got to be somewhere. She didn't show it to you?'

'She may have.' The tone was now more calculating than irritated.

'You mean you don't remember?'

'She was very excited when she came to see me. It was late Thursday afternoon. I was about to leave. She had a great bundle of papers. She was full of what she'd been up to. Surprise, surprise, and all that.'

'While the idea of having the Round House protected was not the sort of surprise you needed. Mark you, the news spurred Seawell into action. So it suited Denis.'

She shrugged, but made no comment.

'Lady Brasset didn't leave any part of that bundle of papers with you? Some intentionally, some by mistake?'

'I don't understand.'

'She took a lot of photocopies at the library, most of them, it seems, to mislead Sims. He told me as much. He was quite philosophical about it. Understood she wanted to keep everything dark until the last minute.'

'There were photocopies, yes. She dropped some of them in the waste basket.'

'Nothing else?'

She hesitated. 'Yes, I remember now. A sheet of paper in handwriting. Might have been a copy of a letter. Didn't look like it.'

'It wasn't her prize exhibit?'

'Oh God, it might have been. Does it matter? And do get me a drink.'

He got up and took her glass. 'And did she leave this piece of paper with you? On your desk perhaps? By mistake? Didn't she ring you from my office when your students were out to lunch — or working from headphones? Didn't you say you didn't think you had any such paper, but you'd have a look? And didn't you find it?'

'Yes, yes, yes.'

His questions had been intelligent invention. The call must have been made. Lady Brasset had effectively said so to Jacks. Still, it had been a long shot.

'If you knew all about the wretched letter, or whatever it was, why didn't you say so in the first place? It wasn't my fault Louella left it behind.'

Treasure wondered about that: aloud he said, 'It was thoroughly inconvenient for Lady Brasset not to have had it with her in London. Made the difference between strangers having to take her word it existed, and reading it for themselves. Naturally, we believed her.' He handed Cynthia her glass. 'It was mostly because of what she said was in the letter I rang Sheikh Mhad Alid. That was what set Seawell moving in such a hurry. But I don't believe the people at the DoE were so impressed that Exhibit A was missing.'

'You know that?' she asked, too searchingly.

'Lady Brasset implied it. That letter is pretty crucial . . .'

'To the Round House being listed?'

'Mmm. More, now Marshford's own copy has gone missing. There's the suggestion, of course, she invented the whole thing. Would you credit that?'

'Entirely. Louella was ruthless. Unscrupulous in what she considered a good cause.'

'You think she composed the letter she left with you?'

Again she hesitated. 'If it was a letter. I didn't read it.'

'And she didn't read it aloud to you?'

'I told you, she was excited. She came bursting in with this garbled story about the two architects. What she'd found in the Marshford Papers. She was quoting from things. Yes, probably letters.'

'Did you realize what her day in London might start? That she could be scuppering the Sandy Lane project entirely?'

'Certainly not. One is so used to Louella's causes. Many came to nothing. This one sounded specially futile. Until later.'

'You didn't tell her right away protecting the Round House would do you and Algy out of a small fortune?'

'How could I without . . .'

'Without doing you and Denis out of another small fortune? Without blowing his little scheme, though, as you say, you aren't party to that. Just a sort of delayed beneficiary.'

'You can be very hurtful when you choose, and quite unjustifiably smug. You and your business friends have just as much interest in seeing the Sandy Lane scheme through as we have.'

'All three of you. True, though it seems my business friends are likely to pay twice for the privilege. Tell me, when did you deliver Lady Brasset's copy letter to her cottage?'

'I don't know what you mean.'

'I think you do. I think you knew exactly how important it was to her case. Did she leave it on your desk by mistake, or did you arrange that it got left behind? Of course you were too astute to destroy it right away. When she rang from London the first time, I believe she was certain she'd left it with you. That's why on balance, and on advice later in the afternoon, you decided to give it back to her. Or you tried to.'

'I tell you, I didn't know it was a letter.' She was now sitting bolt upright. There was more than anger in her voice: it was fear she was permeating. 'I realized it was the paper she was looking for.'

'So you stuffed it into an envelope.'

'I was busy.'

'After she called the first time.'

'Yes.'

'And dropped it in to the cottage . . .'

'Yes. Uh!' Her teeth dug into her bottom lip.

'At around four-thirty on Friday afternoon. Meaning to demonstrate to Lady Brasset how conscientious you'd been, thinking she might return on the early train. So you were at the cottage after all?'

'I'd forgotten. I . . . I came up to make Algy some tea, but he'd gone out. I slipped the envelope in on the way back.'

'You went in the cottage?'

'No,' she almost whispered. 'And I didn't smell gas.'

'But Lady Brasset rang again later, about measurements. And then it was obvious she wasn't coming back early. And that's when you had second thoughts—or someone put second thoughts in your mind. What if Marshford's letter—the original—had disappeared? If that happened, had you done something unspeakably stupid? Preserved the only copy? So did you then go back to the cottage . . .'

'No, I didn't. I . . . I . . .'

'You've forgotten again. Someone saw you driving out of the gate . . .'

'Not Jacks, he'd . . .'

'Gone? That's right. He saw you the first time. Was he paid five hundred pounds later to forget it?'

Her jaw tightened, but she said nothing.

'The second time it was someone else. But you were there all right to get back that envelope.'

'But why . . . ?'

'On the strong chance that by six last evening enough interested people knew the importance of the original. That one of them might have decided to do something about destroying it.'

'I couldn't have known.' Still the voice was quiet, uncertain.

'Something better than intelligent surmise on your part. Anyway, the thing's gone. You're too bright to miss chances—especially ones you can engineer for yourself.'

'Chances?'

'Your friend Louella had trusted you with her secret. By lunch-time yesterday even Sims's assistant knew what she was doing. You made it your business to spread the word. You scared stiff all the people likely to benefit from the Sandy Lane development. Except Denis Pitty. Once he'd got his money, of course, both of you knew it made no sense to support Louella.'

She was stroking her brow with both hands as though trying to relieve the tension there. 'I didn't go into the cottage. I didn't get the letter back. Denis promised to get it today but . . .'

'You didn't have your own key to the cottage?'

'Never. It's why I *couldn't* get in. If I'd smelled the gas I'd have switched it off. I couldn't have turned it on. I know Jacks thought it was turned on later . . .'

'Denis told you?'

She nodded. 'If there's an investigation . . . because Jacks died. If it comes out I was there.' She shook her head slowly. 'I would have saved Louella's life, but I never had the chance. I never could have harmed her. People will think I went in. I always went in. But this time I couldn't, don't you see?'

'Because the key had gone already. The one under the flower-pot,' Treasure confirmed.

The relief on her face was instant. The tears in her eyes this time were genuine enough. 'You know that? Oh thank God. You can prove it? Tell them if it comes up?'

He nodded but knew he yet lacked the justification.

'Thank you, thank you.' The weeping was now uncontrolled. Then, in a single spontaneous movement she folded her arms around his neck and pressed her cheek to his. He could feel her whole body quiver with each great sob. He tasted the salt in the tears as she kissed him, not particularly expertly, but with feeling. People had different ways of expressing their gratitude after all: he decided it would be churlish to seem insensible.

CHAPTER 18

' 'Evening, Mr Treasure, sir. Thought it must be you.'

'Hello, Mr Stock. Late patrol?'

The banker had earlier parked his car on the rough verge some distance from the Trings' house to stop any noise disturbing the Canon. He was glad he had done so, particularly since he had stayed longer than he'd intended. The policeman, pushing his bike, had come up to him as he was unlocking the car door.

'Ah, well, it's a bit tricky, sir. Why I'm out. Glad of your help. It's this envelope, see?' He withdrew the object from under his cape. 'Addressed to Lady Brasset from Mrs Tring, it is. The one my wife came on this morning, at the cottage.'

'That disappeared in the hall?'

'That's the one, sir. Well, it didn't. Disappear I mean. The wife's that ashamed. Put it in her pinny—the pocket of her pinafore—*meaning* to put it on the hall table. Had it on her all the time. She was in such a rush to be back to get my dinner. That was the trouble. Football being early, see? She's not usually out on a Saturday morning. Routine all to pieces, that's what it was.' He paused. 'Oh dear, she's that upset.'

'And she's just found it?'

'Few minutes ago. She was sorting out the wash for Monday.'

'Well, there's no harm done, surely?'

'Could have been. If it had gone in the machine. *And* Mr Pitty's been looking for it. Like I said, I'd meant to ask Mrs Tring if she'd taken it back. Then I heard the Canon was poorly so I didn't like to bother her. Same as now. Don't know whether I should knock or push it through the letter-box or what. I telephoned Mr Pitty. No answer. I see you just come out, sir. How is the Canon?'

'Not too well. Needs to sleep. Best not to risk waking him. About the letter. Can we walk down to your house? You won't book me for parking here?'

The constable smiled. 'No, I won't do that, sir. You're well off the thoroughfare, and a Rolls-Royce adds a bit of tone to the village.' He nodded approvingly at the car as the two walked away together. 'You were saying about the letter, sir?'

Ten minutes later Treasure was sitting in the kitchen of the Stock home, consuming excellent hot chocolate and buttered homemade speculo biscuits under the approving gaze of Matilde.

'It's irregular, sir. It's irregular without any doubt,' said Stock, pulling on a bushy eyebrow. 'If what you say is right, I should be getting on to the Station. CID work this is, and no mistake.'

'But if I'm wrong, a lot of police time is going to be wasted, plus a lot of law-abiding people may be put under suspicion. A lot of them friends of ours.'

'I see that too, sir. What you're asking is . . .'

'We delay reporting you've found the letter till tomorrow morning.'

'A few hours only, Clifford. That's all *monsieur* demands. And really it's 'is letter anyway,' put in Matilde. She had heard only part of what Treasure had said to her husband, and she was unclear about why the CID should be involved over her stupidity. One thing she knew for sure: Treasure — who looked like all her favourite actors rolled into one — said Lady Brasset had told Eddy to send what was in the envelope to him in London.

Matilde was happy to accept the word of an obvious English gentleman in such a matter. It also made her feel a good deal less guilty.

'And if we opened the envelope, sir, you know exactly what we'd find in it.' Stock was weighing his words while considering the short time left before his retirement.

'A copy of a letter in Lady Brasset's own hand. Yes. But I don't suggest we open it. Or do anything that might be considered in the least unlawful or improper.'

'There,' uttered the constable's wife. It followed whatever Treasure said was in the envelope was surely so.

Opening it would have been not so much unlawful as a challenge to integrity.

'Could I have some more chocolate, love?' Stock's tone signified preoccupation with more important matters without reflecting on the quality of the beverage. He turned to Treasure. 'And phoning these people, then you and me sitting it out, as you might say. You reckon that'll be according to Judge's Rules?'

'Undoubtedly,' replied Treasure. He had the slimmest memory of the rules referred to but worked always on the premise that any law which didn't comply with common sense could ultimately be challenged with impunity. 'All we're doing is deciding not to wake the Trings to tell them we've found a letter Mrs Tring hasn't even reported lost.'

'Ah, there is that,' put in Stock with a speculo half way to his mouth. 'I could have just shoved it through the letter-box, though.'

'It may be splitting hairs, old chap, but in the circumstances—' he smiled at Mrs Stock who beamed broadly in response—'I don't believe it'd be characteristic of you to have done that. You'd want to explain how the thing turned up.'

'Without doubt, Clifford,' agreed Matilde with a pointed sigh.

'That's right enough, sir. Take it round in the morning, I would.'

'So, that's settled. And you and I can spend an off-duty hour or so sitting in Lady Brasset's grounds.'

Stock showed less contentment on this point, but his mouth was too full of buttered biscuit for immediate disputation.

'Let's say we're going badger-watching,' added the banker hurriedly.

'That's every poacher's excuse, sir—and burglar.' But the comment came lightly.

'And we could hardly be mistaken for either. Now if

you'd rather I made the calls from the box up the road . . .'

'Not at all, sir. They're only local anyway. Phone's in my office at the front.

Matilde went ahead and had carefully polished every part of the instrument, and the seat beside it, with a new duster, before Treasure was allowed to begin his calls.

'Apparently, Mrs Stock said you were looking for it this morning. She's very embarrassed, her husband said,' Treasure explained.

'It's just that Cynthia mentioned it. I said I'd pick it up. I don't think it's important,' Pitty replied in an over-casual tone on the other end of the line. 'On the mantelpiece in the living-room, you say?'

'That's right. Mrs Stock thought she'd put it in the hall. She remembered later it was the living-room.

'Good of you to let me know. I'll pick it up in the morning.'

'Could I meet you there? Shall we say nine-thirty?'

'If you like.' The lawyer sounded surprised, and not in the least enthusiastic.

'How was Brighton?'

'Er . . . windy. Only got back a minute ago.' It was ten to eleven.

'I know. I tried you earlier'—but only a few minutes earlier. It was fairly certain Pitty hadn't been in touch with Cynthia—unlikely he would telephone at this hour and disturb the Canon.

'You called on the Trings. How was Algy?'

'Poorly. I had a long chat with Cynthia.' Treasure paused. 'A pretty frank chat.'

'I see.' The uncertainty in the voice implied the speaker was awaiting rather than enjoying illumination.

'About the copy letter in that envelope. Lady Brasset meant it for me. She told Jacks to post it to me.'

'I'm sorry, I don't follow.'

'Jacks told me so himself.'

'You saw Jacks?'

'We had a confidential talk this morning, yes. Before lunch. Before he came to you. I gave him a certain amount of advice. I'm sorry I couldn't tell you when we talked. Not without risk of compromising others.'

There was a long pause. 'I think I owe you an explanation,' offered Pitty eventually.

'I think so too. It's why I suggested we meet in the morning.'

'Tonight would be . . .'

'Less easy for me.' He could make what he liked of that. 'Good night.'

Treasure had replaced the phone before the lawyer's collected thoughts had found proper expression. Next he called the Petworth number. Tony Quaint answered.

'Has Ali left yet?' Treasure asked.

'Just going. He's washing his hands. D'you want him?'

'No.'

'You put the cat among the pigeons there, all right. Something he's not letting on about too. Something about the sale of the Round House. Is that insurance company on the up and up?'

'I think that's Seawell's business, don't you?'

'I suppose so,' though there was no disguising Quaint didn't mean it.

'There's been a development with the Marshford letter. The one you said didn't exist. Well, it does. At least the copy Lady Brasset made.'

'Or dreamed up. How does it read? She was old enough to get the style right, I suppose. Probably went to school with all the Marshford daughters.'

'She wasn't quite that old. Anyway, I can't vouch for the style, or anything else in the letter yet. I haven't seen it.'

'Has anybody else?'

'It's in the living-room of Lady Brasset's cottage. In an envelope addressed to her. It'll have to stay there till the morning. I'm picking it up then with Denis Pitty, the lawyer.'

'You said the original's lost. That's assuming there ever was an original.'

'That's right.'

'Must you have a lawyer around when you get this copy?'

'Yes, as it happens. Remember it's not addressed to me.' It was tempting to add the lawyer in question would be as happy as Quaint himself to see the document quietly destroyed.

'How did it get where it is? In an envelope. Wasn't it supposed to have been stuffed in her coat pocket? Jumped out, I suppose. That gardener didn't see it.'

'It was put there later, in error.' Treasure lied in a good cause.

'Sounds fishy to me.'

'We'll see when I've read it tomorrow. What effect it'll have on the DoE.'

'Oh my God,' came as a sort of muted, hopeless supplication for divine partiality in the cause of Roxton International.

'Sorry, didn't catch that.'

'My back's hurting.'

'Bad luck. Talk to you in the morning. Good night.'

Treasure wondered how well Tracy was doing. He had called her first.

'Are you sure it's OK for me to go, Mr Daws? It's only quarter to.'

'Absolutely, Tracy, you captivating creature.' The proprietor of the Beachcomber leered at her from the customer's side of the bar. 'I'll lock up the booze. Another drink, either of you?'

Daws was addressing the Commander and Mr Elderberry. Both had drifted in during the previous hour as they sometimes did on ordinary Saturdays in winter. This Saturday in a curious way encouraged clannishness. Looking on the bright side, none of those present might need to endure the bleakness of Sandy Lane night-life for even one more week.

'Is Mrs Daws all right?' asked Tracy as she emptied the till. The takings were small. There had been seven people in the dining-room for dinner—including the Misses Catchready-Taunton. All had since left. There were just the four of them in the bar.

'Esta all right? Oh, tip-top, thanks, love.'

'She hasn't gone to bed?'

'No incentive with me still here, eh?' He glanced about for appreciation. The others hadn't been listening. 'No, she's in the office. She'll put that in the safe.' He nodded at the small pile of notes, coins and one Visa slip. 'Unless she throws caution to the wind, rushes out and paints the town red with it.' He wrinkled his brow in a sign of despair. 'Who'd run a seaside hotel, eh? I'd make more with a jellied eel stall. Might do that next.'

'It's just she looked a bit upset . . .'

'When you came back from talking to Mr Treasure, sweetie,' Elderberry chipped in. 'We were all a bit upset. Perhaps it'll all come right, though.'

'As I see it, whatever's in that letter of Louella's, Seawell are committed to buying us out on Monday,' said the Commander.

'But Treasure said he'd be handing it over to the DoE,' put in Daws.

All three men exchanged pointed glances.

'He doesn't really have any option.' This was the Commander.

'Being an honourable man,' commented Elderberry.

'Being an honourable man's all very well if you're a rich banker with no mortgage and no pile of debts dragging you down,' Daws mourned.

'Well, good night, Mr Daws, Lancelot. Don't wait up, Daddy. I'm going for a blow along the front. May drop in on Sally for coffee.' Sally was a friend who lived at the other end of town.

'Wrap up, and take a stick,' ordered the Commander.

'In case I have to beat a handsome man into submission!' she joked as she left the room.

Tracy crossed the empty hall, and made for the office behind the reception desk. The door was closed, but she heard the ting of the telephone being replaced. She knocked and entered without waiting for a summons. Mrs Daws was sitting at the desk. She was holding a crushed handkerchief to her nose. Her eyes were red with weeping.

Treasure hadn't purposely collected Dung. The brown dog had joined him unexpectedly in the bushes opposite the front door of the cottage, refusing to be sent away. They were crouched together, waiting for action. Specifically, it was Treasure who anticipated stirring events: Dung simply harboured a vague expectation about a newly conceived mealtime. The relationship between man and dog had become easier when Dung spotted the Thermos flask and moved downwind of the banker to be close to it. Dung had been in a cow field: quite recently.

Constable Stock was some distance away. He was waiting behind a low, well-spread young oak, its leaves withered but not yet fallen. The tree was close to the drive exit high on Treasure's left.

The Rolls was parked out of sight behind Stock's house.

The policeman's bicycle was hidden at the side of the cottage.

The rain had held off, and there was a strong breeze. And suddenly there was Tracy Mane in the middle of the drive.

'Cuckoo! Cuckoo!' she cried, looking about her.

'Shut up, you're out of season,' called Treasure in a low voice, parting the cover in front of him. 'Come in the bushes, quick.'

'I've had better propositions,' she giggled. 'You should be ashamed, luring innocent young girls . . .'

'Keep your voice down.'

'Aye, aye, sir.' She cuddled up beside him. 'Your dog pongs.'

'He's not my dog. His name's Dung.'

'You're kidding?'

'I'm not. How did you get here?'

'Last bus. Stops at the crossroads.'

'Anyone you knew on it?'

'Only Bill Watts, the driver. It was empty.'

'You needn't have come.'

'I guessed you'd be here. Fancied a ride home in the Rolls.'

'It may be a long wait.' He zipped up the weatherproof golf jacket. 'Mr Stock is at the far gate.'

'I know. He came out and waved while I was cuckooing.' She pressed up even closer to him. 'Anyway, I'm the only one with a key to the cottage. You might need one.'

'How d'you come to have . . .?'

'Our back door key . . .'

'Fits this front door. I'd forgotten. Your father did tell me. Did you get the story over to everybody?'

'Mmm. Including Daddy.'

'I didn't mean . . .'

'I know you didn't. But he ought to have as much

chance as everyone else to prove he's straight.'

'That's a point.'

'It isn't just for the letter, is it? There's more. It's more serious than the letter.' The unusual, earnest note remained in her voice.

'Maybe. If anyone comes after the letter tonight, it could be someone's in deeper trouble than . . . than people have guessed.'

'Except you. You know who's going to turn up.'

'I have an idea, yes. I could be totally wrong.'

'I doubt it, Mr Treasure, sir,' said Tracy with confidence. She was a discriminating reader of detective fiction. 'If we're in for a long wait, could we have some of whatever's in that Thermos now?'

'Hmm. May not be enough for two,' he said sternly. Dung shuffled on his other side. 'Or three,' he added.

It was just after midnight when it happened.

Later Treasure couldn't recall which registered first—the constable's shout or the sight of the firey torch.

'Stop the bike,' yelled Stock, but the swish of the wheels on the drying tarmac was then already echoing off the house.

Treasure and the girl broke cover as the hooded figure on the racing bike hurtled past. They saw the crude, flaming petrol bomb fly accurately at the living-room window. The bottle bounced hard against the wooden frame but didn't go through the glass. It shattered with a blinding flash. In a second everything outside seemed to be alight.

'Garden hose round the corner,' shouted the policeman pounding down the drive.

'Get inside. Phone the fire brigade. Then come out quick.' Treasure had to make a fast decision. Tracy already had the key in her hand.

Dung had been asleep. He leaped up to follow the

others, scrambling into the open. Terrified by the fire burst, he scuttled up the drive and tripped up Stock, who came down heavily.

'Bugger,' cursed the policeman. He got to his feet and hopped painfully towards Treasure who was already advancing with the turned-on hose. 'Give chase, sir. She and I can handle this. Not as bad as it looks.' He snatched the hose. 'Take my bike. Not the road,' he added breathlessly. 'The footpath. I saw. Go left at the top. Oh, my ankle.' He was standing on one foot directing the hose with one hand while beating at the radio attached to his tunic. 'Bust most probably. Bloody dog.' But Treasure was already too far away to hear.

CHAPTER 19

The footpath was narrow, straight for some distance, and overgrown. The surface was uneven. There was a ditch at the side—and the bomber was in it. Stock had been right about the route: pursuit was worth the try.

The police bicycle was built for endurance not speed. But Treasure covered half the distance that separated him from his quarry before the other had remounted and got moving again.

It was years since he'd been on a bike. They said you never forgot. He hadn't—except about the gears. The going was easier after he found he had three speeds. The fancy contraption ahead would have five, perhaps ten gears. They couldn't be much help on this short cut. He felt the straggling bramble tear his cheek, then claw across his jacket. He hardened his grip on the handlebars. Keeping your balance here was all.

He saw the chestnut branch in time, ducking quickly. When he looked up the bike ahead had disappeared. He pedalled harder. Then he could see it was a bend ahead.

He knew the road where the footpath joined it. It was on the hill down to Tophaven, a quarter of a mile below the crossroads.

Now he was certain, too, the fugitive was the same cyclist who had passed the phone-box after lunch. The racer was well in sight. There was no mistaking the black clad rider and the yellow machine. The fitful moonlight had been enough. And now there were street lamps. The built-up area had started.

Soon the going was flat. The distance between the two bikes widened—but not so much as he'd expected. The rider in front had the faster machine. But Treasure sensed he was fitter. If he could count on his own deduction, the banker knew he was the fitter of the two. He crouched lower over the front wheel.

As yet he couldn't vouch for even the sex of his quarry, let along true identity. The cover-all track suit, the Balaclava, the goggles—the outfit had looked just seriously sportive in the day: now it was plainly sinister.

The terrace houses and corner shops, the billboards, side streets, parked cars and pedestrian crossings—they were all there, lining the way, the standard fitments of the urban scene. Only the people were missing: only the responsible human beings he needed to shout out to bar the way, call for assistance, summon the police.

But in all the distance he had come not a solitary figure had appeared along the way: not one. And it was Saturday night! If provincial Britain withdrew at seven, the population of Tophaven might have emigrated en bloc at midnight

'Stop thief! Help! Police!' he hollered. At least it liberated an inhibition: it did nothing else. Whoever he was chasing glanced back once. There were perhaps three hundred yards between them. He had to close the gap.

He wasn't losing—but he'd gained nothing either over the last half-mile.

In a minute or so they'd be in the town proper. He didn't know the layout well enough. A local could lose him—shake him off in the back streets near the centre.

The grassed and rose-bedded roundabout ahead was huge. There were five exit roads leading off it. He ignored the direction signs. Concentrate on the racer, the rear light: was he closing the gap now? He thought so.

Then he saw the lighter bike mount the roundabout itself and streak across the centre. It slowed slightly at the raised middle, then raced smoothly between the flower-beds, bumped on to road level again and spurted down the High Street.

He couldn't imitate that circus act. There was nothing else for it—just keep pedalling like mad; hope to make up the lost distance. At least he knew which exit. He was nearly there. He swung across the road with a dangerous rake. It was then the pedal scraped the tarmac. He thought he was coming off—wobbled, lurched, then righted the machine. Now he too was in the High Street.

Marks & Spencer, Tesco and Currys welcomed him in lights. 'Say the Leeds and you're smiling' flashed the sign in the building society window. But nothing else was moving: no cars, buses, vans, lorries—worse, there was no other bicycle in sight either.

The two policemen emerged from checking the doorway of Barclays Bank. Treasure braked. 'Chasing a racing bike. Incendiarist. See which way?' he shouted, starting to pedal again.

'Second left,' responded the cadet constable as surely as if he were directing someone to the post office. His voice and features suggested early promotion from the boy scouts.

'Your name, sir?' demanded the senior officer. Both

the men in blue were now incongruously sprinting beside him. He was moving well.

'Treasure. Can't stop,' he called as the distance between them began to increase. 'Come from Colston. This is Cliff Stocks's bike.'

The older policeman fell back, talking into his radio.

'That road's closed lower down, they're . . .' It was all he heard of the cadet's earnest intelligence as he too gave up the unequal challenge from a Sturmey Archer top gear on a 27-inch-wheeled Raleigh Roadster determinedly propelled.

Adare Street, the second turning, was indeed closed half way along—except that hardly anything stopped a bike. There was a planked walk-way up some steps on one side. 'Pedestrians Only' the notice read. He could see all this from the end—also the fugitive dropping the racer, from a shoulder carry, back on to the road the other side of the excavations.

He waited only to mark his quarry's subsequent turn to the right before carrying on himself down the High Street. He had no chance if he tried humping his heavier machine over what looked like fifty paces. Better to take the next turning—a wide one: it was the Parade, the shopping street that ran parallel with the Esplanade. The sea was only a hundred yards south.

He must have covered the distance from Adare Street in the same time as the criminal if they were on parallel courses. If the other bike was making for the sea it had to cross the Parade in the next second. The banker raced along it: nothing crossed in front of him. Half way down he turned left.

He had walked through the section between Adare Street and the Parade on his way back from the library. It was the oldest part of town. Alleys and lanes crisscrossed between the two thoroughfares. Treasure did the same. Whoever he was following was counting on local knowledge now. What else was left for the pursuer than getting it right by accident?

If the fugitive lived here then all was lost: even a familiar bolt hole . . .

The collision happened at right angles, at one of the completely blind corners. Treasure had been moving fast and was hit broadside. He came down with both machines on top of him.

There was no chance to grab his assailant who, still upright, threw a dustbin at him and ran.

Treasure was dazed by the fall, and he took a glancing blow to the head from the lid of the bin. Dizzily he got to his feet. He covered one smarting eye with a hand. Through the other he watched the black-clothed figure dash south down the lane and across the well-lit Parade.

Where were those policemen? 'Police!' he shouted.

His hand was moist. He pulled it away from his forehead. Water, not blood: he was seeing through both eyes. There was nothing else for it. He pulled the racing bike upright, got on, and started pedalling. A light came on in an upstairs window: what was the betting it wouldn't open? He didn't wait to find out.

He was unsteady for a few moments. After that, compared with his experience on PC Stock's mount, he felt nearly jet-propelled.

The policemen weren't in the Parade when he crossed it. He dared not divert to look for them. The running figure was still in view, crossing the Esplanade. The big house on the left was Pitty's. He passed it at top speed.

And there on the sea front was a moving police car: a white Rover with all the trimmings—facing the wrong way, already a quarter of a mile off and moving well in the general direction of New York.

He might be on his own but he was damn nearly on top of the enemy who was now at a side gate to the pier. It had to be locked surely?—except it was being opened with a key. He could even hear the click.

Time later to question whether local ratepayers got value out of the local constabulary. He shouldered the bike up the steps to the wide promenade, jumped on again and pedalled hard straight for that gate. It was made of stout steel bars and it was slammed hard on to the front wheel as he got to it.

He was shaken by the sickening jar: his head just missed one of the bars. But this time he was still upright, able to force the bike forward. He'd stopped the gate slamming shut on its lock.

'You can't get away,' he rasped huskily at the figure pushing on the other side. His throat was dry as parchment. His heart was beating to burst. 'Police are behind me.' For the moment the claim was self-evidently metaphorical—but they had to be here soon.

'Police!' he shouted, making a nonsense of his last statement.

Suddenly the pressure from the other side gave way entirely. The bike was going through. Too late he realized it was a feint. A split second later the gate was swung back at him with terrible ferocity. He pulled his hands back in time to stop them being squashed.

'Swine!' he swore at his retreating assailant.

He lost precious seconds disentangling the front of the racer from the gate. The mangled wheel had temporarily jammed the closure—but the lock was still open.

He clambered over the useless machine on to the wooden broadwalk. At the same moment the moon went behind cloud. There had been bright lights on the Esplanade, but none on the pier, save for a red navigational beacon set high at the very end. Sydney Marshford hadn't legislated for the pier.

The best Treasure could do was jog into the blackness. He should soon get used to the dark: so should the fugitive, of course.

Was a pier a dead end for a felon? In the films, it was high buildings that signalled the terminal retreat for fleeing criminals. You knew they were trapped when they started to climb. He jogged on. Come to think of it, piers were different half the time. You could get off a pier—climb down to the beach, where he had been today—half the time. Right now there'd be no climbing down. Right now there was angry water lapping below him, and not far below him. The tide was right in.

He jogged faster, and now he could see his quarry. The figure was further ahead than he'd expected—abreast of the open-air theatre built on the bulge of the pier at half-way point. There was a roofed stage, that was all, with an area in front for a deckchaired audience.

The sighting had been fleeting. The fugitive had disappeared behind the stage. There was a way of escape with a head start if the banker went the wrong side.

'Police!' he shouted again, but he was only checking. As he expected, the wind carried his voice in the wrong direction—far off to the right.

He lifted the metal inset from the slatted wooden trash basket fixed to a stanchion. With all his might he hurled the canister to the left of the stage, then raced hard to the right.

He heard the clatter of the metal as it hit the decking on the other side. He rounded the stage. The decoy had worked. The two came nearly face to face—and the one being chased was armed.

The narrow wooden board should have caught the side of Treasure's head. He ducked at the right moment and kicked out at the wrong time. The crack to his knee was excruciatingly painful. He rolled over massaging his leg. For heaven's sake, why was he here?

He picked himself up. The board was under him: it was split at one end. There was painted lettering on it that he could easily decipher. It bore the legend GENTLEMEN: they'd need a new one for next year.

In a way he was winning. The villain had gone on, not back. The red beacon was casting an eerie light ahead. The dark figure was running for the shelter of the enclosed theatre at the very end of the pier—passing a line of side-show shacks.

So it would be hide-and-seek again, but this time he had the weapon. And he didn't intend to be surprised, hit or handicapped ahead of any race back to the Esplanade. He could leave now of course without risking the ignominy of getting locked up for the night on an empty pier—and probably losing the criminal in the process. Bitterly he considered the chances of help being at hand as definitely remote: he had come this far, so . . .

'Skittle Alley' proclaimed the sign over the first narrow building, positioned dead centre where the pier broadened out for the last time. The tarpaulin front was firmly battened down. 'Five balls for 20p' read the blazoned message at the side. And there were the balls; dozens of them. They looked like rubber cricket balls and they were stored in boxes against the first window Treasure came to.

He smashed out the glass with the wooden sign, pulled out one of the boxes, and tucked it under his arm. Then he helped himself to another—they were cardboard apple boxes; easy to handle.

Hurrying along to the right of the skittle alley, he darted across at the end to check the other side. The east wind was blowing hard so far out from the land: this time it took his breath away as he came from cover.

The enemy wasn't in sight behind him: there'd been no doubling back. Moving as well as he could, clutching his boxes, he passed an amusement arcade that was glazed on both sides down to the deck. All the time he watched for movement on the far side.

The shuttered dodgem car arena came next: plenty of cover on two blind sides here. He spurted round two of them ready to drop everything except the wooden board if it was a case of confrontation or pursuit.

The figure jumped back into the darkness—well ahead. Treasure was just quick enough to see.

Only the concert party theatre was left now. It was big and it was wide—and it offered the best escape cover yet. He'd planned for this, without being certain they'd get so far.

The open deck on both sides of the building was narrow. He dropped one box of balls on the windward side and ran with the other, well covered, to the right-hand corner of the theatre.

Immediately he heaved the contents of the box he was carrying along the boards towards the end of the pier. Fifty hard rubber spheres bounced fast down the deck. He was counting on their echo in the sheltered area to sound like someone advancing in a hurry.

Three seconds later he was emptying the second box of balls down the windward side. The noise would be obliterated by the wind—like the sound of his own movement right behind them.

Could he count on his adversary now making the dash down the apparently clear, windy side?

A moment later, Treasure knew he had got it right.

The figure in black came as though from nowhere. He was sprinting towards the banker and then, in the same second, he was flying through the air as one foot, then the other, had come down unevenly, disastrously, on a scatter of rolling, unyielding rubber balls.

Treasure had five yards to cover. Heroically, he leaped the last two—to land flat on his face on the empty deck, empty except for three skittle balls, all in uncomfortable places.

The enemy hadn't gone over the side as he

thought—though the disappearance had been almost magical. The tell-tale gap in the balustrading marked the top of a straight steel staircase. He grasped the handrail and humped his aching self down the steps.

Below he could just make out an angler's gantry. It circled the end of the pier at the lower level. It was slippery: there was lashing spray everywhere, and a weird howling.

The figure in black must have rolled to the bottom, then struggled upright and now, pursued by Treasure, was blundering along with one leg trailing. An icy wave whipped by the wind roared across the gantry—blurring everything, freezing movement, soaking the exhausted adversaries.

There was a matching steel staircase on the leeward side. The fugitive glanced back, tearing off the useless goggles. Treasure was too close. The steps were too far. There was no fight or energy left.

It wouldn't have been a dive—just a jump from the rail: possibly a jump to freedom for an immensely strong swimmer—certainly a plunge to a battered demise for one that wasn't.

Treasure was in time to grasp the expended, unprotesting figure round the waist, pulling them both down to the open steel decking. Another wave hit them as he tore at the Balaclava.

Breathing hard, he stared down at the white, soaked face.

'Your daughter and the money,' he shouted over the tumult around them. 'Were they really worth all this?'

The man caught nothing of the words. He shook his head. 'Let me jump. No chance in this,' he shouted back. 'Better in the end.' He was sobbing.

CHAPTER 20

'It's a sin to believe evil of others, but it's seldom a mistake. Have another cucumber sandwich,' said Canon Tring from his bed. Treasure helped himself.

It was tea-time on Saturday, two weeks after the arrest of the Tophaven Chief Librarian on a charge of double murder.

Treasure's wife was still in New York. He had driven down to play golf at the invitation of Commander Mane. As promised, he had called on the recuperating clergyman before returning to London.

He had talked briefly to Cynthia Tring in the kitchen upon his arrival, and while she had been making the tea. Relations between them had been more embarrassed than strained by events. Some things that had needed saying had been said. Cynthia had then gone out on some invented errand leaving the two men alone.

'In the case of Sims, I should have followed suspicion with action a lot quicker,' said the banker between mouthfuls.

'No one suspected the chap of anything. None of us even thought to tell you he was Esta Daws's father.'

'No one needed to. They're so alike in looks—not to mention temperament. I remember guessing at the relationship as soon as I met him. It simply went out of my mind for a bit.'

'Out of mind for a bit. Obsessional neurosis, our doctor says. Sims felt he'd failed his daughter, especially after his wife died. Convinced her husband had too. Right there, I'd say. Then he was certain, quite certain, Louella was spoiling her chance of ever getting any money. Will they plead some kind of mental imbalance, d'you think?'

Treasure shrugged, then picked up his cup from the little Victorian table beside the chintz-covered armchair.

The room was small and spartan — and overpowered by a massive walnut wardrobe. The chair had been brought in from Cynthia's pretty boudoir next door. There were serious-looking books in a solid, glass-fronted case. A black and white print of Holman Hunt's 'Light of the World', in a heavy gold, pedimented frame, bore sombre witness from the wall opposite the bed.

'I suppose they might try temporary insanity,' said the banker, absently stroking his still bruised kneecap. 'He's confessed to everything in sight, apparently.'

'Everything in sight,' repeated the Canon. 'Well, I'd say he'd been possessed by devils.'

'Mmm. Diabolically clever, certainly.'

'An apposite corollary.'

'Burning down the cottage could have been just as effective as breaking in for his purposes.'

'To eliminate the letter. Louella's copy letter?'

'Which wasn't there, of course. But he didn't know that. He thought he was taking less risk. In case the place was being watched. He could have got away. And he didn't have long to work it out either.'

'Extemporizing, he came up with the unexpected?'

'That time, yes. But Lady Brasset's egg saucepan was a piece of improvisation that didn't come off in the end.' Treasure paused. 'And it was the lady herself who first made me suspicious of Sims, when he over-elaborated.'

'Louella did?'

'He made great store to me of what were supposed to have been her last words to him. Delivered in the hall, outside the library. Where she could smoke. That's what he told me. Something about getting behind the new library project. But the following afternoon Lady Brasset had told me Sims hadn't wasted a second seeing her off, let alone engaging her in small talk in the hall. He'd been so frantically anxious to read the Marshford references she'd fed him.'

The Canon shook his head. 'Wouldn't have alerted me. But then . . .'

'It just seemed inconsistent, that's all. The whole yarn he spun me about his being worried about Louella and the new library was a total red herring, too. Simply wanted to camouflage his deep concern over the Round House the day after he'd done for Louella. More tea?'

Tring refused. The banker poured some for himself before going on. 'And they didn't have their last words on Thursday, either. Jacks said she'd told him on the phone she'd rung everywhere else about the lost letter. That had to mean she'd rung the library.'

'He's said so since?'

'Yes. I'm afraid the significance was lost on me at the time. But it came back later. His assistant took the call first. That's how she came to know why Lady Brasset was in London, something he'd actually mentioned to me. The girl had passed the phone to him, though.'

The Canon was chuckling. 'Lesser Council employees in this town would never treat with Louella on business. Not if they could find a superior handy,' he observed drily.

Treasure smiled too. 'Curious how some people can't suppress their prejudices. Not in any circumstances. Sims simply couldn't resist telling me the lady was a slave to tobacco. It was something he obviously deplored. Yet it was the habit he'd relied on to kill her.'

'Sooner rather than later,' the Canon offered gravely. 'He'd have done better to swallow his prejudice, and not advertise his strategy.'

'Precisely. He told me she never smoked in the car. It followed she lit up as soon as she got out of it. At first it seemed a long shot to me. Counting on your victim, as it were, to light the fuse.'

'Light the fuse. Cynthia insists it was totally predictable. He needed only to know about the volume of gas in the air doing the trick. Quite small, they tell me. Hmm. Librarians are full of useful information. And poor Jacks saw him call at the cottage. Didn't name him, but described him to you obliquely as an intimate of Louella's.'

'Only because she spent so much time at the library. A lot of other people thought the same. About the supposed friendship. I gather there were even suggestions of a romance in some quarters, despite the age difference.'

He noted the twinkle in his companion's eyes, and wished he'd left out the gratuitous report.

'She never looked her age,' said the Canon quietly.

Treasure nodded. 'Sims found the spare key, of course. That wouldn't have been difficult if you knew there was one about somewhere. Everyone did.'

'Everyone did,' echoed the priest. 'Poor Louella. So trusting.'

'Keeping it afterwards was astute. It stopped any other caller going in. Smelling the gas. Someone could easily . . .' This time he purposely abandoned what he had been about to say.

'Cynthia would have gone in. She was there after Sims,' supplied the Canon flatly. He looked up. 'Feels very badly about it all.'

'It wasn't her fault the key had gone.'

The other man seemed not to have heard. 'Volunteering to us all at lunch that day she hadn't been to the cottage.' He paused. 'You know Denis gave Jacks five hundred pounds not to tell anyone he'd seen Cynthia? It was all so unnecessary.'

'Probably it seemed not at the time.' Treasure cleared his throat. 'Only the four of us know where the money came from. Jacks was a regular gambler.'

'Gambler. Horseracing.'

'Yes. The police are satisfied the money could have been winnings. There's really no point in it coming up again.'

It had been Cynthia's decision to tell her husband the facts on that episode. She had held back on other particulars—on her actions and relationships—not to save her own face but to avoid upsetting him. This much she had admitted to Treasure. It seemed to him she had become a singularly chastened woman—and perhaps a wiser one.

'She feels it was her fault Sims knew Louella had gone to London, and why she had gone,' added the Canon. 'It could easily have been so, of course.'

But she'd been tempting him to steal, not to kill, Treasure believed. Aloud he said, 'Quite a few people knew on the day through Louella herself. Sims was one. We can't know when he decided to murder. He says he doesn't. Her call to the library certainly prompted him to take Marshford's letter.'

'And his sole motive was to protect the money from the Sandy Lane business.' The Canon sighed.

'Afraid so. Not to benefit himself. Only his daughter and her husband. He'd given them his own savings already.'

'But how could he have believed murdering Louella would stop her plan? The scheme to have the Round House protected?'

'He didn't know it would necessarily. He was desperate, and he didn't know she'd got as far as she had. He saw an opportunity and took it. That's what his daughter believes. Chances are he went to the cottage in the first place to plead with Lady Brasset. Commander Mane did just the same. But she wasn't there. Sims was demented over Mrs Daws's situation. I believe he arranged the murder right then. On impulse.'

'On impulse. Letting fate play half the hand. There

was no certainty. Not in Louella's case,' said the Canon. 'And he hoped what looked like her accidental death would nip her plan in the bud.'

'That's about it,' Treasure replied. 'It was dark when he got to the cottage. So far as he knew, no one had seen him. He came in his car — an old, nondescript Mini.'

'The bicycle and the elaborate . . .'

'Headgear? He didn't use them till the next day, which, incidentally, started well for him.'

'You mean people did accept Louella's death as accidental?'

'That and the fact that I told him there was no trace of the copy of the Marshford letter. He'd already purloined the original by then, although, you know, he hadn't actually destroyed it.'

The Canon smiled knowingly. 'Ah, the transcending conscience of the scholar. Louella had left her copy on Cynthia's desk.'

'Who had meantime found it and dropped it in at the cottage, not really appreciating its significance.' Treasure thought of this as the authorized version. 'It was the news about Jacks that spoiled the picture for Sims. In the circumstances he had to silence him, and very quickly. The murder itself wasn't difficult. Just took the determination — and a strong stomach. He must have come up behind Jacks covered by the noise of the cutter, then . . .' He drew his hand across his throat.

The Canon winced. 'They tell me it was his daughter who warned him he'd been seen at the cottage. But how did she know?'

'She overheard Jacks talking to me at the Round House. She's volunteered that to the police.'

'Eavesdropping?'

'Unintentionally as it happens. She'd hoped for a private word with me. When she saw me with Jacks she was too shy to show herself. Then, after what she heard, she was too scared. She knew her father had been to the cottage the day before. Now she thought he could be suspected of . . . of arranging the accident.'

'Although she assumed he was innocent?'

'Difficult to be sure.' Treasure helped himself to a homemade cup cake. He deplored the passing of the English tea as an institution: he was making the most of this one. 'You know Mrs Daws is in a nursing home? Nervous breakdown.'

The Canon nodded. 'You saw Sims near here that day, after you'd brought me back from Chichester.'

'On the bicycle, with his face covered. I didn't connect that with Jacks's death until it looked as though there might have been two murders. The track suit is what Sims normally wore at the youth club, I gather. He helps run it one night a week.'

'Voluntary work. Responsible, public-spirited action,' chanted the Canon quietly. 'The bicycle is one of three belonging to the club. I remember it was Louella persuaded the Tophaven Council to provide half their cost. The rest of the money she gave herself.'

Neither man spoke for a moment.

'To use the letter as your bait was very astute. You put yourself in grave danger.'

Treasure shrugged at the compliment. 'Whoever did the murders really had to have that copy or everything might have gone for nothing. And PC Stock was along to protect me, you know?' he added lightly.

'By all accounts he saved the cottage from taking fire. As to protecting you . . .'

'We had only the one bike,' put in the banker wryly. 'Also, like most nightmares, while that chase seemed to take hours, it was really only a matter of minutes. There were policemen all over that pier seconds after I stopped the chap jumping in the drink. Our real problem was communications. Stock broke his radio falling over a dog.'

'Falling over a dog. I heard. I know the animal well. Answers to the name of Dung, and not without reason.'

'Having no telephone at the cottage was more of a set-back,' Treasure went on. 'Sims had cut the wires as a precaution . . .'

'Ours into the bargain.'

'So I gather. He did it a long way back up the road. Wasn't difficult. Wires cross over a wall somewhere. And as you know, he put most of the phones in the village out of action in the process, including the public one at the crossroads. It took Tracy Mane ten minutes to find a house with a line working. That's why the fire brigade arrived long after Stock had the fire out.'

'And why the police were so slow getting to you.'

'Mmm. Touch of farce there. Nobody figured we were on the pier because it's supposed to be impregnable. Even the police don't have a key to it.'

'But the Chief Librarian does? Mmm. A perquisite of office, no doubt. Sounds like something out of Gilbert and Sullivan.'

'Or Sydney Marshford,' added Treasure drily. 'Thing is, the gate slammed to behind me. The cops had to scale a freshly installed anti-vandal barrier.' His amusement turned to concern. 'Here, I'd better go. I'm tiring you.'

'Stay a little longer. I've had no other visitors today.' The plea was genuine. 'It was a very little coronary, you know I'm only allowed little ones nowadays.' There was a glint in the older man's eye. 'Something I wanted to ask you . . . Denis Pitty.' He sighed deeply. 'I feel he comes out of the affair, shall we say, diminished? I'm sure my wife is of the same opinion. Loath to express it, perhaps.'

Treasure hesitated before commenting.

The Rackburn & Claremont had repurchased the freehold of the Round House from Seawell for precisely the sum they had been paid for it. There had been no publicity or explanation. Treasure had personally arranged this curious transaction. A substantial offer by Seawell for the same property had subsequently been accepted by the Trings. There had been no quibbling by anyone involved over who legally owned the freehold after Christmas.

Outsiders were left to conclude Lady Brasset's researches had led to the revelation of Marshford's ruling about the lease. Cynthia's insistence about keeping the college going to the bitter end was still regarded as evidence of her strong sense of moral duty.

The question of any collusion between Cynthia and Pitty to sell the Round House twice had not come up. The Canon freely admitted he'd never read the lease: he assumed his wife hadn't either. He regretted Pitty had delayed doing so (part of the diminishing process), but charitably believed he would have done before it expired — or before he, the Canon, did so, whichever was the soonest.

Just as the Trings had now become reasonably well off, it was equally certain Pitty was a good deal poorer through the Round House affair. Treasure, who knew all the facts, was inclined to take the last one as mitigation of a kind.

'I believe Pitty's had business problems,' he said carefully. 'I had a word with him on the phone yesterday. He's pretty subdued. Knows he's been careless — even foolish.'

'Foolish?' The Canon examined the small hump made by his feet under the bedclothes. 'Foolish. Yes.'

'Jacks went to see him because Mane and I had separately told the poor chap to contact the people he'd seen at the cottage. He didn't like to go to Cynthia direct. That's why he went to Pitty, knowing he was her lawyer and friend, to ask if he'd speak to her.'

'Speak to her! Instead he produced a bribe. On the spot.' The feet were given an involuntary wiggle.

'Also planted the thought in my mind he'd been one of the visitors himself. I learned later he didn't know who the others had been. He rang Sheikh Mhad Alid to warn him visitors had been observed *in case* the sheikh had been one of them—which he hadn't. So it followed Jacks hadn't consulted Pitty as a lawyer on his own behalf, as both Mane and I had suggested. If he had, there'd have been no need for Pitty to contact the sheikh. He'd have known the name of the other caller.'

'In some ways, Treasure, he was moved entirely by concern for others.' The Canon's observation came more as an apology than as evidence of conviction.

Treasure was content to impress the sentiment. 'He's been very helpful over a favour I was begging for someone. Something a bit sensitive.' The letter to Louella about Elderberry had been dealt with. 'But certainly he still has problems.'

'Problems. Dr Brasset, who arrived last week, says he's a rogue. Privately makes no bones about it. Taken the family estate out of his hands. Cynthia's inclined to move our own affairs to another lawyer.' He missed the lift of Treasure's eyebrows. 'Very awkward. We've been friends a long time.'

'The five hundred he gave Jacks to keep her name out . . .'

'Over-reacted, as I said,' the Canon interrupted. 'She was perfectly innocent. Why not say so? Infinitely preferable to a web of deceit. Also cheaper. I don't like it one bit. Anyway, Cynthia's reimbursing him.'

'Mmm. At the same time his action was precipitate, perhaps, but it was to save her embarrassment. He probably now regrets the impulse. I know Cynthia's sorry she condoned it. But it's easy to be wise afterwards.'

'I've said something of the sort to her.' The old

clergyman was now evidently tired, but the gaze he fixed on Treasure was still penetrating. 'I'm sure he had her best interests at heart. Source of great relief to me that after I'm gone she could rely on his friendship as well as his professional advice. They'd become increasingly close. I've encouraged that.'

The last words were delivered slowly and deliberately. He continued to fix the banker closely, his stare augmenting the verbal message in a way no words could have done.

'Do you think I have been unwise?'

'No, I don't.' He had expected some such question. 'Pitty's over-reached himself. He's indulged in living beyond his means and, I suspect, his intellectual capacities. I don't believe he's a rogue. He's been misguided and he's made a lot of mistakes. There's time for him to draw back. The last two weeks have brought him to his senses pretty brutally.' He paused. 'If I were you, I wouldn't try to influence Cynthia in their . . . their future relationship. She's quite capable of working such things out for herself.'

'Working things out for herself.' The eyelids closed, then reopened for a moment, but sleepily. 'Goodbye, Treasure. Thank you for coming. Cynthia will be sorry not to have seen more of you. I'm glad about the Round House. Poor Louella . . .'

The banker was already on his feet. He took the tray gently from the bed and quietly left the tiny room.

'So the Department of the Environment, *and* the town council *and* you didn't think the Round House worth preserving, so that was it,' said Tracy Mane, aggrieved.

She was sitting beside Treasure in the Rolls, enjoying a free ride to London. The Manes were living at the Beachcomber since vacating their house and while the cottage the Commander had bought was being refurbished.

'In the first place, I personally think it's worth saving . . .'

'But Daddy said you told the DoE it shouldn't be allowed to stop the development. Couldn't be justified.'

'Sometimes one's personal inclinations clash with one's corporate . . . er . . . obligations.'

'How absolutely foul. I shall have to consider withdrawing all offered privileges.' She pulled down the sleeves of her cardigan in a symbolic gesture which he unfortunately missed.

'I suppose I didn't phrase that very well. But I'll suffer being underprivileged with fortitude.'

'I only said consider withdrawing,' she added hastily. 'And since you're not a consistent Philistine, I'll try to overlook the lapse. Daddy did get his money, after all.'

'So did the others.'

'So the development's on. The famous Marshford letter didn't prove anything.'

He turned the car left on to the main Dorking and London road. 'No, that wretched letter proved nothing conclusively. I chose to think, though, Lady Brasset was right. That the W.B., the architect addressed by Marshford, really was William Butterfield . . .'

'Of mathematical title fame.'

'Of economical habit. Yes. The house he built was certainly designed by Soane.'

'So you're vandals to knock it down. Just like Louella said.'

'It's really a question of balance. The place isn't that good or important. For instance, if we weren't allowed to remove it, and it stopped the project entirely, would you mind your father having to give the money back?'

'Knock it down! Knock it down!' she cried. 'Philistines of the world unite, you have only your integrity to swallow.' She looked across at him. 'Daddy couldn't be made . . . ?'

'Of course not. The Round House might have been demolished. In fact, I'm surprised you haven't heard, it's going to be preserved.'

'But isn't it in the way?'

'Preserved but resited. To be precise, we're shunting it forward about a hundred feet. It's timber-framed. It'll come apart and go back together again fairly easily. It's going to be a first-class restaurant—the one that was scheduled to be in the apartment block, only better.'

'The kind that gets in the Egon Ronay guide?'

'Exactly. There's certainly room for another one in this catchment area. We'll get rid of all the nasty wartime additions to the original building, of course. When it's re-erected it'll look as it did when new. The kitchens will be in a half basement at the back. The upstairs will be the bar.' There was no disguising the enthusiasm in his voice.'

'You sound like you're in charge. You said the development was nothing to do with you really.'

'Only remotely.'

'And won't it cost a lot to move the place? You said Sheikh Ali and the other one . . . the one who beats his wife . . .'

'Tony Quaint. You don't *know* he beats his wife . . .'

'Or worse. Yes, that's him. You said he and Ali were very uptight about increased costs.'

'It happens this little operation isn't costing them a bean. It's the whim of a very rich man. The Emir of Abu B'yat. That's why I'm sort of in charge.'

'Ali's brother. But what does he need with a restaurant in Tophaven?'

'Good question.' He frowned at the driver of the BMW overtaking him as well as exceeding the speed limit. 'The Emir is fascinated by British stately homes. Ali says he collects castles. That isn't true, but when he's here he goes sight-seeing, incognito. Last year he went to Woburn Abbey which he liked very much. He liked the hotel he stayed in nearby even more. It's called Milton Ernest Hall in, as you might expect, the village of Milton Ernest, Bedfordshire. Incidentally, it's a very good hotel. Ever been there?'

'No. I'm free tonight, though,' she offered solemnly.

'Nonsense, your cousin is expecting you on Campden Hill for the rest of the weekend. I heard you tell your father. You never give up, do you?' He chuckled. 'Anyway, the Hall is new Gothic. It's the only complete country house William Butterfield ever designed. It was commissioned by his brother-in-law in 1852.'

'So the Emir bought it?'

'I gather he'd like to have done, but it wasn't for sale. I didn't know, but since then he's been making a careful study of Butterfield's work. Of course, that's mostly churches, colleges and schools. Then two weeks ago he rang me. He'd heard a bit about our little adventure. It got in *The Times*, as you know.' He spoke as though he wished it hadn't.

'Intrepid banker braves all,' proclaimed Tracy.

'That must have been some other paper. The Emir wasn't all that impressed, as it happens, until I came to mention the Round House was possibly by Butterfield.'

'And he sort of owns it. Through Seawell.'

'Right. And his brother was about to knock it down.'

'Crikey.'

'Right again, Miss Mane.'

'So all systems reverse for a happy ending?'

'That's about it. First the Emir wanted the house as an English residence. Eventually he accepted it was too small, wrong place, difficult for security. I was in Abu B'yat a few days ago and explained what might be done. The restaurant idea. We'd had some rough plans put together. The people at the Society for the . . .'

'*Protection* of Ancient Buildings?' she cut in with emphasis.

'That's right. They helped enormously. We had to work very fast.'

'You told me protection was more important than preservation.'

'That's true. In the case of an old building protection is still the primary consideration.'

'Like with a young lady's honour?'

'Er, yes. That's fairly analogous,' he replied carefully, with what he considered the sage addition. 'Both could involve a priceless treasure preserved.'

'Pom, pom, pom,' she teased. 'Or a delightful . . . pleasure . . . deferred?' She moved closer. 'By the way, that cousin's in Paris. How far's Milton Ernest?'